SPACE

STATION

DOWN

TOR BOOKS by BEN BOVA

Able One

The Aftermath

Apes and Angels

As on a Darkling Plain

The Astral Mirror

Battle Station

The Best of the Nebulas (editor)

Carbide Tipped Pens (coeditor)

Challenges

Colony

Cyberbooks

Death Wave

Earth

Empire Builders

Escape Plus

Farside

Gremlins Go Home
(with Gordon R. Dickson)

The Immortality Factor

Jupiter

The Kinsman Saga

Leviathans of Jupiter

Mars Life

Mercury

The Multiple Man

New Earth

New Frontiers

Orion

Orion Among the Stars

Orion and King Arthur

Orion and the Conqueror

Orion in the Dying Time

Out of the Sun

The Peacekeepers

Power Failure

Power Play

Powersat

Power Surge

The Precipice

Privateers

Prometheans

The Return: Book IV
of Voyagers

The Rock Rats

The Sam Gunn Omnibus

Saturn

The Science Fiction Hall of
Fame, Volumes A and B (editor)

The Silent War

Star Peace: Assured Survival

The Starcrossed

Survival

Tales of the Grand Tour

Test of Fire

Titan

To Fear the Light
(with A. J. Austin)

To Save the Sun
(with A. J. Austin)

Transhuman

The Trikon Deception
(with Bill Pogue)

Triumph

Uranus

Vengeance of Orion

Venus

Voyagers

Voyagers II: The Alien Within

Voyagers III: Star Brothers

The Winds of Altair

SPACE

STATION

DOWN

BEN BOVA

and DOUG BEASON

A TOM DOHERTY ASSOCIATES BOOK  NEW YORK

This is a work of fiction. Characters in the book are entirely fictitious and are products of the authors' imaginations—with the exception of George Abbey, Mike "Mini" Mott, Bill "Shep" Shepherd, and Fred Tarantino, whose names are included with permission, for purposes of verisimilitude.

SPACE STATION DOWN

Art by Michael Ferraiuolo

A Tor Book
Published by Tom Doherty Associates
120 Broadway
New York, NY 10271

www.tor-forge.com

Tor® is a registered trademark of Macmillan Publishing Group, LLC.

The Library of Congress Cataloging-in-Publication Data is available upon request.

ISBN 978-1-250-30743-9 (hardcover)
ISBN 978-1-250-30744-6 (ebook)

Our books may be purchased in bulk for promotional, educational, or business use. Please contact your local bookseller or the Macmillan Corporate and Premium Sales Department at 1–800-221-7945, extension 5442, or by email at MacmillanSpecialMarkets@macmillan.com.

First Edition: 2020

Printed in the United States of America

0 9 8 7 6 5 4 3 2 1

To the men and women who are helping humankind

expand civilization to the stars

The laws of politics:
1. Get elected.
2. Get re-elected.
3. Don't get mad, get even.

Senator Everett Dirksen (R. Illinois)

International Space Station

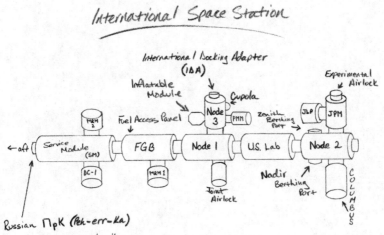

International Docking Adapter (IDA)

Inflatable Module

Fuel Access Panel

Cupola

Node 3

PMM

Zenith Berthing Port

Experimental Airlock

JLP

JPM

MRM 2

Service Module (SM)

FGB

Node 1

U.S. Lab

Node 2

← aft

DC-1

MRM 1

Joint Airlock

Nadir Berthing Port

COLUMBUS

Russian ПрК (Peh-err-ka) "transfer chamber"

Flattened "Roadkill" view — does not reflect modules extending into/out of page

D A Y   O N E

JAPANESE MODULE (JPM)

Kimberly Hadid-Robinson floated upside down in the International Space Station's Japanese module—or JPM, as she and the other astronauts called it.

Her wiry dark hair was frizzed out to the size of a football helmet, but that didn't matter, she thought. Normally she'd tie it back into a ponytail if there was even the slightest chance that she'd appear on TV. And it didn't matter if the live broadcast was being streamed down only to the Johnson Space Center, because invariably some PR genius at NASA Headquarters would decide to shoot a portion of the feed to the national news outlets. They loved to show the public that a female astronaut was serving as the senior ranking American on board the ISS—for the same reason that Public Affairs was using one of their up-and-coming women on the ground to narrate today's docking. The "Voice of NASA" was usually some over-the-hill bureaucrat who should have retired years ago; Kimberly welcomed the young Hispanic addition, a minority like herself.

Kimberly was a slim, slight sylph of a woman with skin the color of burnt almonds, a little snub of a nose, big dark eyes, and a smile that could light up a room. She wasn't smiling at the moment.

Much as she'd like to be on hand to meet the new arrivals, the experiments running in the JPM demanded Kimberly's attention far more than greeting the crewmen coming on board.

The JPM was the farthest module from the docking port in the MRM-2, the Russian airlock, where the newbies were arriving. It was only a hundred yards away from the JPM, but she knew she couldn't leave the module for more than a minute; it wasn't worth the trouble—or the headache, for that matter—if she left the experiments just to be there to glad-hand the new arrivals.

After all, she reasoned to herself, support for the work we're doing here on the ISS doesn't really come from congressional funding: it comes from the public's interest in what we're doing, and that means completing the experiments that even high school kids had thought up. They'd won awards to fly their ideas on the ISS without worrying about the PR benefits of greeting another few space travelers who're about to make a six-month stay on the station. She'd meet them soon enough.

And it wasn't as if the incoming cosmonaut was a total stranger to the ISS. Kimberly knew that Farid Hazood was a retread, a Kazakhstani who'd flown aboard the station three years ago: one of those foreigners whom the Soviets . . . er, *Russians* . . . periodically granted a berth in the ISS. For the Kazakhstanis, it was a sort of repayment for allowing the Russian Soyuz and Vostok launchers to continue to lift off from the Baikonur Cosmodrome in Kazakhstan.

It also served a double purpose: the Russians retained a semifree launch pad that took only thirty days to refurbish after one of their launches, and the Kazakhstanis maintained international stature as a space-faring nation—a pretty exclusive club numbering only 40 of 196 nations worldwide—well worth the payment and cost for both sides.

She'd never met Farid Hazood, and she knew he'd aced his first mission, so it was no surprise he was chosen to fly again. But even with Farid's experience, Kimberly thought it was a little strange to have the Kazakhstani coming up with a total newbie. It had been three years since Farid had last flown, and a paying space tourist was accompanying him in the approaching Soyuz capsule; the station's normal crew of six was being augmented for a nine-day period with this "taxi" crew carrying the tourist. At least the Soyuz's pilot and commander, Colonel Yuri Zel'dovich, was a seasoned longtimer. This would be his fourth flight to the space station, so Farid and the tourist had some solid experience flying them.

But Russians were Russians, and as eagerly learning capitalists they were happy to accept cash from just about anybody. It cost tourists over sixty million dollars a pop for training, launching, and spending a week on board the ISS, where they were exempt from any responsibilities except to sightsee—and spend the rest of their lives back on Earth bragging about the experience.

The Russians were so hungry for cash they'd even flown up three dozen multimission radioisotope thermoelectric generators, or RTGs, for the U.S. on the last Progress resupply mission; they'd temporarily placed them in MRM-1, at the Russian side of the station, until they could be moved outside the ISS during an extravehicular activity, or EVA, and stored at the end of a boom for safety.

The U.S. would never have been able to launch the plutonium RTGs to the ISS, as *any* mention of radioactivity ignited hysteria—even though the compact nuclear power sources were absolutely necessary for powering the sensors, rovers, and living areas needed for exploring Mars and beyond, where solar panels are impractical. But the Russians didn't have environmental activists or an independent press to publicize a risky launch; they just didn't tell anyone, and took NASA's money without fanfare. So Kimberly had to admit, compared to the sexy role RTGs had in ISS's next phase in the space program, some of her efforts at advancing humankind's knowledge had more to do with the public relations side of NASA, looking after zero-gee ant farms, growing larger-than-life asparagus, and measuring the viscosity of weightless Jell-O.

But she kept that gripe to herself. The money they made from launching the RTGs and tourism was of particular interest to the Russians, especially since the U.S. would soon stop paying $82 million apiece for every American astronaut launched in a Russian Soyuz capsule to the ISS. The U.S. hadn't had a human-rated spacecraft since the Space Shuttle retired, but thank goodness several newly licensed capsules—Boeing's Starliner and SpaceX's Dragon—were just coming into service. Kimberly grimaced as she thought of her last return flight in the Soyuz: a horrific four-gee descent that squeezed your guts and usually hit the ground at some isolated farmland in the Kazakhstani wilderness.

If you were lucky.

She never complained about the landings, knowing that one of her more famous fellow astronauts had come down smack in the middle of the Iraq war zone some twenty years earlier.

So while she regretted not being present to meet Farid Hazood and the Qatari tourist, Adama Bakhet, at the docking port, Kimberly told herself she'd make it up soon enough after they'd entered the ISS and started integrating with the crew. Besides, two of the Russians and the other Americans aboard the station couldn't make the docking, either; Al was manning the control center and Robert was with the Russians, who had just borrowed three of the four JPM laptops and were now readying a pair of EVA suits in the Joint Airlock.

So Kimberly kept one eye on the experiments percolating along, and the other on the webcast video she'd put on her laptop as the basketball-shaped Soyuz slowly approached the Russian MRM-2 docking compartment, or DC. The capsule floated gently toward the ISS, no faster than one foot per second as the new female "Voice of NASA" spoke quietly over the comm link.

She could see in the background of her laptop's monitor stars moving slowly, silently across the black infinity of space. Even though she had witnessed dozens of dockings, the scene still made a heart-stopping view: mating with the million-pound ISS while it and the Soyuz capsule both hurtled through space at 17,500 miles per hour brought a lump to her throat. It was an incredible human achievement, accomplished some 250 miles above the Earth's surface.

Reluctantly, Kimberly turned away from the laptop and peered through the confocal microscope at the crystal she was monitoring. It was visibly growing, slowly but unmistakably, like a diamond glittering in the microscope's glareless light. Floating in front of the experimental chamber, she was careful to position herself away from the portable microwave projector that was beaming its 98 GHz radiation into the crystal specimen.

The novel experiment was something she'd never expected to come from the Air Force Academy, but with Scott Robinson pushing heaven and earth to overcome the Academy's trade-school reputation, his alma mater was evolving into a world-class research organization.

Now where did *that* come from? Kimberly hadn't thought of Scott in what? Minutes?

Focus on the experiment, she commanded herself. Stop thinking about Scott: you're divorced, it's over.

But her ex-husband was CAPCOM today, serving as their astronaut lead at the mission control center, MCC at Houston, commanding the space station's communications link with the ground. It's been eighteen months since the divorce, Kimberly told herself, a near eternity in today's stop-and-shop world of one-relationship-after-another. And besides, his ego was so large it probably filled every corner of the MCC.

Still, she saw Scott's handsome, smiling face in her mind.

She shook her head to get clear of Scott's memory and peered through the eyepiece while her right hand delicately adjusted the Helium-Neon Zeeman laser to measure the crystal's growth. So far, so good. As the scientists had predicted, the 98 GHz waves from the microwave projector actually accelerated the crystal's growth over what had been measured back on Earth in a one-gee environment. Score one for zero-gee, Kimberly thought. No, better. It was a hat trick: a home run for the science community, the Air Force Academy, and the ISS.

And for Scott Robinson, as well. Scott was the one who put his old alma mater in touch with NASA's chief scientist and got the experiment onto the ISS.

Enough about Scott! she told herself. She looked over at her laptop and saw that the airlock hatch in the MRM-2 was swinging open. The newbies were arriving.

JAPANESE
MODULE (JPM)

Floating between the crystal growth experiment and her laptop, Kimberly watched the inner airlock hatch swing open and the jumpsuited body of the Soyuz spacecraft's commander, Colonel Yuri Zel'dovich, drift slowly into the ISS, headfirst. Smiling broadly, Cosmonaut Ivan Vasilev, the one-man welcoming committee, reached out for his approaching comrade.

Zel'dovich's shoulder bumped gently against the hatch's metal framework, making his feet slowly rotate upward in the zero-gee space. Small, vibrating globules of bright red blood pulsed in the air, more of them oozing out from a slashing wound in the colonel's neck.

His eyes wide with shock, Vasilev grabbed at Zel'dovich's lifeless body and started yelling hoarsely in Russian while Kimberly watched the scene on her laptop's screen, frozen with sudden terror. Vasilev grabbed a handhold on the side of the module and pulled forward, toward the hatch.

Kimberly saw a knifelike object—it was actually thicker than a knife and looked as if it had a retractable blade—suddenly fly from the Soyuz and embed itself in Vasilev's eye with a sickening thud.

The cosmonaut screamed and jerked away, pawing at his face, frantically trying to pull the blade from his eye, his body twisting in the air, spherules of blood spewing from his face.

A blue jumpsuited body shot out of the Soyuz from the airlock, hurtling toward Vasilev. Kimberly recognized the man from the publicity photos and media releases she'd seen: Farid!

She'd never met the Kazakhstani, and from everything she'd heard, three years ago he'd been a valuable member of the ISS crew. She'd been looking forward to getting a computer scientist up to the station, to help reduce her own brutal research schedule.

But now, muttering something in a guttural language, Farid reached for Vasilev with outstretched hands and caught the Russian as he was trying to pull the blade from his eye. Farid put a hand to the back of Vasilev's head and pushed as hard as he could against his chin, snapping his head back. Then he twisted Vasilev's neck until Kimberly actually heard an audible *pop* as the spine snapped.

Vasilev went limp. Farid shoved him away. The dead cosmonaut spun slowly in midair and bumped into the metal structure of the compartment as he floated inertly in zero-gee.

In the Japanese module, Kimberly tightly grasped the handhold she'd been clinging to, too shocked to react to the murders she had just seen. As she started to unconsciously rotate around, her free hand suddenly felt an incredible searing pain, as though the hottest oven in the world had just opened in front of her and she'd stuck her hand smack into its middle. She jerked her hand back. The 98 GHz microwave beam, she realized. Even though her skin wasn't even reddened, it hurt like hell. No wonder some Academy geeks were working on developing such microwaves to protect embassies overseas.

Wringing her hand in pain, Kimberly saw a second person emerging from the Soyuz airlock, wearing a blue jumpsuit identical to Farid's. She recognized Adama Bakhet, the Qatari tourist. Bakhet floated out slowly, hesitantly, taking his time, obviously quite new to zero-gee.

Kimberly remembered watching a video about the young billionaire tourist from Qatar. He'd paid $60 million for the opportunity to stay aboard the ISS for nine days. But she didn't focus on him. He was a newbie, and as a tourist he might not even adapt to the station's zero-gee environment before it was time for him to leave.

To Kimberly, the real threat was Farid.

Farid moved out of the monitor's view, disappeared from the screen. Where's he heading? What was he going to do?

Kimberly jerked forward and slapped a hand on the emergency alert button on the caution and warning panel. Klaxons started blaring all through the station. The signal should not only get everyone's attention, but the crew should rush to their emergency stations. Farid and the fake tourist would hear it, too, and know that they'd lost the element of surprise.

Gingerly, her hand still throbbing from its exposure to the microwave beam, she jabbed at the monitor control, her feet rotating in midair as she moved. In addition to warning the two Russians and the American in the Joint Airlock, she needed to quickly alert Al Sweeting to what she'd just seen. Al was one of her American colleagues who was manning the station's control center, next door to the Russian SM module, during the docking. Unless he'd been watching the docking he wouldn't know what had just happened.

Farid was probably heading for Al. Kimberly's fingers flew over the controls and the monitor blinked and switched to Central Post. She turned up the volume—

And she saw Al and Farid grappling in the zero-gee compartment, rotating around in the air, bouncing off the metal shelving, monitors, computers, and white-sided insulation as they clawed at each other.

I've got to do something! Kimberly knew. But what? NASA couldn't even help, as this view was internal to the ISS, and not being broadcast.

The SM was at the far end of the ISS, and the Russians or the remaining American should be able to get to it faster than she could. Still, Kimberly couldn't just stay in the JPM and watch. She flicked her eyes from the monitor to the array of white cloth bags Velcroed to the compartment's wall; they held tools and equipment that she might be able to grab and use.

With the Klaxon continuing to hoot throughout the station, she turned back to the laptop's monitor, her breath quickening as she watched Al and Farid battling. Al fought furiously, arms pummeling wildly, but Farid was bigger, more solidly built, obviously more experienced.

A scientist like Kimberly herself, Al was small in stature and had a feral appearance: the other astronauts called him Rat, although Kimberly kept their relationship strictly professional and always referred to him as Al.

But that didn't do anything to help Al now.

Farid was holding Al in a choke hold with his left arm. Kimberly could see the dark hair on his wrist in the high-resolution clarity of the laptop's monitor. His arms bulged in his cosmonaut's blue uniform. It looked as though the man had spent the three years since his last ISS mission lifting weights and working out. This certainly wasn't the quiet Kazakhstani that the psychological profilers had analyzed. Had he undergone some sort of physical training for this radically different behavior?

As they gyrated in zero gravity, Farid twisted Al to the left and brought his right hand up and placed it against the back of Al's head.

Al's face turned beet red as he struggled for breath. Gasping, he used both hands to try to pry Farid's massive left arm off his throat. He thrashed and kicked with both his legs, jerking violently back and forth, desperately trying to work free. The two started rotating in midair, bouncing off the consoles. Just as they floated out of sight of the video, Farid viciously twisted Al's neck . . . and he went limp.

Kimberly pounded at the comm link to NASA, wanting to make sure that the ground was aware of what was happening. How much had they seen? They should have seen Colonel Zel'dovich's dead body floating from the Soyuz and Vasilev being murdered, but they hadn't responded in any way. She was sure they were shocked, probably too stunned to respond. She knew they wouldn't be able to do anything from the ground to help her at this moment, but they had access to the most creative minds in the world: *somebody* should be able to come up with a workable countermeasure.

But Kimberly realized that at this moment it was up to her, the two Russians, and one other American. They couldn't rely on NASA to do anything in the station that they couldn't do for themselves.

The comm link to NASA Headquarters was out, she realized. Not responding. Then she remembered that the link had been working just moments before, when Scott's voice had been broadcasting over the monitor in his official duty as today's CAPCOM while the Soyuz had docked.

She knew that the feed was being sent out over NASA TV, and in addition to being picked up by the Russian space program, every major network and news channel back on Earth would have someone watching the feed, even if it was only a lowly summer intern. Their only job was to watch for anything that might occur aboard the ISS that might be worthy of shooting to the newsroom—or even breaking into their regularly scheduled broadcast, if it was important enough.

None of the big guys wanted to be scooped with breaking news by their competitors. Being first meant being able to charge more for commercial airtime, and that meant more bucks. Which was the real name of the game, not news just for the altruistic sake of news.

Kimberly quickly ran through the alternate links emanating from the ISS. One after another they showed that nothing was being transmitted or received. Running her fingers over the touchscreen, she called up the backup satellite-to-satellite relay. That too was dead.

This wasn't just a technical malfunction; it was a deliberate severing of the entire station-to-ground communication links.

She felt her pulse racing faster, her heart beating so hard it seemed to be trying to burst out of her ribs. Farid. He must have cut the links. He was a computer scientist; he knew exactly how to do it. With his past six-month tour on the ISS he had more than enough experience to control the entire station.

Looking around the crowded compartment, Kimberly kicked out and shot through the air, reaching for one of the white cloth bags secured to the JPM wall that held a potpourri of tools. Her feet glided upward as she grabbed the bag and unfastened its Velcro strap. Fumbling inside, she pulled out two foot-long wrenches and an oversized screwdriver.

Guns were prohibited aboard the ISS. The purpose was to prevent any violence that might occur from people crowded together in an inescapable environment for months—even years—at a time. Bullets would only punch holes in the station's thin aluminum siding, letting the air escape and killing everyone inside.

For the same reason the Russians had decreed that knives were not allowed on the ISS either, although Kimberly knew there was an ultrasharp utility knife stowed away in Shep's toolkit—the grab bag of various odd tools Bill Shepherd had brought up with him when he had served on the ISS. Nobody but Shepherd, a free-spirited ex-Navy SEAL, could have gotten away with such a flouting of the rules. Several crew members had used the knife when they needed it. Nobody complained about it and HQ didn't know it existed. Kimberly was pretty certain Shep's bag—and the knife—were still in the JPM where Shepherd had stored it, but she couldn't find it.

From what she'd just seen, Kimberly wasn't thinking about using an approved, standardized weapon to defend herself, or following any international rules that had been negotiated and talked to death by chair-bound bureaucrats. These madmen would be coming after her. She was totally focused on survival.

Kimberly knew she didn't have time for discussions or new age, touchy-feely, get-in-touch-with-your-emotions, hand-holding séances. These bastards were coming for her, and she had to be able to defend herself. They'd already murdered three men; what were they going to do next?

She thought she knew. Farid and his companion were out to kill everyone on the station.

Sooner or later they would come for her.

Sooner, she realized. Not later.

She began to tremble. They want to kill me!

But then she remembered her father, all those years ago. And the fear inside her subsided. It did not disappear altogether, but now it was overlaid by an icy, pitiless resolve.

Those murdering sons of bitches, she thought. I'll kill them. Both of them.

But how?

FLASHBACK: KIMBERLY, AGE 10

Her eyes nearly blinded with tears, ten-year-old Kimberly fled out of the schoolyard, stumbled across Porter Road, and ran all the way home.

My dress, she kept thinking. My new dress. They ruined it.

Her mother was in the front yard, working on her bed of chrysanthemums. Once she saw Kimberly she dropped her trowel and ran to her only child, her normally placid Japanese features wide-eyed with sudden alarm.

"What happened?" her mother shouted. "Your dress is filthy!"

Kimberly rushed to her arms, still crying. She tried to explain between gasping sobs. "They said I was too dark to wear a white dress! They threw mud at me! Five of them!"

Mama brushed the tears away, wrapped a protective arm around her daughter, and led her into the house. Kimberly's father was at the door, his lean, ascetic face worried, alarmed.

It took several minutes for them to get Kimberly soothed down. Mama led her upstairs, helped her take off the ruined dress, and cleaned her up.

"There were five of them," Kimberly told her, calmer now. "Marla Kingston was the leader. I hate her!"

It was the first day of the new term. Kimberly had been advanced one whole grade, she was so bright. But some of the older girls did not like their new dark-skinned arrival.

"Five of them," Kimberly repeated. "They threw mud at me. They said I was too dark to be with them."

By the time Mama led her downstairs again Kimberly was almost calm. But she could feel the anger burning inside her.

Her father was waiting at the foot of the stairs. "Come with me, Kimberly," he said, leading her into his office.

Dr. Harold Hadid was a third-generation Saudi Englishman who had emigrated to the United States to pursue a career in neurosurgery. Tall and reserved, he'd had to face the inborn, unconscious intolerance of the British class system and decided to move to America. There he had met his California-born, Japanese American wife, excelled in school at Johns Hopkins, and settled in the Washington, D.C., area.

He sat Kimberly in the big leather armchair that was usually reserved for guests and listened patiently to her story about the other girls' bullying.

"I hate her!" Kimberly concluded. "Marla Kingston. I hate her!"

Sitting on the rocker next to her, Papa raised a slim finger.

"Hate is a vicious emotion," he said softly. "It can lead you to do things you'll regret later on."

"But she—"

With one of his rare smiles, Papa said, "Let me give a word of advice, Kimberly. An American politician, a U.S. senator, in fact, once said, 'Don't get mad, get even.' Think about that."

Kimberly did think about it. When she returned to school later that day, she went straight to the principal's office to explain that she had gone home to change her dress, which had somehow gotten begrimed with mud.

She kept to herself, avoiding most of the other girls in her class, and everyone forgot about Kimberly's muddied dress . . . .

A few months later, she won the top score in the class's state exams. And somehow Marla Kingston's paper disappeared and she had to retake the test after regular class hours. Even then, her paper was rejected by the computer scoring device because of illegible handwritten sections.

And years later, when Kimberly and Marla Kingston were seniors at Johns Hopkins University, Marla's cell phones, laptops, and other digital devices malfunctioned so often that Ms. Kingston was reduced to tears.

Don't get mad, get even.

JOHNSON SPACE CENTER, ISS CONTROL CENTER, HOUSTON, TEXAS

Although he was on the ground and not in space, Lieutenant Colonel Scott Robinson took the initiative, as he'd been trained. Shocked and incredulous, he was sitting in front of the new, organic LED panel with the CAPCOM sign atop it, his earphones dangling around his neck.

Four years of astronaut training, three six-month tours aboard the ISS, five years flying the F-22, two years of pilot and fighter training, and four years at the Blue Zoo made him react without thinking—the one thing he'd mastered after years of preparation for this one instant in time that would affect nearly every one of the seven-plus billion people on Earth.

For the first time in history, he killed a live video feed to the public being beamed from space, immediately after Vasilev was murdered. No way in hell was he going to give these terrorists any publicity by showing ISS personnel being slaughtered.

Broadcasting over NASA TV, Roscosmos, the Space Channel, and other channels picked up by every major network in the world, the public feed of the live coverage from the International Space Station suddenly went dead. Channel screens went dark and nothing, not even a sign apologizing for the inconvenience, appeared on the networks.

But the feed was still being broadcast over NASA's closed channel, and he knew that every person in the U.S. government would instantly start working to help any way they could.

And the media went apeshit. Especially after just seeing Zel'dovich's dead body and witnessing the brutal slaying of an ISS crew member.

Scott didn't ponder the public relations crisis that might erupt from NASA's press dweebs, and he didn't wring his hands over the possible—and now, certainly probable—exponential drop in funding the space program would see from irate congressmen. He couldn't care less; it was the last thing on his mind, as it should be. He was one of the last, true astronaut fighter pilots NASA still employed in the dwindling astronaut corps, and like the rest of the astronauts, he had been trained not to react but to *anticipate*, to stop the problem, fix it, and ensure that it didn't happen again before it erupted into anything big.

Every person in the room manning the communications consoles that oversaw space station operations, their sensors and data feeds, was among the most highly qualified people in the world. They just didn't get better than this. Even after years of neglect, the space program still attracted the world's top talent.

And Scott wouldn't want anyone less qualified in the communications center, either with him here on the ground or if it was him up on the ISS, undergoing what the American and Russian crew was experiencing . . . as Kimberly Hassid-Robinson was now.

And *that* escalated the stakes even higher, because he and the people in this room weren't only trying to assist the ISS crew to survive whatever-the-hell the whole world had just seen; now it was personal, as far as Scott was concerned.

But as good as everyone on the floor was, he was still the only person who'd recently been to space. That gave him the creds to pull off what he'd just done—and they still had comm with the station through their closed link.

But seconds later, the remaining NASA-only comm channels with the ISS blinked off, as if someone on the ISS had killed the emergency visual and voice links streaming from the station.

The noise level in the room was approaching that of a jet taking off on afterburners. Everyone was standing, yelling into their throat mikes as they stretched the wires from their headphones as far as they could reach, gesticulating to unseen listeners, turning to their neighbors and trying to yell over the escalating noise.

For some reason Flight, the ISS Flight Director, wasn't taking control and trying to focus everyone back on helping the astronauts and cosmonauts on board. Scott realized this was Flight's first solo and the poor kid was badly rattled. So as today's senior astronaut liaison serving as CAPCOM, Scott needed to take the bull by the balls.

He yanked off his headphones, kicked the black, government-issue swivel chair out of his way, and climbed up onto the console. He started clapping his hands and yelling as loudly as he could, "Hold it! Stop! Quiet down!"

He kept clapping, now and then pointing to a person to silence her neighbor so they could all focus their attention on him. Someone bolted from the control center, leaving their post. Within seconds the noise in the room dopplered down considerably, al-though a few people still gabbled on excitedly. The chamber was quiet enough for Scott to speak, not in a shriek but in a strong, measured tone designed to let people know he was in charge and get them to listen to him.

Now that the command center was quiet, Scott held his hands over his head and said firmly, "Listen up! Everyone in here knows Zel'dovich and Vasilev are dead, and there's nothing we can do about it. Now that the ISS's comm links have been cut, we need to be trying everything we can think of to contact our people on the station. *Everything.*

"You know what that means. We need creative solutions on overriding the blackout. We need innovative ways to contact the crew and let them know that we're actively looking for solutions. The main thing is to keep focused on contacting our folks and figuring out what happened—by any means possible. Monitor the onboard sensors, the experiments, anything that may give us a clue as to what's going on and what happened. Understand?"

The comm techs exchanged glances with one another; some turned to get back to their consoles. Others looked uncertain; they needed additional encouragement.

"All right," Scott boomed. "Get on it. Help our folks. They're depending on us. Now move it!"

The room was almost silent now, except for the sounds of the technicians returning to their consoles. Scott waited a few heart-beats, scanning the room until he was satisfied that everyone had a grip on their emotions.

Then he hopped down from the console and looked around the room for Flight. The rookie Flight Director was still sitting at his console; his face was flushed as his fingers slid across his touchscreen. It was his first time as flight director and the poor kid was shocked, numb. Scott realized he'd have to stay in charge, at least for the time being.

Scott felt his stomach tightening. It was always this way after a pressure situation, from his first F-22 flight and his first combat emergency, to being accepted for the astronaut corps. Even with his first flight in the manned version of SpaceX's Dragon capsule to the ISS.

But this time he knew the sick feeling in the pit of his stomach wasn't from the pep talk he'd just given; it was from wondering if Kimberly was still alive.

For as bad as things had gotten before the divorce, the one thing he realized after it was how big a jerk he'd been, bringing the whole fighter pilot, astronaut machismo pose into the marriage. You should have checked it at the door, asshole, he berated himself. For once he was single again and back on the street he realized how shallow he—and the lifestyle he'd led before he'd gotten married—had been. Especially since it took so long for him to accept that Kimberly now commanded the ISS, a position he'd recently had himself; it had shocked him to think that a scientist could ever have the same coolheaded, no-nonsense skills needed in pressure situations, but like it or not, his ex-wife was in the hot seat now, and there was nothing he could do to help her.

He walked to the Flight Director's desk. The man had his head down, staring at his console, looking overwhelmed. Scott hesitated, and then put a hand on his shoulder. When he didn't acknowledge, Scott leaned over and whispered, "Pull it together."

Flight nodded, but still didn't respond.

Scott returned to his monitor and put his headphones back on. He knew that the others in the room would be trying every channel, every data port, every other entry portal into the ISS, so his trying to call the station as CAPCOM wouldn't make any difference at this point.

He needed to call the NASA Administrator right away. He knew he couldn't trust that the Administrator had been told about the emergency just yet. He knew she was a busy lady and even though she was a former astronaut herself, Patricia Simone didn't have enough time in her crowded schedule to be continuously watching NASA TV. He knew her staff should have gotten to her and immediately brought her up to speed on the situation, but he himself had to actively close the loop and make sure she'd heard.

JOHNSON SPACE CENTER, ISS CONTROL CENTER, HOUSTON, TEXAS

Sophia Flores bolted up from behind her Public Affairs Officer console, shocked as she and the mission controllers saw Farid cruelly twist Vasilev's head. The young PAO gaped at the oversized screen, barely believing what she saw.

Blood foamed from Vasilev's mouth as he and Farid floated out of the camera's view—and Sophia kicked into high gear.

Her public affairs training overwhelmed her shock, crashing through the numbness brought on by the brutal attack. Her PAO classes had thrown scenario after scenario at her in realistic simulations with the press and in the mission control center, drilling her to *expect the unexpected*, so she'd remain calm and not frighten the public.

She immediately checked the NASA TV link being fed to the

public. Good, it had been severed. JSC and HQ would clean up the public fallout.

And there *would* be incredible fallout with this . . . brutality broadcast all over the world.

Turning, she squinted up at the glass-enclosed viewing area that overlooked the floor of the control center. She saw hands pressed against the glass, mouths open in amazement. Sophia yelled up at the overlook and waved for the senior PAO accompanying the VIPs to *get them out of the viewing area—now!* No one moved or paid her any attention as an uproar reverberated throughout the control center.

She stood on her tiptoes and tried to see into the darkened overlook. Where in the world is the senior PAO?

Suddenly, a commotion broke out behind the VIPs, and several of the gapers turned to congregate around something behind them. A few of the people who turned away squatted down on their haunches; someone must have fainted.

Underneath the overlook, two mission controllers pointed at the front of the control center. Sophia turned as the oversized display blinked and the words *Transmission Terminated* scrolled across the screen. The closed NASA-TV link had been severed from the ISS, and CAPCOM was standing on his console, clapping his hands to get everyone's attention.

Sophia glanced back at the overlook; people still milled around in shock, attending to whoever had fainted. She ripped the headphones from her head. Someone had to clear the viewing area!

She squeezed her way past a crowd of mission controllers and exited the MCC. Sprinting up the stairs, she entered the overlook and saw a group of VIPs clustered around someone lying on the floor. "What happened?"

"I don't know," someone said. "He was fine just a minute ago."

She pushed through the gaggle of people and recognized the senior PAO. He wasn't moving.

Did he have a heart attack? No one in the group was helping, so there were obviously no medical personnel in the room. She pointed at the man who had answered her. "You—call 911 on that red phone by the door. And you—" she pointed at another person. "Bring me that AED on the wall." The woman she'd pointed to hesitated, as if she hadn't understood what Sophia had meant. "The automated external defibrillator, now!"

She squatted down by the side of the senior PAO and held her ear to his mouth and nostrils; she couldn't detect any breathing and she couldn't find a pulse. She looked up as a woman handed her the portable AED. Opening the case, Sophia felt a flush of anger when she saw a solid red X on the battery indicator. It was dead. She didn't have time to replace the battery.

Straightening her arms and interlocking her hands, she immediately started CPR. She spoke while she worked. "Everyone! Step away from the window! Exit the overlook and go down the stairs, then line up against the wall in the hallway. If you see another AED, then bring it to me. Otherwise, direct the emergency personnel up here when they arrive. But most importantly stay out of the way! Understand?"

The VIPs looked at one another, taken aback by such terse orders given by someone so young.

She raised her voice. "Does everyone understand?"

They murmured and started to file out of the overlook, not making eye contact with her.

The man who had called 911 said, "They're on their way." He hesitated, and then started to join the people filing out.

"Wait," Sophia said, nodding for him to join her. "Stay here. I'm going to need some help."

"Right."

Sophia directed her full attention to pushing against the senior PAO's chest. She hoped that nothing else bad would happen today, but she had a dreadful feeling that events would only cascade and become worse . . . much worse.

JOHNSON SPACE CENTER, ISS CONTROL CENTER, HOUSTON, TEXAS

Scott glanced at the clock. Only four minutes had passed since he'd cut the live feed from the ISS to the public media. They're probably screaming bloody murder right now, and wondering if they'd really seen that on the ISS, some 250 miles above the Earth. Scott bet that some TV execs might think the NASA feed had been hacked by jokers.

He ran his fingers over the touchscreen and set up a link with the Administrator's office at NASA Headquarters back in Washington, D.C. The phone was picked up on the first ring.

"Mike Mott."

"Mini, Basher," Scott said, using their old fighter pilot handles. His nickname had stuck with him, as had Mini's. An ex-Marine Corps pilot, Mini Mott was just barely tall enough to qualify for flight training. And even though he had failed to enter the astronaut corps, he had been picked by Patricia Simone to be her executive officer at NASA Headquarters. His buzz-cut thatch of light brown hair was well-known throughout the agency. Small but deadly was the word about Mini Mott.

"We just heard," said Mini. "Trying to get ahold of the Administrator now. How about you? Do you have contact with the station? How are our folks?"

"Don't know. We're out of communication. All links and relays to the ISS are down."

"What about NASA TV?"

"I severed the live feed to the public right after Vasilev's murder."

"Good call."

"Someone on the ISS took down everything else; probably Farid."

"So we don't know if anyone else was killed, right?"

"Roger that." Scott pulled in a deep breath, trying to calm down. "Where's the Administrator?"

"Scheduled to be in a cabinet meeting, briefing the cabinet on the implications of the cut in our budget."

"Crappy timing."

"Deaths are crappy timing. We're trying to pull her out now and get the word to her, but the White House staffers are being their usual pricks."

Scott's mind raced. "I'll stay on the line if you need me. We're doing everything we can to get back in contact with the station."

"Well tell everyone to try harder—" Suddenly it sounded as if Mini was holding a hand over the speaker, muffling it. Seconds passed, then, "Basher, we're patching you in to the cabinet meeting. One of the President's aides just whispered the news to him and all hell's breaking loose. You'll be going over the speakers to the President's cabinet. Tell them what you saw, what the status is, and what you're doing to help. Can you handle it?"

"Copy that," Scott said, leaning back in his chair. He kept his eyes glued to the monitors at the front of the room displaying the status of the ISS's systems. He may not be able to communicate with the ISS, but from here he'd be instantly able to relay any changes in the ISS, from the onboard sensors to even a change in altitude.

He blinked. *Change in altitude.* Now why did that cross his mind?

"Basher, Mini. Stand by one. We're patching you through to the White House communications agency."

The line chirped and suddenly sounded tinny, as though its digital signal was somehow being analyzed and encrypted.

"Lieutenant Colonel Robinson?"

Scott straightened in his chair. "Speaking."

"Sir, the President of the United States."

JAPANESE
MODULE (JPM)

Carefully grasping the wrenches and screwdriver, Kimberly flew out of the JPM. Once in Node 2, she took a hard right and headed for the opposite end of the station by grabbing the hatchway's inner handrail, changing her linear momentum to angular. The Klaxon still wailed throughout the ISS, and as she rounded the corner she didn't see anything at the far Russian end. Her field of view to the Russian SM module, roughly a hundred yards away, was constricted by both the size of each successive module's hatch, as well as her path as she propelled herself to the aft side of the ISS.

She soared into the U.S. lab, taking care not to hit the metal vestibule opening. Holding the makeshift weapons in front of her, she exited the aft end of the lab within seconds and thrust her hands down, causing her legs to rotate in the opposite direction. As she passed into Node 1 she kicked out, hitting the vestibule, which shot her toward the Joint Airlock entrance, like banking a pool ball off the side of the table.

She flew into the airlock, where Alexi Lashin and Viktor Ol-off, the two remaining Russian cosmonauts, and Robert Stafford, her American colleague, had been preparing the EVA suits. They quickly grabbed handholds and pulled themselves out of her way as she zoomed in. Careful not to hit her wrenches or screwdriver, Stafford reached out and clutched her by the arm as she shot by, twirling her around and stopping her in the middle of the module instead of allowing her to whiz past and crash into the hatch.

One of the bulky EVA suits was rocking in its cradle, looking as though someone had been in the process of donning it. Four of the three dozen RTGs stored in MRM-1 were lashed together, floating near the outside hatch. Oloff swam to the vestibule and poked his head out, looking down the long series of interconnecting modules.

"Get back in here," Kimberly snapped. "Now."

Viktor jerked his head back inside the Joint Airlock. Pushing against the metal vestibule edge, he slowly floated back into the module and twisted around to look at her, his darkly stubbled face looking puzzled.

Robert's pale blue eyes were also perplexed as he steadied her. "What's going on? We heard the alarm—"

"You weren't watching the docking?"

Hanging upside down relative to Kimberly, Alexi shook his shaved head. "*Nyet*. We were helping Robert into his suit. We're moving the RTGs outside the station."

"Here." Kimberly shoved the tools at the three men. With quizzical looks on their faces they took the makeshift weapons, but instead of peppering her with questions, their cosmonaut and astronaut training kicked into high gear and they waited for Kimberly to explain, understanding that instead of wasting time asking questions, Kimberly would quickly bring them up to speed.

She glided to the module's vestibule, which opened to Node 1, and peeked outside. Quickly pulling back, she spoke in a hurried half whisper, briefing them on what had happened.

"They killed Colonel Zel'dovich?" Alexi asked, his voice half an octave higher than normal.

Kimberly nodded. "And Al. And Ivan." Something inside her wanted to break down and cry, but Kimberly pushed the possibility aside. Not now. Not ever. At least not 'til we get the bastards.

His face grim, Alexi gripped the wrench like a battle-ax and pushed off for the exit leading to Node 1.

"Alexi, stop!" Kimberly ordered.

He ignored her. He kept going until Viktor grabbed him by the foot. Alexi tried to shake off his grip, but he rotated toward the hatch. Turning, he glared at Kimberly, his face white with fury.

"We cannot allow those mad dogs to live," Alexi said. "I will stop them."

"No, not alone," said Kimberly. "You didn't see them. They're too well trained, extremely coordinated."

"The new one is tourist and unable to function in zero-gee. I kill him first." Alexi was built like a weight lifter, his chest and arms bulging inside his flight suit.

"And if you fail?" Kimberly challenged.

"I will not fail," Alexi muttered. He turned to go.

Viktor said, "Listen to Kimberly. You are right, comrade, but *we* will stop them, not just you. We work together." Turning to Kimberly, he asked, "You have plan?"

"Yes, I do." She moved up so she could keep an eye out the exit, to detect the intruders if they tried to surprise them. "They've cut off the comm links with Earth, so I imagine whatever they have planned, they're going to see it to the finish. Like I said, they looked well trained, so we'll have to surprise them, catch them off guard so we can stop them before they reach their goal, whatever it is."

"You mean we ambush them and then kill them," said Viktor. "So we hide."

"That's right," Kimberly agreed. "Viktor, you and Alexi wait in Node 3, then rush out together to surprise them. Robert, you hit them from the side, coming from here. I may be the smallest on board, but I'm faster than any of you. I can draw them out, make them chase me to Node 1."

Robert followed her gaze out the exit and frowned. "But what if they catch up with you?"

"They won't. I'll make sure of that. Farid's still getting his space legs back, and like Alexi said, the new guy, Bakhet, the Qatari tourist—he's still fumbling around, although that doesn't make them any less dangerous."

Viktor asked, "So how will you do it? What you say, 'Draw them out'?"

"I bet they're moving from aft to bow," Kimberly replied. "Probably methodically searching the entire ISS, hunting us down, module by module. Which means they'll be searching as a pair. So I'll start working my way aft, down by the SM module. When they spot me I'll shoot back here, toward Node 2. But I'll stop in the U.S. lab and incite them. When they enter Node 1 that's your signal to converge and spring the ambush."

"And kill them," Alexi said grimly.

Kimberly raised an eyebrow. "It would be nice to be able to question at least one of them, find out what they have in mind or if they're just insane." She hesitated. "But yes, after seeing what they've already done, I think our top priority is not just stopping them, but killing them." She looked around. "Any questions?"

The three men shook their heads.

"All right, let's go. Be sure to hide in your respective modules. As soon as they're in Node 1, go for it. I'll try to yell when they're there, but don't wait for me if you see them. I may not be able to give you a signal—I may be trying to survive myself."

"Right." The two Russians pushed off, Alexi and Viktor across the module, to Node 3.

Kimberly waited until they were out of sight, then started out. Robert grabbed her arm. "Good luck, kid."

"Thanks."

Following Kimberly to the hatch, Robert said, "Basher was serving as CAPCOM. Does he know what's going on up here?"

"He must have seen what I saw on the monitor, so hopefully he dropped NASA TV's feed to the public; but one of those murderers must have cut our comm to Earth. So Scott probably doesn't know we're still alive. *No one* may know."

"So if we don't succeed, then as far as NASA's concerned we were taken out when those guys docked."

"Yeah." Kimberly wanted to get started for the SM module, but Robert still clutched her arm.

He asked, "If we don't get them—if they kill us instead—what do you think those guys will do next?"

"I don't know," Kimberly said as she pulled free of Robert's hand and started aft. "Maybe they'll just kill themselves; maybe this is some sort of twisted suicide mission. In any case, let's not let them get that far."

NODE 1

Kimberly tried to get her breathing under control as she entered Node 1. Her heart was pounding wildly against her ribs; it seemed as though the *thump-thump-thump* could be heard throughout the ISS.

There was no sign of Alexi or Viktor. They were already hidden, out of sight and hopefully ready for the ambush. She tried to steel herself, knowing that if either of the murderers still had the knife Farid had used on Ivan Vasilev, they'd probably use it as soon as they spotted her. Which meant that she couldn't get too close, and she'd have to take evasive action so they'd never have a clean shot.

She'd have to make sure that they'd miss. Otherwise it might be the last thing she'd ever do.

Scott used to call it jinking, she remembered, when he told stories about trying to break the lock of a missile's radar on his F-22 and he'd have to whip the fighter back and forth, slamming the stick as far as it would go and maxing out the gees.

Now Kimberly knew she'd have to jink herself, careen from wall to wall off the sides of the modules as she tore back to Node 1 with the two murderers at her heels. Otherwise they'd find an open shot and she'd be as dead as Al Sweeting and the two Russians.

Or would they try to rape her first? Kimberly shuddered at the thought.

Panting, she looked down the long passageway of interconnected modules, from the closest—the Russian FGB—to the farthest, the SM. In the distance, a thick silver cylinder, one of the RTGs, dislodged from its mooring in MRM-2, tumbled slowly across her view. Behind her was the U.S. lab, where she'd be waiting while the guys sprang their ambush.

Since they'd killed Al in the SM, that meant they were probably going through either the DC-1 or the MRM-2, she reasoned. She didn't want to be trapped away from the guys, so she thought she'd barely venture into the FGB and hopefully flush them out there.

She'd turn and hightail it back here. The distance wasn't that far, barely thirty meters, but it was far enough for them to gain the advantage and kill her.

Which is *not* going to happen, Kimberly told herself firmly.

Now that her heart rate had slowed, she whispered loud enough for the guys in the modules at right angles to where she floated in Node 1 to hear her.

"Heading out to the FGB. Wish me luck."

She floated backward, looking for a place to plant her foot and push off, when Alexi popped his bald head out of Node 3. The hotheaded idiot was showing himself, and if the two intruders spotted both Alexi and herself it wouldn't take much for them to surmise that a trap was being set.

"Alex," she hissed. "Down."

At that instant the two intruders rotated into the Russian SM module from DC-1, located at the far, aft end of the ISS. They'd probably been searching the DC-1 module, located perpendicularly to the SM, and from the time they'd taken must have done a thorough job, trying to ferret out any crew member who might have been hiding. They really were being methodical, moving from aft to bow and leaving no compartment unsearched.

Alexi spotted the two at the same time as Kimberly. Grasping the hatch with a massive hand, he swung out of the vestibule and kicked off after the intruders. His face contorted with rage, he bellowed something in Russian, holding the foot-long wrench in front of himself as he flew from Node 1 into the FGB.

"Alexi! No!" Kimberly felt the words come out as a scream, terrified that by jumping the gun he would only get himself killed.

She heard a commotion as Robert scrambled out of the Joint Airlock. Half a moment later Viktor shot out of Node 3; both men were holding their makeshift weapons out in front of them. They flew past Kimberly looking as if they'd been mainlining adrenaline.

Robert's eyes were wide, his face flushed. He twisted in the air and hesitated. "Where . . . where are they?"

"There!" Viktor pointed his long wrench down the modules as he kicked off to join his Russian comrade.

Without a word, Robert planted a booted foot on the wall and took off, following him.

Kimberly didn't know what she should do. She had to help the guys, but couldn't think of anything right off that would target only the two intruders and wouldn't affect all of them. She was certainly no match for them using another makeshift weapon, and if any of the big lunks didn't keep on the offensive and instead tried to protect her, it might end up getting one of the guys hurt.

But what could she use to help them, other than one of the tools? She could duck into the JPM and pull out one of the lasers, but they were all eye-safe and relatively harmless. There were plenty of toxic chemicals stored on board but using them could end up harming herself and the ISS more than the intruders if she tried to spray them around indiscriminately.

Watching from across the distance of the two modules she heard Alexi roar like a bull as he dashed into the FGB, his hands outstretched. Viktor and Robert were no more than a couple of feet behind him, also brandishing their weapons and bellowing madly.

Alexi flew straight toward the tourist, Bakhet. The man didn't move; it was almost as if he'd given up any hope of defending himself.

Kimberly realized it was a trap.

"Alexi!" she screamed. "Watch out!"

Farid suddenly shot out from the left, knife in hand. He slammed into Alexi as Bakhet ducked, allowing Farid to bowl over Alexi. They spun through the air with wild, slashing thrusts. Farid sliced open the side of Alexi's throat. The bald Russian spun around in the module, blood spurting from his veins in tiny, pulsating spheres.

Bakhet slipped out of Kimberly's sight as Viktor and Robert flew into the module. They both tried to use their tools on Farid, but Kimberly heard a loud grunt as Robert was suddenly struck by Bakhet in the middle of his back.

They started clawing at each other, but Bakhet grabbed one of Robert's ankles and jerked him deeper into the module, like a fish being yanked out of the water. Bakhet wrapped both arms around Robert, then slid one arm up around his neck. He jerked violently, once, twice, and Robert suddenly went slack. Bakhet pushed the body away and they both floated apart.

Blood was spurting from Viktor's arm as he and Farid continued to spar. Bakhet joined the fight and the two murderers backed Viktor deeper into the module, moving out of Kimberly's field of view. An instant later Viktor's body spun out of the module's hatch, limp, lifeless.

Kimberly was gasping hard, furious with herself for not having joined the melee. Maybe she could have helped, at least distracted the two intruders while the guys worked together to defeat them. That had been her plan in the first place; if Alexi hadn't jumped the gun they might all three be still alive.

As she might not be in an extremely short time if she didn't get away and find something to defend herself with.

The first thing she had to do was regroup and find a weapon. She could analyze the situation later. Right now she had to survive.

NODE 3

Kimberly kicked out with her leg, hitting one of the containers secured to the ISS wall, and rapidly pushed off for Node 3. Entering the module, she shot across the spacious volume, not knowing if Farid and his partner had seen where she'd gone. The vestibule to the inflatable Bigelow module was on her left, and she could hide in the Bigelow—but since the unit was nowhere near as large as the other modules and wasn't storing much equipment, they'd quickly rummage through whatever was in there and spot her. Worse, if they didn't kill her they might lock her inside the inflatable module by bolting the hatch shut.

And then what could she do? She'd be trapped without any way to get out or even to fight back. There wasn't even a spacesuit in there, like the EVAs stored in the Joint Airlock or the smaller, second-generation suit she'd temporarily moved to the JPM.

Desperately swinging her head, scanning everything in sight, she spotted a stack of white container bags tied together in a bungee jail at the far end of Node 3, next to the node's commercial spacecraft docking port and the Cupola that gave an unobstructed view of Earth as they orbited around it.

She didn't have time to unzip one of the bags, empty its contents, and try to squeeze into it. The bag's contents floating around the node would be a dead giveaway to what she'd done. But she did have time to hide behind the stack of bags. Maybe.

Kimberly pushed over and started pulling apart the bungee cords that held the bags to the module's side, one eye on the hatch where the intruders would soon appear. She yanked the cords apart and pried open a slit just large enough for her to squeeze through and wriggled into the opening, then wedged herself in behind the bags. She turned and smoothed the cords back into place, then pushed herself deeper into the bungee cord jail that typically flexed enough to allow pulling the bags apart.

It was like slipping behind the living room sofa when she was younger, playing hide-and-seek with her friends. Most of the bags were filled with soft stuff, like clothing supplies and dehydrated foods. She edged those out of her way as she burrowed deeper into the pile. Other bags felt hard, metal objects such as spare parts and equipment. Kimberly tried to use them as a buffer between her and the softer bags, in case the intruders started poking through the pile with something sharp.

Pushing to the back of the stack, she pressed against the white insulation covering the module wall that kept in the station's heat while protecting its innards against the vacuum's deathly cold, bare inches away. Her heart was racing again and she deliberately slowed her breathing with deep, steady breaths, trying to breathe without making a sound.

She waited. She could hear the hum of the air changers working in the background and the creaks and barely audible groans of the space station as it slightly expanded and contracted from the temperature gradients caused by having one side of the structure exposed to harsh sunlight, the other to the cold darkness of shadow.

She didn't move.

She thought she heard the sounds of the two intruders as they made their way through the modules. After disposing of her crewmates—no, after *murdering* her crewmates—disposing was too dispassionate, too technical a term, one that can be used at arm's length. They've murdered six men, Kimberly thought, and now they were hunting for her.

They weren't just intruders, they were cold-blooded butchers who were intent on slaughtering the entire crew of the ISS for some unknown, bizarre reason. There was no way to justify what they had done or what they were planning to do—if they even had a plan. And the more she confronted the reality of what had happened and the real possibility that they'd kill her as well, the better chance she had to accomplish her number one priority—survival.

She heard one of the killers enter Node 3 and held her breath. It sounded as if he bumped against the aft wall, next to the inflatable Bigelow module. The other one was apparently staying outside Node 3, probably standing guard in case Kimberly tried anything else from elsewhere in the ISS. She heard the sounds of containers being opened and equipment shoved from one location in the Bigelow module to another, Velcro straps being ripped apart, the clinking of metal against the Node 3 hatch.

Kimberly couldn't hold her breath any longer. She let it out in a long, slow, quiet sigh.

No reaction from the murderer searching the module. She felt a wave of gratitude surge through her. The two killers didn't speak much as they went about their search, just a few short, curt words in Russian. Which made sense, Kimberly reasoned. Even though Farid was a Kazakhstani and Bakhet from Qatar, they'd both had to be able to speak fairly fluent Russian during their cosmonaut training.

Was Bakhet really from Qatar? Kimberly wondered. That's

what his biography claimed. But it didn't make any difference if he was from Qatar or Mars, right now. All that mattered was that they were both trying to hunt her down. Kimberly decided that if she survived the next few minutes, after the two of them left Node 3 she'd make a break for their Soyuz capsule.

At least she'd be able to hole up there and see what they were up to while staying safely away from them. And if necessary she could use the Soyuz as an emergency escape vehicle and return to Earth, leaving the two murderers alone on the ISS.

She'd make that decision later, she told herself. Perhaps much later. Right now she concentrated on staying alive.

The one in the Node 3 module moved closer to the stack of storage bags. He rattled the mesh of bungee cords that held the stack together, then pushed a hand through an opening on the side and rummaged through a few of the containers. Kimberly kept absolutely still and held her breath.

The intruder moved away from the bags. Kimberly heard him going through the equipment that was fastened to the other side of the module, banging the equipment around carelessly.

The other man came into the module and the two of them exchanged a few words. Not in Russian, Kimberly thought, trying to puzzle out the language they used. Were they satisfied that she wasn't hiding among the bags? Or would they now try to open up the bungee mesh and start going through the MO bags one by one? If so, they'd discover her.

On the other hand, if they left the module, then she could quickly bolt for the Soyuz. When they didn't find her anywhere in the station they'd eventually return and start their hunt all over again.

She thought she heard them start to leave, but suddenly there came the sound of someone pushing off from a foothold. An instant later she was pushed violently back and hit her head against the insulated wall. She tried to keep from gasping as the air was shoved out of her lungs and she momentarily lost her breath.

A ripping sound sliced through the module, and Kimberly realized they were using something long and sharp to try to pierce the bags. It must be the titanium prybar that the Russians used to open stuck hatches, she realized. Time after time she heard the white canvas cloth rip as they repeatedly stabbed the meter-and-a-half-long bar through the pile of bags. Every few thrusts she heard a sharp metallic clang as their weapon hit equipment stored among the other supplies.

The murderers jabbed the stack in a random pattern, sometimes pushing the prybar slowly through the pile, other times taking a leaping start from across the module to fly across Node 3, impaling several bags at once. They laughed and chattered at each other. They were having fun!

Kimberly pressed back against the insulated wall as two jabs in quick succession came close—one near her hip and the second just inches from her right eye. Clenching her teeth hard to keep from crying out, she caught a quick glimpse of the prybar and felt sweat beading her brow. The long slender rod was curved at one end and tapered to a blunt point at the other. The metal could easily slice her into pieces.

The killer jabbed the prybar through the stack, then after a seeming infinity of time he stopped, apparently satisfied that Kimberly wasn't there.

She heard the two men exchange a few words, then their voices drifted away. Minutes passed, and when she didn't hear anything more Kimberly assumed they'd left Node 3.

Since they were advancing down the ISS from the aft, or Russian side of the station, toward the bow at the opposite, American end, she knew that they'd either be searching the U.S. lab or Node 2 next. Then she could make her move.

She silently counted a few more minutes to make sure they weren't still in the module, hiding, waiting for her to reveal herself. After another minute, she thought she could make out sounds from beyond the hatch of them searching another module. Slowly, cautiously, she inched forward and slid between the shredded bags.

The module was littered with plastic mesh and what was left of the contents of the bags. Shards of tattered cloth, ripped clothing, torn pieces of food, even broken electronic equipment floated weightlessly in midair, slowly rotating, bouncing off the insulated walls of the module; one of the thick cylindrical RTGs had drifted in. The module looked as though a herd of wild, starving cats had been thrown into a zero-gee compartment laced with catnip.

Quietly, Kimberly pushed through the floating debris and coasted toward the Node 3 starboard hatch, which led back to Node 1. She hovered in the vestibule, just inside the module, listening for any sign that the killers were near. In the distance she could hear the two of them talking. And laughing. *Laughing*, Kimberly thought, an icy resolve settling over her like a coat of armor.

She started to head out of the module when she noticed, secured to the wall, an American toolbox. One of the guys must have moved it here temporarily when they were bringing in some equipment from the Bigelow module.

She quickly floated over and rummaged through the fastened-down equipment. There it was! Shep's knife, a folding lock, tanto-style blade. She unfastened the ultrasharp knife from its holder, her spirits soaring. Shep's knife didn't have the reach of that titanium prybar, but after Bill Shepherd had smuggled the sharp Ernie Emerson blade on board the ISS during the Space Shuttle era, the Americans had kept the unofficial tool aboard for those extratough jobs when their official, and much duller, blades just couldn't get the job done.

Kimberly held Shep's knife in one hand as she returned to the hatch. She waited a moment.

The murderers had stopped talking. She couldn't detect any sign of their presence. Maybe they were already searching the JPM, where she'd been when they'd docked. If that was the case they'd be at the far bow of the ISS, which would allow her plenty of time to get to the Soyuz, perhaps even undetected.

PURSUED

Kimberly hesitated another moment, and then decided it was time to go. Holding Shep's knife in her right hand, she grabbed the edge of the Node 3 starboard hatch with her left as hard as she could, pushing away at the last moment to keep her momentum from swinging her around. She flew headfirst into Node 1, and once clear of the Node 3 hatch she kicked at the vestibule to change her direction and head down the ISS to the far, aft end.

She'd tried to be as quiet as she could, but one of the two must have seen her. As she soared through Node 1 she heard an excited shout come from behind her.

Crap! She felt as though she'd been doused with a bucket of cold water. She flew through the air with her hands out in front of her, still holding the knife. She didn't dare look behind her, but she figured that they must have already pushed off in hot pursuit.

Time seemed to slow to a crawl. Although she was flying quickly through the air, to Kimberly it seemed as if she only crept toward the Russian FGB module.

She knew she was moving much too slowly. She hadn't been able to kick off as aggressively as she normally would; she wanted to get out of Node 1 as quickly as possible because although she'd thought the two intruders had been in the JPM, they might actually be much closer.

And they were.

Time seemed to slow even more and it took almost forever to reach the FGB.

Finally. Just another few feet through the Russian FGB module and she'd be in the SM. Then she'd be able to make a sharp upward turn to the zenith, into MRM-2 where the Soyuz was docked. She reached out with her fingers, wanting to claw her way through the empty air of the zero-gee environment, but there were no handholds or places for her to kick off so that she could travel faster. She was stuck with her tortoise-like movement through the air.

She felt a surge of adrenaline as she finally approached the SM hatch—

Something sharp, fast, and hard whizzed past her. Her hip suddenly flared with pain. Kimberly doubled over and brought her free left hand to her hip. It felt warm, sticky blood.

And something was clanging out ahead of her. She spotted the Russian titanium prybar bounce off the side of the hatch and come twirling back toward her, spinning end over end.

Kimberly ducked and the long, sharp-edged metal bar barely missed her. But her motion in midair had rotated her body and instead of slipping through the SM hatch and kicking off for the Soyuz, her torso slammed against the metal vestibule between the FGB and SM.

Gasping with pain and fright, she looked up and saw Farid hurtling toward her, his arms stretched out as if he was aiming straight for her throat. Still rotating, Kimberly stuck out her bloody hand and grabbed the metal edge of the vestibule and yanked herself back into the FGB. She spun head over heels along the sidewall, at an angle to Farid and now hovering just below him.

Farid's forward momentum prevented him from stopping or

turning around. He hit the vestibule where Kimberly had just launched herself. She knew she couldn't get to the Soyuz now; she either had to hide or somehow barricade herself into one of the modules. But that meant she had to get past Bakhet. She could see the tourist slowly, carefully making his way toward her; he was already in Node 2 and would soon be entering the U.S. lab.

She took her eyes off Bakhet as she bore straight toward the caution and warning panel of the FGB. If she timed things right she could get to the U.S. lab before the Qatari and hopefully before Farid was able to untangle himself and spring back in her direction.

Kimberly rotated in the air, and just before she hit the metal panel on the side of the module she twisted up, slamming her feet against the plate so she could push into Node 1 at an angle.

She flew across Node 1 and zoomed into the U.S. lab, hoping she could fly underneath Bakhet as she had done to Farid seconds earlier. But as she approached the Qatari, a searing pain flared down her arm, and instead of moving at a good angle toward the wall she headed straight for the blue European Space Agency storage bag.

She reached out and grabbed the container. The Velcro fastener ripped open and a potpourri of electronics hardware flew out, spilling everything from batteries, wires, solid-state lasers, and other lab equipment across the module. She twisted around and spotted a high-power flashlamp, used as an energy source for one of the old Russian solid-state lasers. She grabbed the device out of the air and groped to set its repeating mode.

Bakhet tumbled into the module and careened off the aft wall. Kimberly heard him grunt as if the air had been knocked out of him. She frantically looked for a place to kick off, but she still wasn't at an angle that would give her a good vector back toward the JPM and away from the Soyuz.

There was no way she'd be able to get past the two of them and be able to lock herself inside one of the three Russian modules. But as she quickly ran through her options, she got the gut feeling that if she could get back to the JPM she should be able to jury-rig some sort of device that would allow her to come back and punch through both the murderers.

She heard a sound behind her. Turning, she saw Farid soar through the portal, aiming straight at her. Desperately, Kimberly held up the flashlamp, squeezed her eyes shut, and stabbed at the power switch.

She felt a staccato of hot flashes on her face and through her closed eyes sensed a bright red pulsating flare. The afterimage glared in her vision as she opened her eyes and bounced off the far wall of the module.

Farid screamed a loud, guttural screech, his hands clasped over his eyes. Bakhet was bent over double, wailing and pawing at his eyes. Kimberly twisted and kicked out, trying to get past Farid while he was temporarily blinded.

He randomly flailed out with both hands, trying to grab her. Trying to make herself as small as possible, Kimberly ducked beneath him, but as she flew past she felt his clawlike hands rake down her back. Her momentum changed, and for an instant she thought she wouldn't reach the vestibule. She reached out and hit the hard metal edging of the hatch and bent her body through the portal and into the next module.

Now inside Node 2 she made a hard left into the JPM, still blinking at the searing afterimage of the flashlamp. Behind her she heard Farid and Bakhet talking; calmer now, they were regrouping, starting after her again, only seconds behind.

As Kimberly entered the JPM she realized she'd never be able to jury-rig a weapon quickly enough to stop them. She'd have to hole up, somehow barricade herself inside the Japanese module until she had the time to gather her wits and prepare for another tangle with the murderers. And this time, she hoped, she'd be better prepared.

As she flew through the vestibule into the Japanese module she spotted a VAJ—a vacuum access jumper—rolled up and secured by the hatch. It gave her an idea, and she rapidly raced through the pros and cons of it. At first she dismissed it out of hand, but the more she thought about it the better it sounded.

Her entire decision-making process took less than a few seconds, but she knew exactly what she had to do. She reached out and grabbed the tie that held the VAJ.

BARRICADED

Clutching the VAJ to her chest, Kimberly pulled herself into the Japanese module. She quickly unfastened the vacuum access jumper and unrolled its metal hose. It spread out in midair, writhing slightly like a weightless snake.

Kimberly turned to the vestibule.

There was a two-foot clearance between the hatches of Node 2 and the JPM. If she could evacuate the air in the vestibule after closing the hatches on either side, there was no way the intruders would be able to get to her. Kimberly mentally calculated that with the size of the ISS hatch, the 14.7-psi air pressure pushing against the 176,400 square inches of hatch area would exert nearly *twelve tons* of force, keeping the hatches closed.

She raced through the checklist attached to the VAJ, knowing that she had only a few seconds to act. Better get it right the first time, she told herself.

First she closed the Node 2 hatch. She unstowed the crank handle, rotated it out, and started twirling the lever like crazy. When it stopped she moved it back, then went through the JPM's hatch and shut it by grabbing the quick release handle. It closed with a satisfying clang.

Okay. Next step is to evacuate the vestibule.

Kimberly uncapped the pressure equalization valve, grabbed

the VAJ, and connected its green fabric-covered metal hose to the experimental vacuum manifold, leading to the vacuum of space.

Through the small viewport in the hatch she saw Farid suddenly appear. She hoped the seals were tight, but she didn't have time to worry. If they got in they'd kill her, she knew, and she thought she'd rather die in the cold vacuum of space than have those two bastards slit her throat.

She pushed off for the laptop and rapidly typed in the necessary commands, calling up a schematic of the JPM module and opening the valve to the vacuum outside.

With a barely audible *whoosh* the air in the vestibule connecting Node 2 with the JPM was released to space.

Kimberly saw tiny crystals of ice swirl around the outside exit as the humid air expanded and instantly froze in the cold grip of vacuum. They looked beautiful, like a sprinkling of fairy dust. She thrilled at the sight, and even more so at the realization that her plan had actually *worked*.

In the back of her mind she felt grateful that the ISS was the first complex vehicle designed from the ground up to be operated through computer graphical interfaces instead of hardwired mechanical control panels, allowing any laptop to operate the station. Maybe I'll be able to take advantage of that to gain control of the station again, she thought.

She realized she was hurting. Dull, sullen pain throbbed in her hip and her arm. She saw Farid still at the Node 2 hatch. He pounded against the glass but she couldn't hear anything across the vacuum interface of the vestibule. He glared through the thick window, his eyes wild. Spittle spewed from his mouth, his nostrils flared.

Kimberly was too tired to face him. She hurt too much. She floated up and away from the hatch's viewport. She was effectively barricaded from the murderers; she was safe in the JPM—for the time being. They couldn't open their hatch to get to her, and even if they got themselves into an EVA suit, the spacesuits were much too large for the JPM airlock, which was designed to expose small experiments to vacuum. It was barely big enough for the second-generation suit Kimberly had stowed in the module.

She caught a glimpse of movement in Node 2, down where the pressure release valve to the vestibule was located. Floating slowly upward to get a better view, she saw that Farid was trying to open the pressure equalization valve. Kimberly drew back, wondering if the idiot wanted to kill all of them.

He could certainly try to open the valve, she knew, but the air would have to rush completely out of both Node 2 and the entire ISS before they could even open their own hatch. And even if they did that, they *still* couldn't open her hatch to the JPM: try as they might there was twelve tons of pressure pressing her module's airlock hatch against the vacuum.

Kimberly realized that there was a slight chance they could get through, though. Not impossible, yet an incredibly small chance, and they'd have to be awfully quick—and lucky: The viewports were 8 inches in diameter, ¾-inch-thick glass, with two panes separated by 2 inches. If they tried to smash the viewport on her hatch they would have to shatter their Node 2 window first, probably using the titanium prybar. That would repressurize the vestibule while the air in the entire ISS would start escaping via the VAJ hose. Then they'd have to smash the JPM hatch window, which would rapidly decompress the JPM while they attempted to enter the module and go after her.

The decompression would happen so fast that it would probably kill them before they could accomplish whatever they had planned for the ISS.

So they'd kill her but they'd also end up dying themselves. In the time it would take them to get into the JPM most of the air in the whole space station would be forever lost to space, and they would *all* end up dying.

So why would they even try?

Unless their real purpose for this insane attack was only to kill everybody on board, including themselves.

But why try to do that? It would have been much easier just to sabotage a few resupply rockets than to go to all the trouble of getting two radicalized cosmonauts on board the ISS. It just didn't make any sense.

On the other hand, Kimberly thought, with two murderers imperiling the whole ISS by trying to evacuate the air in the vestibule, nothing made much sense.

She saw both Farid and Bakhet gesticulating wildly in Node 2. She still couldn't hear what was going on, but it looked as though they had discovered that the air in Node 2 was escaping into space. They probably also realized that by the time they'd be able to get to her, the air supply throughout the ISS would be totally gone.

Again Farid turned to the hatch. He pounded angrily on the thick glass plate, but Kimberly still couldn't hear any sounds. His eyes bulged out and his face turned so red it looked as if all the blood in his body had welled up to his head. He shook a fist at her.

Kimberly slowly floated down until her nose nearly touched the JPM's viewport. They were only two feet apart, but separated by the tons of force clamping the two hatches shut.

As Farid raged on, his face red and contorted, his arms flailing, Kimberly's mind raced, trying to think of what she could do to stop the two, no matter what they had in mind. They wanted to kill her, she knew, but what else? What was their final objective?

Before she turned away from the viewport she kept her face stone cold, showing no emotion except icy, frigid contempt as she stared them down.

Then as slowly as she could she moved her right hand in front of her face, gradually closed it into a fist, and then, millimeter by millimeter, raised her middle finger until it stood fully upright.

She pushed it to touch the viewport. As Farid's eyes widened at the obscene gesture, Kimberly mouthed a silent *Fuck you.*

ASSESSMENT

Obviously furious, Farid pounded harder on the viewport but Kimberly couldn't hear a sound because the vestibule was in vacuum. If the situation weren't so deadly serious, she thought, this could be a great physics demonstration to beam down to school-kids, showing the need of an atmosphere to transmit sound waves.

Kimberly turned her back to the viewport, realizing that she had little time for speculation. She pressed her hand against her hip and winced. The bleeding had stopped but it hurt like hell. The hip was bruised as well as cut. Her arm was bruised, too, and she knew that it was going to be sore.

She pushed off and found a small first aid kit. While bandaging the hip, she tried to assess the situation.

She was safe for the time being. As long as she kept the VAJ attached to the bleed-off port, the vestibule would remain in vacuum, and the enormous force of both Node 2's and the JPM's 14.7-psi atmosphere would keep the hatches tightly sealed.

She glanced through the JPM for a quick inventory. She had plenty of air, electrical power, and heat to survive. There was only one laptop in the module; she remembered that the guys had borrowed the other three for Robert's EVA. But from the one, she could control nearly all the functions of the ISS's systems. Farid shouldn't be able to cut off any of the JPM's vital systems, she thought. Kimberly remembered from Farid's bio that he had been a computer specialist, and she assumed that he had kept his skills current. He might even know the onboard systems better than I do, she worried.

Her eyes rested briefly on the water and meal pouches that she'd kept in the JPM for when she was too involved running experiments to go out and eat with the rest of the crew. I'm set for food, she told herself. And she'd be able to use nearly any of the sealable experiment containers to hold her bodily wastes when she had to relieve herself.

In a perfect world she'd be able to think of some way to over-power the two intruders, but she realized that in reality she might be in this situation for the long haul—maybe even as long as it took for the next mission to reach the ISS. Or sooner, she mused, if the people on the ground were considering a rescue flight.

Which reminded her that now that she had the basics to sur-vive, her top priority was to communicate with NASA.

She floated over to the American laptop and tried to access the comm link.

Nothing.

She tried various options, individually accessing each of the four downlinks, but couldn't get a response from any of them. She tried to connect with the satellite cross-link. Still nothing.

Kimberly drew in a breath. Farid must have already disabled the system. Probably his first priority, after murdering the crew. So does that mean that NASA doesn't even know I'm still alive? They probably don't even know that the rest of the crew's been murdered.

So what are Farid and his fake tourist cohort, Bakhet, trying to do? she wondered. None of this made any sense. She'd under-stood that Farid had been a valuable member of the crew on his last mission three years ago: quiet, bright, quick to learn. He must know every system and computer network on board. Kimberly understood that she was facing a true insider, one who knew the ISS as well as she did. Maybe better.

Three years ago Farid must have suspected that his stint on the ISS would probably be the last time he'd be in space. The missions didn't come cheap, and if it hadn't been for the Russians throwing the Kazakhstanis a token bone of allowing them a flight every so often, Kazakhstan would never have had a man in space.

So why would the Kazakhstani cosmonaut turn on them? Neither Farid nor his comrade Bakhet had spewed any religious ranting. Had he been radicalized in the past three years? Was that why he'd turned into a cold-blooded killer?

And who was this supposed billionaire Qatari tourist, Bakhet? He and Farid are obviously in cahoots, but what are they up to? What are they trying to do?

And what can I do to stop them?

They'd physically dominated all the Russians and Americans aboard the ISS, so she knew she'd have to use her brains to defeat them rather than brawn. She had to come up with a plan to either best them, or give herself enough time to make it to the newly docked Soyuz—or perhaps even their escape vehicle, the extra Soyuz—to get back to Earth.

But whatever their motivation, whatever their purpose, Kimberly knew there would be no reasoning with them. She'd seen what they could do and knew full well that no amount of logic was going to change their minds. She mentally raced through the probabilities and kept getting the same, inevitable answer:

It was either her or them.

JOHNSON SPACE CENTER, ISS CONTROL CENTER, HOUSTON, TEXAS

Low, urgent voices swirled all around Scott Robinson as he sat at the ISS CAPCOM console. He'd just been patched through to the President's cabinet meeting.

Spread around him, the ISS control center looked like a barely controlled bedlam. Next to Scott a hundred men and women were busily, frantically working their consoles, each person desperately focused on understanding what had happened aboard the space station and what was currently going on.

Scott tuned out all that commotion and focused his attention on the phone, unconsciously tightening his earphones as he spoke into his throat microphone. "Mr. President, this is Lieutenant Colonel Scott Robinson, today's CAPCOM—NASA's astronaut liaison to the ISS."

The President's voice came through Scott's headphones,

sounding rushed, impatient, not at all like what Scott had previously heard at the State of the Union or other speeches.

"Colonel, Administrator Patricia Simone tells me you can bring us up to speed on exactly what happened on the International Space Station."

"Yes, sir," said Scott. "I can relate the activities up to the moment that communications were cut." He quickly summarized the events that he remembered, drawing out the details of cosmonaut Ivan Vasilev's brutal murder, as well as his decision to cut the public feed to NASA TV.

The President asked, "Has anyone else died?"

"We're working on that, Mr. President. All four comm links and the satellite relay have been cut, but we're still receiving information over the data links used for onboard science experiments."

"Do you know if there are any survivors?"

"Not yet. We're trying to patch into the ISS systems through the data links—basically hack into the sensors that are located throughout the station to find the location of any astronauts or cosmonauts. These are sensors such as temperature—"

"Will you be able to distinguish between the astronauts," the President interrupted, "and these . . . terrorists?"

Scott shook his head. "No, sir; that's highly unlikely. But we may be able to tell how many people are on board and where they're located. We may even be able to tell from the amount of carbon dioxide present if the individual is large or small, depending on the amount and rate that CO_2 is being generated— but those readings may also be an indication of a high level of exertion."

The President didn't respond, although Scott heard a muttered discussion on the other end of the line; low murmurings in measured voices.

A familiar voice came over his headphones. "Scott, Patricia

Simone here. Were you able to identify if *both* Farid and the tourist, Adama Bakhet, were responsible for the murders over the video link, or was it just Farid?"

Straightening, Scott replied, "We're not sure, ma'am. We didn't get too much footage before the link was severed, but we've already sent what we have to NASA Headquarters. And our folks in the image analysis group in Building A here at JSC are poring over what didn't appear on NASA TV's public feed; we'll shoot HQ a copy of the details as they come up."

The President came back on the line. "And I assume that Johnson Space Center knows of no motivation for this attack."

"That's correct, sir. We were caught just as flatfooted as everyone else. We're sending all the psychological data we have on the two to Headquarters, as well as working with our colleagues in Russia."

"So we don't know why this happened, how they pulled it off, or even if there is anyone still alive on board the ISS."

"That's correct, Mr. President. But again, we're working on it."

The line was muffled as another discussion appeared to take place among the cabinet members. Then the President resumed, "I'm ordering other agencies to work with NASA, to determine what happened, to recommend possible options for bringing communications back to the ISS, and to recommend any other action. The NSA and DoD will be contacting your center shortly for the latter two, and the CIA about the former. I've directed that all their tools be placed at NASA's disposal. In the meantime, you are to keep Patricia informed of any changes on the ISS, or if you discover any motivation for this heinous crime. My top priority now is to find out if there are any astronauts or cosmonauts still alive on the ISS and what it will take to help them. Understand, Colonel?"

"Yes, sir," Scott answered, suddenly aware that he'd been

tasked to speak for NASA. But he knew that *that* wouldn't last long. As soon as Patricia Simone was out of the cabinet meeting he'd get his marching orders from Headquarters. NASA took its chain of command seriously, as did he—especially as a military officer. But be that as it may, he wasn't about to argue with the President; that would all be sorted out later.

"And one more thing," the President added. "I want to know the second that communications are reestablished with the station."

"Yes, sir, Mr. President. I understand completely—" Scott stopped in midsentence.

"Excuse me?" said the President.

The control center's giant monitor suddenly blinked.

The control room fell dead quiet, as if all one hundred people across its floor had been frozen in a block of ice.

Stunned, Scott spoke slowly. "Mr. President . . . you'll get that last order you gave me fulfilled sooner than you'd think."

Sounds of chairs shifting. "How's that?"

"The link with the ISS . . . it's just been brought up."

JAPANESE MODULE (JPM)

Kimberly's hands flew over the keyboard, trying to determine exactly where the two killers were located in the ISS, when the monitor suddenly blinked and the ISS logo came up on her screen.

Her eyes went wide. One of the downlinks to Johnson had just been reestablished! Something was about to be transmitted.

Stunned, Kimberly's hands flew to her face. She didn't know what to think. After all her efforts to hack into the four downlink channels, and being thwarted every step of the way, this suddenly came out of left field. Had the link been brought up by Farid?

As if working on their own, her fingers raced across the keyboard once more, trying to send a message down to MCC, the NASA mission control center.

But her efforts were in vain. A visual image of Farid and his cohort Bakhet filled the screen. Once again, Farid's computer skills had overridden her efforts to send a frantic message down to NASA, to tell them she was still alive and she was going to do everything in her power to defeat these SOBs.

As she desperately tried to circumvent the digital quarantine that Farid had created against her, it dawned on Kimberly that this couldn't be just the work of one individual. Even Farid, with his profound working knowledge of the ISS, his insider know-how about how all the station's systems functioned, could never have managed to circumvent her efforts so quickly. This *had* to be more than one person working against her, and from the professional manner in which all her efforts had been circumvented, she realized that this had to be a highly organized endeavor.

This had been a well-planned attack on the ISS, to take total command and dominate every one of its functions, after first exterminating the station's crew. That meant they wanted absolute control of the station for some major, preplanned purpose.

As she came to this conclusion, Farid's voice, with his proper British accent from his Eton and Cambridge days, spoke over NASA's video and comm link to the world:

"Today marks the beginning of Dabiq, the Final End of the Folly. The glory of Al-Qahhar will dominate, and the world will see His victorious glory."

Kimberly drew in a breath. She remembered from her father's Islamic background that Al-Qahhar was the *Subduer,* the Supreme One and Irresistible—*not* the Compassionate and All Understanding, the Allah she had been brought up to trust and understand.

This was an incredible sharp turn from everything she'd been taught and led to believe since a little girl. Even worse, this was incredibly more dangerous. What did he mean, the Final End of the Folly? The *final?* Was he about to announce a harbinger to the Final End?

The view on the laptop's screen switched from Farid to an aerial view of New York City, taken either by Google Earth or perhaps the space station itself. The picture's resolution was so fine and detailed that Kimberly could see individual cars on the streets. Farid's voice came over the speaker.

"In four days the infidel city will cease to exist. The flaunting cesspool of wealth, the so-called International Space Station that keeps the downtrodden subdued, will hurtle from the heavens and crash into New York." A cartoon image of the ISS's thousand-mile path across the ground blinked next to the view of New York City; the path ran from Florida to New York.

"As a vengeful meteor from above, their godless monument of steel and technology will obliterate their center of depravity, their so-called financial center of the world, the fount of all evil. The one-million-pound space station will impact New York City with far more energy than the atomic bomb that devastated Hiroshima." The computer-generated graphic of the ISS's impact trajectory enlarged to fill the screen. "And as the ISS breaks up in the atmosphere, it will spew radiation in a path a thousand miles long and hundreds of miles wide, poisoning your country forever with plutonium. Your loathsome city will be destroyed, your contaminated east coast will be uninhabitable, and millions more will die.

"New York City—in four days, meet your death."

The video feed switched off.

For several shocked moments Kimberly stared at the now-blank laptop screen. She realized that her hands were trembling, shaking. Stop it! she commanded herself, and began to tap at the keyboard once more in an attempt to break into Farid's brief broadcast, to let NASA know that she was still alive, and to try to somehow stop this unbelievable insanity.

What was Farid thinking? Why would he do this? If his TV feed had been broadcast to the public, not only would the media go nuts, but there might well be rioting, terrified people by the millions trying to get out of the city, away from the coast, with car wrecks and traffic jams up and down the whole Eastern seaboard.

Did Farid *really* think he could somehow deorbit the ISS and crash it into a specific location, such as New York City? It was crazy to even think he could be that accurate. And spewing a radioactive path of plutonium? What was that about?

She suddenly felt cold. *The RTGs.* The Russians had just flown them up on the last Progress, compact nuclear power sources. It had been all over the news; everyone knew this was the next phase for the ISS in the human exploration of space. Each multimission radioisotope thermoelectric generator carried over ten pounds of Pu-238, or 360 total pounds of highly radioactive plutonium in the three dozen RTGs. Although the radioactivity would spread over a large distance, Pu-238 had a half-life of eighty-eight years and the public might never venture into the contaminated area . . . .

But the final target was so precise a location, and with the uncertainty of where the ISS might be deorbited, it was insane to even think that Farid could ever come close to hitting the city, or even New York state, for that matter. With the way the atmosphere changed from second to second, it would take incredibly good luck to hit anyplace from Florida to Maine.

But on the other hand, Kimberly realized, if the panic didn't come from the fear of impact, it would be the fear of being contaminated by a cloud of deadly plutonium falling from the sky. And if his broadcast had been transmitted to the public there could well be rioting and other acts of fear-driven violence, starting in New York and spreading up and down the coast, as well as inland. The average American didn't have a clue about radiation, how aerodynamics really worked, or even basic orbital mechanics. So although the threat of hitting New York and contaminating the eastern seaboard might be small, it was the panic and rioting that would cause all the damage.

And that nonsense about the station's one million pounds creating more carnage than an atomic bomb: the ISS's aluminum modules were thin-skinned. They would mostly burn up in the atmosphere, along with the solar panels and other pieces of equipment. Only about 5 percent of the million pounds would survive the burning reentry, resulting in no more than fifty thousand pounds impacting the ground. And even that wouldn't be all concentrated at one impact point, but rather would be spread across tens of hundreds of miles, just like the plutonium.

But try selling that to the general public. All they'd know is that the sky is falling, and they'd trample their own grandmothers to get away, *anywhere*, to be safe.

Kimberly felt her cheeks grow warm as she now realized that Farid's insane plan had a nugget of reality at its heart, and that she had to reprioritize her whole existence to one all-important goal: stop these SOBs.

JOHNSON SPACE CENTER, ISS CONTROL CENTER, HOUSTON, TEXAS

Déjà vu, all over again.

The mission control center erupted into a madness of yelling as the link from the ISS was cut. Monitors at the MCC started showing projected impact points if the station was to really be deorbited in four days, but the error bars on each of the locations spanned half the continent.

Scott felt his chest constricting as he realized what had just happened. The ISS had been overrun for the sole purpose of crashing the station into a populated area—New York or Los Angeles, it didn't matter, so long as it caused mass hysteria and the wild violence of millions of people seeking survival; and spewing plutonium as it descended was just icing on the cake. A terrorist threat that dwarfed anything ever attempted before.

His headphones clicked as he now heard frantic babble from

the White House: Everyone there was just as rattled as everyone here, Scott realized. The phone connection was no longer muted, but he still couldn't make out any details of the shouting. And with the noise in the control center ratcheting up as well, Scott couldn't even think.

He stood up and started clapping his hands again, as loudly as he could,

"Again, stop it! Quiet down!"

This time the control center quieted almost instantly. Most everyone looked angry, their faces red with the frustrating knowledge that there was nothing they could do to help. A few people sobbed. Tears filled some faces.

Scott spoke rapidly, knowing that at any moment he might be called to answer questions from the White House. He was thinking out loud, rehearsing what he'd say if—no, *when*—the questions from Washington started flooding in.

"You all know your jobs and I don't have to tell you how to do them. We're going to need to know the precise altitude of the ISS as a function of time, and couple that with the best information we have on the atmosphere, to keep an updated projection on the point of impact and the ground trajectory as it deorbits."

He made eye contact as he spoke, and he glanced at the placards above each console as the people turned to hear him.

TOPO, who tracks the ISS orbit

ADCO, ISS attitude

ETHOS, life support

RIO, U.S.-Russian activities

SPARTEN, power and solar panels

CRONUS, space communications and video

GC, ground control

BME, biomedical engineer

OSO, mechanical repair

PAO, public affairs officer

Where *was* the PAO? It hit him that the new female Voice-of-NASA had been the one who had bolted from the room. But he had more important things to worry about now.

Scott drew in a breath. Then, "In addition, we'll need every idea you can come up with on how to stop those bozos from carrying this out. I don't care how crazy an idea you might have, *everything's* on the table. The White House will be asking Administrator Simone to give them everything we've got, so start inventing, people!"

He stopped abruptly and put a hand to his headphones.

"Scott, Patricia Simone. We saw the feed, but did any of it go out to the public?"

Glancing down at his console, Scott saw that the kill switch to the NASA TV still glowed red.

"No, ma'am. CRONUS is keeping the public feed down. JSC and the White House are the only ones who saw the transmission."

"Finally, some good news." Simone sighed. "We're extending the press blackout, and the President has ordered that no one at NASA have any contact with the news media. I know that Johnson traditionally has the PR lead for the ISS, but I can't emphasize strongly enough how critical it is for Headquarters to be the focal point for interacting with the public. Brief your PAO, ASAP."

Scott glanced at the empty PAO console; the young Public Affairs Officer was still not at her post. Why had she left the MCC? He looked over his shoulder to the glassed observation balcony, searching out the senior PAO who had been escorting a gaggle of VIPs.

The VIPs were gone. Frowning, he saw the young PAO who had deserted her post directing emergency responders at the back of the balcony. It looked as though they were carting someone away. What the hell was going on? He turned his attention back to the Administrator. "Copy—I'll let him know."

"The media is already speculating about the murders," Simone continued, "and they're playing what little footage they have over and over again on TV all across the world: talk shows, Internet— it's saturating the news. They're reporting that everyone on the ISS must be dead, so let Headquarters handle this."

"Yes, ma'am."

"Thanks to your quick thinking the public probably isn't aware yet of the incredible disaster that could happen if the station is deorbited—"

"Excuse me, Madame Administrator. Surely you're letting the President and his cabinet know how remote the danger to New York actually is. We'll be lucky if we can project what hemisphere the ISS will hit, much less a specific city—until it's much too late to do anything."

"I understand. I've explained exactly that to him, and he appreciates the point. But it's not the impact he's worried about. It's the radiation, and the panic and rioting before the station hits. *Especially* if it gets out that we don't really have a clue this far in advance about where it could impact—or even what the radioactive debris path will look like. It could affect anyone on Earth."

"Copy," Scott said.

She quickly changed the subject. "Now what about our station partners? What kind of feedback are you hearing from other countries?"

Scott felt his face redden. This was going to be tough, especially with what he'd done to Roscosmos, the Russian Federal Space Agency. They're probably screaming bloody murder at NASA HQ and want his head on a plate. "I made the unilateral decision to cut out all the partners when I killed the feed to NASA TV."

"You mean Canada, ESA, and Japan?"

"Everyone, ma'am."

Simone hesitated. "Including Roscosmos?"

"Yes, ma'am. Even the Russians."

He heard her muffle the phone link with a hand over the speaker, but she quickly came back. "Okay. So we really *are* the only ones who heard the terrorists' transmission. The President will let us know when we can reengage with our station partners, so for now direct all inquiries and interactions no matter where they originate back to Headquarters. Understand?"

"Roger that." Scott felt somewhat relieved: Now smoothing over international relations was Simone's problem, not his. But as a retired three-star Air Force general who was currently NASA Administrator, she'd been doing that all her career.

"So what else do I need to know?"

"I've tasked everyone here in the center to do everything they can to update the projected impact point, from engaging the National Oceanic and Atmospheric Administration for real-time continuous feed of atmospheric density to working with the Air Force Space Command—who've already volunteered access to their classified orbital databases, as well as their Space Fence sensors. Their onsite liaison has been extremely helpful in getting us access."

"Good," said Patricia. "I'll speak to the Director of the National Reconnaissance Office and have them work with Johnson as well. They should be able to refocus their assets on helping us."

"Yes, ma'am."

She hesitated. "There's something else. I can't be getting down into the weeds over here. I've got to work with the White House at a strategic level to coordinate NASA's interactions with the media and our international partners, as well as running the agency. Scott, you were just up on the ISS, and you've done a great job during this crisis. I want you out here as my liaison with the National Security Council, be my conduit to understand what they're planning and what they should be doing. Get to Washington, stat, as fast as you can and head on over to the NSC—I'll have Headquarters pave the way."

"Copy," Scott said. "I've got a go-bag here at the office, so I'll file a flight plan and take one of the T-38s VFR direct to Andrews. I should be there in a few hours."

The Administrator switched off. Because Simone was a military officer during her own astronaut days, Scott assumed that now that she'd given the order there would be no question in her mind that it would be followed to the last detail. Luckily his small overnight "go-bag" was nearby, a habit he'd picked up while pulling alert during his F-22 days.

Next shift's CAPCOM had just entered the MCC and was making a beeline to relieve him. George Abbey, Director of Johnson Space Center, Chief Astronaut Fred Tarantino, the head of the astronaut office, as well as four other astronauts, the head of the flight director's office, and a half dozen staffers followed as well. Scott would brief them all and then be on his way to Washington.

Scott took off his headphones, pushed up from his seat, and moved out to do just that.

FLASHBACK: "NEVER GIVE UP..."

Newly promoted Major Scott Robinson was leading a flight of four F-22s over the ocean, escorting a Navy P-3 intelligence-gathering plane near the man-made islands that the Chinese had built in the South China Sea.

On the last few such intel flights, Chinese fighters had "accidentally" buzzed the unarmed Navy plane, flying close enough to raise the pucker factor even in the highly experienced commanders of the P-3s. Scott's orders were to protect the four-engined "snooper" and avoid any problems.

Contradictory responsibilities, Scott thought. But as he flew high above the steel-gray water he grinned to himself. Free as a bird, he thought. Far away from the cares and worries below. As a black Air Force flier, he knew all the subtle—and some not-so-subtle—snubs and hostilities of his fellow officers.

But up here it was different. Up here it was you and your aircraft, and all that other crap was a world away. Back on the ground, when some punkass cracker slighted him or made him the butt of a practical joke, Scott took it in good humor—until he got a chance to get even.

They started calling him Basher because of his attitude. "Never give up, never give in," was Scott's credo. With a smile.

Ten miles out, Scott was finally able to visually ID the five Chinese MiGs his flight had first tracked over a hundred miles away on radar. With their onboard sensors, he and his wingmen had long since divided up the MiGs between themselves on who would shoot who, should the situation deteriorate; it was time for the merge.

The warning signal beeped in Scott's earphones. His plane was being painted by Chinese air-to-air tracking radar.

Seconds later the Chinese leader buzzed Scott, flying canopy-to-canopy, inverted so close that Scott caught a glimpse of the pilot in his bulky flight suit as he whizzed by. Scott immediately slammed his fighter in a high-gee turn and within moments had the MiG in his sights . . . .

Accidentally—purely accidentally, he later swore—Scott touched his M61A2 20-millimeter cannon's trigger button. A stream of tracers lanced out after the MiG, missing it by a fair margin but close enough for everyone in the air to see.

The Chinese fighters broke off and headed home.

There was hell to pay at flight ops when Scott landed, but the furor died down after the big brass realized that the next intel flight was left alone. Nor were the P-3 missions ever bothered again.

"Never give up, never give in," Scott told himself. Up the ante until somebody folds.

The higher-ups were not amused. They never sent him out on an intel escort mission again. Scott saw a roadblock looming in his career path.

One way to get past a roadblock is to go around it.

The Air Force had no objections when, a few months later,

Scott applied for NASA's astronaut corps. The Air Force promoted him to lieutenant colonel and bid him a cheerful farewell.

Basher became a Space Cadet. But he didn't change. He was always the best at everything he'd tackled, and he made sure everyone knew it.

Then he met and fell in love and married fellow astronaut Kimberly Hadid.

And he still didn't change.

JAPANESE MODULE (JPM)

With her feet floating out behind her, Kimberly desperately tapped away at the laptop's keyboard. She kept her eyes glued on the high-resolution monitor as she typed, her frustration mounting with every passing moment.

She had tried every path she could think of to break into Farid's speech, frantically anxious to override his transmission so she could get out the word that she was still alive, that she had barricaded herself from the two killers, that she was trying everything in her power to stop them.

But every software attack she made—either through a direct, front-door attempt or by a covert, backdoor effort designed to be undetected—was immediately countered and stifled. She was stopped cold, as though they had been anticipating her every action. It was as if they were playing chess and they were reading her mind, keeping three steps ahead of her.

She tried to be more creative, tried altering their transmission to Earth by introducing modulated interference or random increases in power in order to send out distress signals. She even tried overriding the ISS antenna.

Nothing worked. Either Farid and Bakhet blocked her from accessing the subroutines she tried to modify, or they cut her off completely. She felt her frustration grow; nothing she tried seemed to work. She wondered how long the two murderers had trained for this one specific task: anticipating that someone might somehow survive their cold-blooded killing spree, and keeping any effort by that survivor to stop them at bay.

Their transmission blinked off and Kimberly saw that once again all the links to Earth were down.

She banged a fist against the laptop's support. Even with that open comm link to Earth, she'd been unable to reach NASA. So, in all probability, no one Earthside had any idea that she was still alive.

What else could she do? She wasn't about to give up. The fight with these guys had just started. But once they began to deorbit the station, the clock would begin ticking for an uncontrolled re-entry to Earth's atmosphere.

Kimberly knew that once the station's thrusters were fired it would be only a matter of a few days to slow the ISS enough so that it would dip into the upper atmosphere. And once atmospheric drag began slowing the station, it would become harder and harder to boost it back up.

So her goal was simple enough: make sure they didn't deorbit.

One way to do that was to stop them from accessing the thrusters' fuel. Without fuel, the thrusters can't work.

They might eventually circumvent her efforts, and carry out their insane plan to bring down the station, but at least this way she could buy some time, get some breathing space to think about how she could really defeat them.

She turned back to the laptop. Racing through the graphical interface, she used the ISS's Portable Computer System to gain administrative control of the station's external functions.

She didn't have to deal with any fuel pumps because the ISS

used pressure-fed hypergolic propellants: the fuel would instantly ignite when it came in contact with the oxidizer. Helium was used to pressurize the fuel and oxidizer tanks, so she had only to shut down the helium valves. Since that critical command required sending two control messages, Kimberly first removed the command that inhibited shutting the valve, then changed the valve state from ON to OFF.

There. That prevented the bastards from using the thrusters to deorbit, and also kept them from commanding emergency overrides that would bring them back up. Since it's been three years since Farid's been on the station, she figured, it might take him a while to figure out what had happened.

That gave Kimberly a little time.

Now for the longer, strategic plan.

She forced herself to slow her breathing and started coolly assessing her situation. She had to go about this logically, divorce her emotions from her actions, especially since at first she'd been frightened and thought only about her short-term survival.

But now she was really ticked off. Part of her wanted to get even, just as her father had told her all those years ago. No way I'm going to allow these terrorists to deorbit the ISS, certainly not without putting up a fight!

But she knew that she couldn't cloud her planning with anger. Not if she wanted to succeed. From somewhere she remembered an old adage: Revenge is a dish best served cold.

She started to set out her priorities, using the laptop to write them down so she could always go back and never forget what she'd committed herself to do, no matter how bleak things looked. She typed:

1. Stay alive, remain out of the hands of the terrorists, and communicate with NASA.

2. Prevent the terrorists from destroying the ISS.

3. Either render the terrorists helpless . . . or kill them.

So—first things first. She'd already accomplished two-thirds of priority one, but she still needed to get in touch with NASA and let them know she was still alive.

As an experimental physicist, she'd always had to jury-rig equipment to make it work right, no matter who the vendor was or how much they claimed it was "off the shelf" and ready to plug and play. High-tech equipment used for cutting-edge research *never* worked right out of the box, and Kimberly had quickly become adept at finding creative solutions to problems and making things work, even if they weren't really designed to work that way. Her secret was that once she decided what she needed the gadget to do, she worked backward and figured out a way to make it work the way she needed.

Okay, she thought. I've cut the terrorists off from access to the propellants they need to deorbit that station. Good. Now she had to figure out what she had to work with in order to survive, to communicate, and to stop the ISS from deorbiting. As well as neutralize Farid and his partner.

At present she had administrative control of the ISS, so she had plenty of air and power; but that may change, she knew, especially if they find some way to override her control as administrator. They might discover a way to get around her lockouts and cut her power and air. But for now, she'd have to trust that what she'd done would hold—at least temporarily. Time to move on to the next priority and find a way to communicate with the ground.

Mentally she raced through several options. She considered exploiting everything from the comm links transmitting data from her experiments in the JPM to directly accessing one of the numerous relay satellites that NASA had placed in orbit.

But while she considered the pros and cons of each alternative, in the back of her mind loomed the bigger problem: keeping the ISS from deorbiting.

She pushed that problem from her thoughts and focused on communicating with Earth. Nothing fancy, complex, or sophisticated: just a straightforward, simple way to talk . . .

And then it hit her. It seemed so simple that she didn't know why it hadn't been the first thing she considered.

Of course.

ARISS: Amateur Radio on the International Space Station. The ham radios had originally been brought to the station years ago to conduct a simple experiment to determine if it was possible to communicate with Earth via such low power devices. Kimberly knew that the program had succeeded and blossomed: ham operators chatted with the ISS continually. The station's last crew had even moved one of the three low-power radios to the JPM from the SM module.

She pushed to the opposite side of the compartment and started digging through a pile of equipment that had recently been moved to the Japanese module. There! She pulled out the Kenwood TM-D700 radio. Looking it over, Kimberly saw that it had two bandwidths of operation, 144–146 MHz and 435–438 MHz. She knew she'd normally be restricted to 25 watts of power, but she'd try to crank it up so she could contact more operators.

Several of the astronauts had used the old equipment, and although she hadn't used it much herself, Kimberly knew the basic principles of how to operate the amateur radio. Once she had it powered up she'd be ready to go. There was an external ham antenna accessible from the Columbus module and the SM, and hopefully when they'd moved the radio they'd added a patch to it from the JPM.

Five minutes later Kimberly started broadcasting, using

NA1SS as her call sign. It was the call sign for the space station and every ham radio operator knew it; they would immediately recognize its origin.

For the first time since the Soyuz had docked with the station, Kimberly felt as though she might really find a way out of this nightmare.

"Is this frequency in use? This is NA1SS. I say again, is this frequency in use?" Kimberly waited for ten seconds, and when no one replied, she said, "CQ, CQ, calling CQ. This is NA1SS: November-Alpha-One-Sierra-Sierra. Do you read?"

No one answered. She closed her eyes and ran through everything that could have gone wrong. Why wasn't it working? The antenna patch was up, she had the right frequency, and she was using the correct call sign. There should have been twenty or more callers lining up to have a chance to speak to someone on board the ISS. Why wasn't anyone answering?

Opening her eyes, she glanced out the JPM window.

And groaned.

Of course. She really was Doctor Obvious. Ham communications needed line-of-sight to make contact! And there was nothing below the ISS except water, as far as she could see.

The ISS was over the Pacific, and except for Australia, there were very few places that could respond.

She swam over to the laptop and pulled up the station's orbital parameters. They were on a descending node, crossing the Pacific Ocean, and beginning to start the long climb up over South America. It would be a while before they would be in a good line-of-sight for communicating.

She floated backward. She'd try again, but she wasn't about to wait. She needed to try something else.

So what next? Kimberly thought briefly about using the links that transmitted experimental data from the JPM to the ground station at Marshall Space Flight Center. All the ISS experimental data were relayed to the Payload Operations Center in Huntsville. If the links were still up and running she wouldn't be able to transmit voice or anything else, but she could modify the data, just like she had tried to modify Farid's crazy transmission of the threat to deorbit the ISS.

She pushed over to one of the experiment platforms, the same one she'd been using earlier when the station was boarded. The crystal growth experiment used a handheld sub-terahertz, 98 GHz traveling wave tube to accelerate the molecular reactions for crystalline growth. A camera was set up to periodically take pictures through the microscope of how the crystals reacted to the millimeter waves, and those pictures were transmitted down to Alabama for analysis.

Kimberly traced her fingers along the camera interface, and her hopes of disengaging the camera from the optics quickly plummeted. It was hardwired to the device. She knew she could eventually take it apart, change its focal length, and then reassemble it to take a photo of a "Help! I'm alive!" drawing.

But . . .

She realized that before the picture was transmitted she'd have access to the data, meaning that she might be able to embed a message in the picture.

What did they call it? Steganography: embedding information covertly in a picture. But she didn't want her message to be secret and unseen; she wanted people to see it and understand it. She needed to embed an alphanumeric message spelling out that she was still alive and safe—for the time being—and if NASA could think up anything that she could do to stop the terrorists, to contact her.

Kimberly glanced around the JPM. JAXA, the Japanese Aerospace Exploration Agency, had a Ka-band link that could carry voice, but it had to be enabled from the ground. Besides, it was only line-of-sight, and would work only when over a Japanese ground station.

But she also knew that the JAXA Kodama satellites might be able to relay the Ka-band link—and, better yet, if the handshake was right, NASA's Tracking and Data Relay Satellites might be able to allow her direct voice communications with NASA. *That's* what she'd put in her message. That, as well as getting the JAXA to activate their two video cameras in the JPM so they could keep track of what she was doing, and use them as a backup by writing messages to them if something happened to the voice link.

She knew it was a long shot, and she may not know if they even were able to receive her embedded message, but she had to keep moving and give it a try. Then she could go on to the next item on her priority list.

Kimberly had already prevented the terrorists from deorbiting the ISS, at least temporarily.

That left rendering them helpless . . . or killing them.

JAPANESE
MODULE (JPM)

After digitizing the photo of crystalline growth Kimberly inserted a very simple but straightforward message into the data stream, including details of what had happened on board after communications with the ground had been cut, and specific directions of how to establish voice comm with her.

She wrote out the message by hand several times before she was satisfied with the size and length. She'd have preferred to print it out, but the printers were only in the U.S. lab and the Russian service module. And before she took a picture of the message with the confocal microscope, she tried to balance getting the information down to JSC with not having the photo thrown out by any software review that filtered out corrupted data.

She wasn't sure if the experimenters would actually look at the photo or instead rely on automated computational analysis. She hoped they weren't lazy and would do the former rather than the latter, but she feared that this new generation of scientists depended more on technology than intuition, and she didn't want to take the chance. Their software might skip over her message and instead mark the data stream as tainted.

She included directions on how to communicate back to her, by voice-enabling the JAXA Ka-band, so she'd know pretty quickly if her steganography idea worked or not. She'd rather be much more straightforward communicating with JSC, but if Farid or Bakhet discovered that she was exploiting the experimental data links, they'd cut them off in a heartbeat, just as they'd done with the other comm links.

So instead of sitting around and waiting for either JSC to respond to her implanted message or the ham radio to be in line-of-sight, Kimberly told herself that now she needed to track those two crazies down and find out exactly where in the ISS they were located. If she was ever going to render them helpless and prevent them from trying to deorbit the station, she'd first have to find out where they were.

She glided back to the laptop, pulled up a schematic of the station's electrical functions, and traced a finger over the lines connecting the station's modules. Each module contained a slew of equipment, ranging from food warmers to sophisticated astronomical devices. When in use, each piece of equipment drew current and produced a drop in voltage, which could be detected, quantified, and located.

By using Ohm's and Kirchhoff's laws as well as knowing the station's circuit layout, Kimberly could easily deduce what equipment was in use and where it was situated. She'd be able to detect all the myriad equipment in the ISS and exploit them as sensors.

Which gave her another idea. She could send out a simple Morse code message to the mission control center by pulsing currents in the JPM! MCC would be monitoring the currents in the JPM as well as the rest of the station, and she could modulate the current to tell them where to look in the payload image data stream!

She wrote a short routine that monitored various traditional and nontraditional sensors, then quickly isolated the LED screens, carbon dioxide monitors, temperature gauges, the zero-gee toilet, oxygen monitors, and a scad of other equipment.

There. She enabled the routine, then started pulsing the currents in the JPM by switching the lights on and off, hoping that someone at MCC would notice the modulation.

After cycling through her Morse code message she turned to watch the rest of the station's electrical activity as it appeared on the schematic on her laptop's display. She felt her heart rate speeding up as she found that the two terrorists had retreated away from the JPM and separated from each other. One of them appeared to be holed up in the U.S. lab, while the other was down at the Russian end of the station, moving back and forth between the control panel in the SM module and the FGB.

What on earth were they doing? Studying the drain on the station's electrical circuitry, Kimberly deduced that they'd powered up most of the laptops in the modules. Probably trying to get around the administrative lock she'd put on accessing the thruster propellant lines. She assumed that although the two of them were crazy enough to want to deorbit the ISS, killing themselves and taking out who knows how many people, they were both sane enough—and probably competent enough—to hack into the ISS systems and retake control of their functions. Including the propellant valves, thrusters, and whatever other controls they needed to carry out their suicidal fantasies.

Her breath quickening, Kimberly tried to throw up some software barriers to prevent them from gaining any additional access to the station's systems, then once again tried to bring up the comm links with Earth.

But almost as fast as she entered a new command her efforts were squashed, sometimes stopped cold before she could even see if the commands had been executed. It was as if Farid and

Bakhet anticipated her every action, as if they could read her mind and thwart everything she tried.

Were they working from some sort of sophisticated, minutely detailed checklist that predicted all her possible countermeasures, or were they simply that much smarter and more competent than she?

After half an hour of being slammed in the one-sided cat-and-mouse game, Kimberly pushed herself away from the laptop in frustration. She was simply no match for the two of them. Or maybe, she thought, it was only one of them. Was Farid that much smarter than she?

She remembered that in graduate school at Princeton she'd known computer geniuses who had dropped out of college and forgone both academics and industry because they were bored with mediocre normal life, and instead lived on the edge, hacking or pursuing other illegal activities simply for the excitement. They weren't idiot savants who excelled only in one narrow area and were deficient in everything else; they were truly intellectually superior people in every sense of the word, compared to ordinary human beings.

But she also recalled that more often than not, their superior intellects came with a lack of common sense. And if there was a flaw that she could exploit, that was it.

From the physical prowess, depth of computer knowledge, and even the precise diction that both Farid and Bakhet had displayed, Kimberly became convinced that the two intruders were dead ringers for this ultra-normal type of human being. With the exception that their motivation wasn't based on boredom or game-playing, but was at fever pitch, inspired by misguided religious zeal.

Kimberly shared their religion and cultural background, and that frightened her even more, because whether they had common sense or not, she knew that they would stop at nothing to bring their vision to reality.

THE WHITE HOUSE:
NATIONAL SECURITY
COUNCIL

Scott Robinson stood in the narrow, carpeted hallway, waiting outside the Cabinet Room with a dozen other men and women. He'd been the last to arrive, but he'd traveled 1,400 miles farther than any of the high-level participants of the President's National Security Council meeting.

He felt grossly out of place in his blue astronaut flight uniform, and wished he'd included a normal suit, or at least a sports jacket, in his go-bag. But he couldn't picture himself wearing his comfortable khaki slacks and button-down shirts in a meeting of these dark-suited, cabinet-level officials, multistarred generals, and probably the President himself.

His only consolation was that at least his blue bunny suit, as the astronauts called their one-piece flight uniforms, exuded instant credibility that often bordered on veneration. The Secretaries of Defense and Homeland Security, plus the National Security Advisor had introduced themselves when Scott had arrived, recognizing him from his previous trip to the ISS just a few months earlier. No one quizzed him about the station, though: either because that was going to be the topic of the impending meeting, or they somehow remembered that his ex-wife, Kimberly Hadid-Robinson, was currently on board—and probably dead.

Scott self-consciously sipped his third cup of coffee and debated using the side bathroom for the second time since he'd arrived when a slim young man in a gray pinstriped suit and slicked-back light brown hair stepped through the door from the Cabinet Room. "Ladies and gentlemen," he said softly, "the President is ready."

Scott followed the others into the Cabinet Room and was directed to a seat along the wall while the others took the cushioned chairs around the long, gleamingly polished table, chatting quietly among themselves. Within moments the same young man appeared at the door across the room.

"The President," he said.

Everyone stood and the President strode in. He looked grim, and didn't greet anyone as he headed straight to his chair at the middle of the table's far side. Scott thought that the President had aged, but he appeared laser focused. He dispensed with pleasantries as he took his seat.

"I'll get straight to the point. I'm extremely concerned about the damage the space station will inflict before and after it hits the ground. Patricia Simone tells me that although eighty-five to ninety percent of the ISS's one million pounds will burn up in the atmosphere, in addition to releasing a significant amount of radioactivity on its way down, there could be more than fifty tons of metal that will survive reentry. Isn't that right"—he glanced down at a single sheet of paper lying on the table in front of him—"Lieutenant Colonel Robinson?"

Scott hadn't sat down yet. He stiffened into attention, stunned that the President would call on him so quickly. "Yes, sir, that's correct. The RTGs won't survive the fall, so we can expect as much as three hundred sixty pounds of plutonium released along its trajectory. But the station's tankage, solar panels, skin, and much of the equipment are made of aluminum, so they'll most likely burn up before it hits the ground."

The President nodded and started to speak, but Scott interrupted and added, "However, Mr. President, as you correctly noted, approximately fifty tons of metal *will* survive reentry and will cause damage if it hits a populated region. But that's an extremely small probability, as the debris will most likely be spread out over a wide area."

"I see," said the President. Without taking his eyes off Scott, he asked, "Is there anything else, Colonel?"

"No, sir." Scott could feel his face growing warm. He quickly took his seat. "Sorry, sir."

"Excuse me, Colonel." The Secretary of Defense leaned forward in her chair. "Just how certain is NASA that this fifty tons of metal that survives reentry will miss a populated area?"

Shooting to his feet again, Scott replied, "Very likely, ma'am. Although it's almost impossible to predict where the space station will reenter the atmosphere, there's a great chance that it will be over an unpopulated area. The world is two-thirds water, so the probability of it even hitting solid ground is only one in three. And when you consider that most of the dry part of the Earth is unpopulated, then the odds of it not contaminating anything or causing significant damage is very high."

The head of Homeland Security turned in his chair to look at Scott, standing behind him. "It's not the physical damage the impact would cause, it's the psychological terror I'm worried about." He turned to the President. "NASA may give only a small chance to the probability of damage, and they may be right. But perception is reality. And if this leaks out, the perception will be that a million-pound space station will hit New York City, contaminate the east coast, and cause incredible damage. Our analysts envision newscasters reporting that an equivalent impact by a one-million-pound asteroid could potentially be hundreds of times more devastating than the Hiroshima blast—"

Scott blurted, "But, sir, that's impossible!"

"It doesn't matter if it's impossible or improbable," Homeland Security continued, his voice edged with irritation. "All it takes are a few misspoken comments and it becomes real. It will spiral out of control. Public reaction can instantly turn into a bonfire, driven by momentum, fueled by the news media and the Internet. And it doesn't matter if it's incorrect or misguided. Once this hits the media it'll cause a panic that will dwarf anything we've ever seen. Rioting, mayhem, breakdown in authority—our civil law enforcement personnel routinely have their authority challenged now; can you imagine what they'll experience if they try to keep order when it's reported that the entire eastern seaboard may be at risk?"

A half dozen murmured conversations broke out around the table. The President rapped his knuckles on the polished wood and the room plunged into silence.

"Any other comments?" he asked tartly.

Scott's stomach was turning sour. He felt annoyed that these decision-makers were allowing the possibility of people overreacting to the threat cloud their judgment. It was obvious to him that just by looking at the facts, the chances of anyone getting hurt by the station's impact were pretty close to zero. You were more likely to die in an automobile accident or get hit by lightning than be killed by a piece of the space station.

But the Homeland Security secretary did have a point, Scott reluctantly admitted to himself. People's fear for the worst would drive their behavior, not any calm, logical assessment of what would really happen. Fear would spread like an unstoppable disease. Truth would become the first casualty of the crisis and distorted reality would become fact in the minds of millions.

The President looked around the room and asked simply, "So what are our options?" It was a demand, not a question.

The Secretary of Defense cleared her throat and looked at Scott. "Lieutenant Colonel Robinson, so it's possible the ISS could impact the eastern seaboard, correct?"

"Yes, ma'am, it's possible, but extremely improbable. It would more likely miss the U.S. entirely in an uncontrolled deorbit. But if the terrorists were to keep thrusting until the station is deep in the atmosphere, I suppose it could hit somewhere along the east coast. But as far as targeting New York"—Scott shook his head—"that's out of the question."

"But the Homeland Security secretary's point is valid," Defense insisted. "And if perception is reality, then the solution is to mold public perception to a new reality."

Scott sank back onto his chair, flustered at where the Defense secretary was heading. But the others around the table were obviously on her same wavelength.

The President picked up her line of reasoning. "You're saying we need to make the reality of the ISS deorbiting no longer a threat. The media is already speculating about what happened up there, and our silence is only making matters worse."

"Yes, sir," Defense said. "Which means going public that the U.S. intends to bring down the International Space Station so that it's no longer a threat."

"By deorbiting it?"

"No, sir." She shook her head. "By shooting it down with an antisatellite weapon."

Scott went rigid on his chair, stunned that they would even bring up the option of shooting down the ISS. After ten years of engineering design, it had taken fifteen years to build the station, with more than thirty-five Space Shuttle launches and four Russian launches. It had cost more than 150 billion dollars; ten nations had contributed to the effort; more than a hundred astronauts, cosmonauts, and tourists had visited the international facility. It was a monument to human achievement, and would play a pivotal role in the next phase of the human exploration of space. Yet here they were callously thinking of blowing it out of the sky—all because two tin-pot terrorists had somehow managed to find their way on board the most exclusive place in the solar system!

"We've had an antisatellite capability since 2008," the Defense secretary continued, "when we shot down one of our own satellites, USA-193, that was malfunctioning and threatened to crash in a populated area. Operation Burnt Frost publicly demonstrated that ASAT technology is real.

"If the ISS is truly in the hands of terrorists who threaten to deorbit that station into a populated area, then we have to be proactive. We have cruisers equipped with Aegis ASAT missiles already positioned in the Pacific theater as part of our defense against the North Korean missile threat. They can be quickly relocated to optimally target the space station."

"And how long will that take?" asked the President.

"It depends on the ISS orbit," Defense replied. "We can first decide where we want the station to impact and then work backwards to where to position the Aegis cruisers. But it makes the most sense to duplicate the Burnt Frost shoot-down and bring the ISS down over the Pacific Ocean, so that even if it has a large debris path it will all fall harmlessly in the water."

She paused for a breath, then before anyone could comment, Defense added, "And it will probably take three, or even four, ASAT missiles to hit the ISS at various locations to break it up into small-enough pieces for a safe, quick reentry—disperse the plutonium over the Pacific."

Looking at Scott again, the Secretary of Defense said, "Air Force Space Command has current ISS orbital parameters from its Space Fence suite of sensors, but it would help to also have NASA's original astrodynamic models to aid in the calculation of where to optimally shoot down the station. Lieutenant Colonel Robinson, how soon can NASA transmit their astrodynamic models to the Air Force?"

Feeling light-headed, Scott struggled to his feet. This decision process was going much too fast, and in a direction far from what he'd been hoping for. "Ma'am, NASA can get that as soon as I have a contact point in DoD." He wet his lips and turned toward the President. "But, sir, really, does it make any sense to do this, without first at least trying to mount a rescue mission? Launch one of our capsules and at least try to take back the ISS?"

The Defense secretary arched an eyebrow. "They've threatened to obliterate New York and contaminate the east coast in four days, Colonel. Which, according to the NASA Administrator, means they've already started the deorbit process. Can NASA even launch a manned capsule in four days, much less than four months?" She shook her head. "The only rockets that launch that quickly are our ICBMs." She turned to the President. "I recommend that you immediately go public and nip this in the bud. The sooner the ISS is brought down, the less panic we'll have throughout the country."

Scott started to protest, but the Defense secretary stared at him and silently shook her head. Frustrated, he plopped back down on his chair while the discussion swirled around the table.

After ten minutes of listening to his advisors' comments the President lifted his hands for silence. The chatter quickly stopped.

Looking weary but undefeated, the President said, "Generate a presidential directive. The danger is too great if indeed the ISS were to hit a populated area, and from this conversation I'm convinced the danger would be even worse once the public finds out that the ISS has been taken over by terrorists. And the public *will* find out. It's only a matter of time before the news media takes the TV feed they already have and comes to that conclusion."

Scott nodded agreement. The media saw the terrorists murder Vasilev before he'd had a chance to cut the feed from the space station. It was already being played around the world.

"Worse yet," the President continued, "we're running out of time. Pre-positioned or not, I don't know how long it will take our Aegis cruisers to reach their launch points. But broadcasting this to the public would only give that much more time for panic and rioting to set in. We can't let this go public and allow the terrorists to accelerate their timetable, so we need to make positioning our ASAT cruisers our top priority." He nodded at the Secretary of Defense. "Activate the Burnt Frost option and keep the deployment classified."

"Yes, sir," the Defense secretary said. "I recommend making this an unacknowledged Special Access Program and call it Burnt Haunt. The less people that know about this SAP the better, and you can bring it out into the open as soon as the deorbit hits the press, show that we're aggressively working to stop the ISS from injuring or contaminating anyone."

"Good point," the President agreed. He turned to the Secretary of State. "Inform our allies through SAP channels as soon as the cruisers reach their launch points. And before the launch is executed, work through classified channels to request that both Russia and China deploy their own ASAT capabilities as a backup, just in case our Burnt Haunt option fails. Any questions?"

Scott felt a sick queasiness growing in the pit of his stomach. This had really spiraled out of control. The Russian and Chinese ASAT weapons were going to be part of the mix. He suspected that their fail-safe systems for calling off a strike to bring down the ISS were nowhere near as reliable as the U.S.'s.

Which meant that the ISS was going to be destroyed one way or the other—either by the terrorists or by the U.S., Russia, or China.

Which left zero hope that if Kimberly had somehow managed to survive, she might get out of this alive.

Because the President of the United States had just signed her death warrant.

SOUTH CHINA SEA: 745 MILES SSE OF HAINAN, CHINA

The Chinese launch facility for unmanned rockets was located on the southernmost part of the Spratly Islands, one of the most remote spots in the South China Sea. Most of the world was unaware of its existence. And although thousands of miles from any major land area, the bare bones spaceport was located in bitterly disputed territory claimed by both the Philippines and China.

A hundred and fifty-five miles to the northwest a low-pressure system moved across the water, increasing swells. Wind whipped the water into frothy, turbulent waves. The seas were unnavigable and dangerous for all but the largest supertankers and cargo ships.

But twenty-one hundred feet below the surface the water was absolutely still and darker than any place on earth; no light could penetrate through the crushing depth. Although the seabed was relatively shallow compared to the rest of the South China Sea, life took on unworldly, exotic features to survive in an environment where forces were over sixty times greater than atmospheric pressure.

A spot of light pierced the absolute darkness. The intense glare lit up the sandy bottom and swept back and forth in a smooth pattern, as though searching for some elusive feature. Moments passed. The light methodically expanded its search until it illuminated a half-buried length of man-made material.

The beam stopped. It grew brighter as it focused on an underwater cable, completely out of place in the otherwise homogeneous sand.

Minutes passed and the 453-foot hull of the USS *Jimmy Carter* slowly approached the high-speed transmission line. Specially equipped thrusters positioned the massive submarine next to the cable until it hovered near-motionless over the seabed. An opening dilated in the hull; operations initiated for remotely tapping the polyethylene-clad, fiber-optic line that ran from Mainland China to the Spratly Island spaceport.

Three hours later the submarine released a buoy, trailing its own, thin fiber-optic cable as it shot to the surface, twenty-one hundred feet above. The line wavered as it reeled out, moving with the shifting currents.

Popping up from the water, the buoy splashed down; an antenna unfolded and despite the squall, solid-state gyroscopes kept it pointed to a pre-positioned point in the sky.

Within seconds, the USS *Jimmy Carter* transmitted purloined, encrypted data to the buoy, which relayed it to an overhead constellation of satellites. The data bounced from satellite to satellite until it was downlinked to Fort Meade, Maryland.

International Space Station

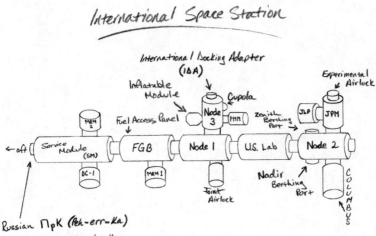

International Docking Adapter (IDA)

Inflatable Module

Cupola

Fuel Access Panel

Zenith Berthing Port

Experimental Airlock

MRM 2

Node 3

PMM

JLP

JPM

← aft

Service Module (SM)

FGB

Node 1

U.S. Lab

Node 2

DC-1

MRM 1

Joint Airlock

Nadir Berthing Port

COLUMBUS

Russian ПрК (Peh-err-Ka)
"transfer chamber"

Flattened "Roadkill" view - does not reflect
modules extending into/out of page

DAY TWO

JAPANESE MODULE (JPM)

Kimberly woke with a start. She was trapped, caught, confined, bound. In a flash, though, she realized that she was wrapped in the bungee-cord restraints that she had wound around herself so she wouldn't go floating across the module while she slept.

She glanced at the vestibule. The hatch was still tightly sealed. Farid and Bakhet had not broken through. Grimly, she realized that if they had found a way into the module she would never have awakened from her troubled sleep.

The only way she'd been able to get to sleep at all—despite her bone-deep weariness—was that she knew it was impossible for them to get in without making a racket, either by depressurizing the vestibule, breaking that hatch window, or even somehow cutting through the JPM module's aluminum side. But the memory of the way they had slaughtered her crewmates haunted her as she dozed fitfully in the normally comfortable zero-gee environment.

She untied the cloth straps and floated free, stretching as she forced herself fully awake. Her hip ached from where she'd been hit by the prybar that they'd thrown at her, and she swam over to the first aid supply to replace the bandage. Preparing the gauze, she reached down and gingerly pulled the wrapping off her hip; a small corner stuck to her skin, but as she exposed the wound she saw that at least it had stopped bleeding. She methodically coated the area with more antibiotic and covered it again, taping the sides.

She'd been lucky to find an extra med kit in the JPM, and would have to somehow raid the U.S. lab if she needed another. But she knew that this would be the last time she'd attend to the wound. If she couldn't stop the terrorists soon it wouldn't matter if the injury got better or worse.

She floated over to the ham radio and started to key the mike, once again trying to establish contact with the ground. Looking at the world map on her laptop monitor, her heart sank: She saw that the ISS was now in the ascending mode, just south of the Middle East. She'd have to wait until she was over Australia or back above the northern hemisphere before she could speak to anyone using line-of-sight. She grumbled to herself in frustration and clicked off the low-power radio.

Still muttering unhappily, Kimberly pushed over to the experiment bench. Trying to cool down, she studied the data links that were still transmitting down to Earth. She hoped she would discover that one of the researchers on the ground had noticed the enormous flow of data that she was sending over the links—or even more obvious—the messages on the digitized pictures she'd been sending.

All they have to do is take a little time and *look* at their damned incoming data, Kimberly groused to herself. There was no way that any halfway awake person could miss her efforts to insert information over the links. But yet, nothing. No response to her messages, nor any indication that any living human being had even looked at the experimental data she had doctored.

Kimberly figured that since Vasilev's murder had been broadcast over NASA TV, that all ISS activity on the ground had probably ground to a halt. As a scientist herself she understood that such catastrophes took precedence over scientific curiosity.

But yet there were some people out there who were more concerned about science than anything else in the world, oblivious to everything around them except for getting the results from their experiments. She remembered one of her fellow scientists when she had briefly worked as a postdoc for the Space Telescope Science Institute, at Johns Hopkins. Her colleague cared about nothing except her science: despite local or national disasters, she never missed a day at the lab, through hurricanes, floods, and even a massive protest demonstration.

Where was she now? Kimberly wondered. Surely there must be *one* researcher who would at least visit her equipment and discover the anomalous data.

She decided to give the data links one last try. Then she had to move on. After all, what could NASA do for her on the ground now that they couldn't have done immediately after seeing the murders? Knowing that she was still alive might give them hope that not everyone aboard the ISS had been killed.

But even with all NASA's collective creativity, could they really whip up some miracle solution to keep the ISS from deorbiting and for her to survive? Nothing short of launching a rescue mission would do the trick, but the next Soyuz resupply capsule wasn't due for another month, and that was the only vehicle that might be swapped out to carry humans to the ISS. And even then, with the terrorists waiting for them, there was no way the Soyuz crew could gain access to the ISS's interior, no way they could live to help her.

Kimberly knew that an unmanned U.S. SpaceX Dragon capsule was scheduled to launch in a few weeks, but that commercial resupply ship was not a human-rated vehicle that could carry astronauts into orbit. And even if it could, it wasn't like the old Apollo capsule where the astronauts wore spacesuits and could go EVA to enter the station. The unmanned Dragon had been designed to dock with a berthing port, not open up to the cold vacuum of space.

So what did that leave her?

The reality was that NASA *might* possibly pull a rabbit out of a hat if they knew that she was still alive, and were thus motivated to come up with some creative solution to thwart the terrorists. She couldn't imagine what they would whip up, but they had hundreds, thousands, of people on the ground they'd be able to utilize. So Kimberly decided to give the data links one more try.

But as she pushed back toward the experiments, she knew that she couldn't wait around for someone else to solve her problems. She kept remembering that she had been trained to anticipate and *direct* the solution, not to react.

That meant that she had to figure out how she could possibly stop Farid and Bakhet by herself.

She floated over to the laptop and started modulating the data links with everything from Morse code to prime numbers to Fibonacci sequences, anything to make someone on the ground do a double take and revisit the information she was sending. Surely no one would think that these modulated data streams are natural. *Somebody* must be inquisitive enough to look at them!

After setting up the links to jump from one modulated stream to another, Kimberly turned back to the Portable Computer System's graphical interface, called up the administrative controls, and once again started trying to take back command of the station.

NASA HEADQUARTERS, WASHINGTON, D.C.

Restlessly, Scott Robinson paced back and forth across the office of NASA's Chief of Staff, still dressed in his astronaut's blue bunny uniform. He'd brought only the one blue flight suit with him, and since the uniform instantly identified him as an astronaut he now wished he'd packed every one he had—it opened doors and allowed him access not only to the higher-ups in NASA but throughout the entire government.

His old friend Chief of Staff "Mini" Mott was hunched over his phone, elbows on his desk, his left hand massaging his forehead. The stubby ex-Marine nodded vigorously and attempted to break into the monologue pouring through his earpiece, but only managed to blurt out quick objections to whatever excuses were being thrown at him.

Whomever Mini was talking to reminded Scott of lots of general officers in the military. Take-charge, Type-A individuals. When you tried to speak with them they told you what they were thinking and you couldn't get a word in edgewise. And when they thought the conversation was finished, they told you that as well.

"Yes, sir . . . yes, sir," Mini was saying.

Three bags full, Scott finished sourly. From Mini's tone and the expression on his perspiring face, it didn't look good. But he had to keep trying. Just because some bureaucrat was trying to save money, or thought the risks were too high, Mini would still keep going.

It was one thing for the President to order that the ISS be shot down with the antisatellite weapons if the station posed a real threat. But as yet they'd seen no indication that the station was descending in altitude. And if it wasn't getting closer to the ground, then it wasn't deorbiting; and if it was staying in orbit then it certainly wasn't a threat and it shouldn't be blown out of the sky.

Scott's idea of attempting a rescue mission had been summarily dismissed at the National Security Council meeting. So the government was lumbering ahead, preparing to blow up a million-pound, $150 billion target flying 250 miles above the Earth at 17,500 miles an hour.

And they weren't even going to do it alone.

He'd sat in the conference room when the Secretary of State confirmed that both China and Russia had secretly agreed to use their own ASAT weapons to join in the effort to destroy the ISS. Scott fumed inwardly. They weren't really concerned that the ISS might come down on their soil and kill some of their citizens. Rather, they saw this as a way to show off their own military capability against a mostly American target, and demonstrate to the world that although the Americans couldn't stop the threat, they certainly could.

The Chinese briefed the National Security Council that they would use their direct-ascent SC-19, a variation of their

Dong-Feng 21 ballistic missile, carrying a Dong Neng-3 non-explosive, kinetic-kill warhead, launched out of their site in the Spratly Islands. The kill would be achieved by intercepting the ISS at 17,500 miles per hour in an orbit head-on to the station, resulting in a direct hit at 35,000 miles per hour, more than enough kinetic energy to pulverize the station. That is, if it hit one of the station's modules and not one of the solar panels. If it hit a solar panel the warhead would fly through the flimsy solar cells, ripping through the station's power source like a hypersonic bullet whizzing through Kleenex.

The Russian ASAT capability was less certain: their kinetic-kill vehicle had yet to be publicly demonstrated. American intelligence sources indicated that they might try to use an old high-power laser system they had developed five decades ago as a counter to the U.S. Strategic Defense Initiative. The CIA reported that the Russians might even use one of their mothballed, explosively powered iodine lasers that they had originally developed to power a laser-driven nuclear fusion system. The massive iodine laser was a relic compared to today's more efficient solid-state devices, but it still might be powerful enough to rip the ISS to shreds.

In any case, Scott thought, the National Security Council considered the Russian and Chinese options as fail-safe backups, which motivated Scott even further to push his proposed rescue mission.

Scott flinched as Mini slammed down his phone. It looked as though the conversation hadn't ended well.

"So Congress won't step in to help?" Scott asked.

Mini's expression could have boiled water. "Not only will they not come up with funding for a rescue mission, but they won't even guarantee emergency funding to purchase a replacement launcher to resupply the ISS, if the mission fails. Which throws the decision back in NASA's court."

"But they didn't say they wouldn't support it, right?"

Mini snorted. "Two negatives don't prove acceptance, Basher. They just hinted that they wouldn't try to stop us if we moved ahead and mounted a rescue mission. So it's in our hands; it's NASA's decision."

A surge of enthusiasm racing through him, Scott burst out, "That's great news! There's a Falcon 9 with a Dragon capsule sitting on Pad 39A at the Cape, due to resupply the ISS next month. You can use that for the rescue flight and move the resupply mission to Boeing's Starliner. Patricia has the authority to accelerate the Falcon schedule to launch in three days, and since the Dragon capsule can carry at least four astronauts—"

"It's an *unmanned* SpaceX capsule on that Falcon 9, Basher," Mini interrupted coldly. "Not rated for humans."

"Then send the Boeing Starliner instead. It's on the adjacent pad!"

"Forget it. It's only carrying supplies. Hasn't been certified for humans yet."

"But the Dragon has. I rode it my last trip to the station—"

"Not this one. The one on the pad would have to be reconfigured, and even if it could, in addition to launching in three days it would *still* take another few additional days to reach the ISS. We don't have the time!"

His voice ratcheting a notch higher, Scott countered, "It takes a few days to reach the ISS because of our mother-loving, risk-averse, two-hour launch window." He glared at his friend as Mini pulled himself up to his full five-foot, five-inch height, but continued, "You know as well as I do that the Russians routinely pull off ten-second launch windows all the time with their Soyuz, and go direct to rendezvous with the station, without changing orbits. Their ships take only a few hours to reach the ISS, not a few friggin' days, like ours!"

"And how many Vostok and Soyuz rockets didn't make it off the launch pad, or blew up after they did? We've already lost crew on the ISS because of those terrorists. If we lose that Falcon 9 trying to hit a ten-second launch window it's another four astronauts killed—not to mention the fifty-million-dollar launcher. How do we explain that to the dead astronauts' families, let alone the American public? And if they fail, forget about that Starliner ever launching; the space program will be over."

Pounding on the desktop, Scott insisted, "Dammit, Mini, we only saw Vasilev being murdered. Robert, Al, and Kimberly may well still be alive, trying to survive but unable to communicate. The terrorists may be dead themselves. Besides, the surviving crew may need medical attention. We just don't know, and that's the whole point! How do we explain it to *their* families if the ISS is shot down without us attempting a rescue?"

Scott realized he was panting as if he'd run a hundred-yard dash. His hands were balled into fists. Mini was glaring at him, his thin face drawn and pale.

"Mini, we've got to try. Or you might as well tell the astronaut corps that their lives don't matter, and the President isn't even thinking about us."

In a low voice Mini replied, "The President is thinking about three hundred and fifty million Americans by bringing down the ISS. That will prevent the panicking, the rioting, and who knows how many deaths."

"But what if Robert, Al, and Kim are still alive?"

Mini closed his eyes briefly. Then, "Okay, what if Robbie, Rat, and Kimberly *are* still alive, and the ISS isn't shot down. How are you going to rescue them if your Falcon 9 blows up on the pad trying to make your ten-second window?"

"Then you simultaneously launch Boeing's Starliner. It's scheduled to the ISS in two months, anyway. It's on another pad, so there's no reason why you can't launch them at the same time. The point is, you never give up, you never give in!"

Before Mini could respond, Scott pressed on, "You never gave up as a Marine, so don't start doing it now. The Associate Administrator for Exploration and Ops will back you, but he has to know it's NASA's top priority. I damned well know that Patricia Simone will think it's a priority: this could have been her up there a few years ago, and not Kimberly. But Patricia's not here and NASA needs a kick in the butt to get the ball rolling and start reconfiguring that Dragon to carry humans. And you're the one to do it, Mini! So start doing your job, Marine!"

The two of them stared at each other from opposite sides of the desk. At last Mini's hard glare relaxed and he muttered, "*Semper Fi*, Basher."

As he reached for the phone he grinned. "You're right. The AA for Explo and Ops is going to have a cow."

"He'll know it's the right thing to do," Scott insisted. "And if *you* don't lead the way it'll set the whole astronaut corps against Headquarters. Might cause a rift that'll last forever."

Mini pointed the telephone receiver at Scott. "Okay. All right. But the instant the ISS starts descending in altitude we're calling this rescue off. Because I guarantee you, when I was on active duty one thing I learned was that when the military was told to accomplish a mission they didn't screw around. Once the Secretary of Defense gives the order to execute their damned Burnt Haunt option and shoot down the station, nothing's going to stop them. Nothing. And the last thing we want is for four astronauts in a Dragon capsule to be in the way. Because as far as the military is concerned, they'd be nothing more than collateral damage. Understand, Colonel?"

Nodding wearily, Scott said softly, "I understand." It felt sort of strange to be addressed by his military title. Since he'd been assigned to the astronaut corps, nobody made a point that many of the astronauts were on active military duty. But here, both at the NSC meeting and now in Mini's office, the honorific seemed to have elevated his status even higher than usual.

Now that he'd succeeded in getting Headquarters to launch a rescue mission, Scott's next goal was to get himself manifested on that launch. Although he'd recently trained on the Boeing Starliner mock-up before being pulled in as CAPCOM for the ISS, he still considered himself the most qualified of any astronaut to fly the rescue mission on SpaceX's Dragon.

He was also the last astronaut to have served on the ISS, prior to the current mission, and he'd had more experience in space than anyone in the active astronaut corps. But all those credentials paled when compared with his real reason for wanting to be on this rescue flight. Kimberly may be his ex-wife but she was still one of the best astronauts and all-around competent people he'd ever known. And for some stupid reason he'd done everything in his ego-driven life to push her away.

Besides that, he realized with something of a jolt, he still loved her.

No one had a better reason for vengeance than he did.

JAPANESE
MODULE (JPM)

Once again Farid had beaten her to the punch. He'd stymied Kimberly's efforts to regain control of the ISS by throwing up roadblocks below the Linux level, the operating system running the computer's graphical interface. It was hard for her to admit it, but the Kazakhstani's systems knowledge of the ISS interfaces was superb, probably even better than the interface designers'. Which meant that Kimberly didn't have much time before they'd discover she had changed the operating state for the propellant pressure valves from ON to OFF so that they couldn't operate the thrusters.

So if I'm going to circumvent the bastard's efforts to use the thrusters, Kimberly told herself, I'll have to use the Portable Computer System in ways he wouldn't expect. Or as Scott would say, I'll have to use the PCS for intelligent preparation of the battlefield. This is a war, she realized; she was going into battle against the two terrorists.

Her face set in a grim mask, she used the PCS laptop to call up the carbon dioxide and oxygen monitors throughout the station.

She scanned the readouts for anything out of the ordinary, trying to find a hint of where the two men were.

Have they slept at all? she wondered. They might be computer geniuses, able to understand the ISS operating system at the machine level, but they were still human. And they'd been through much more physical stress and activity than she'd been through, from the launch of their Soyuz capsule to the murders of the other crewmen. Which meant that even if they were relying on uppers or other drugs to keep them going, they'd eventually crash and have to sleep it off.

Kimberly was hoping that they thought that since she was holed up in the JPM they'd have time to get a little rest before they painstakingly tried to track down why the thrusters wouldn't operate. And she hoped that although one of them might stand guard while the other one slept, the one staying awake wouldn't be operating at a hundred percent; he'd be sleepy as well.

They may have put up computational roadblocks to prevent her from stopping them, but she bet that they wouldn't expect her—a woman—to go at them physically.

She found what she was looking for in the computer's data. There. The CO_2 monitor in Central Post had ticked upward. That meant that at least one of the terrorists was in there. But she also saw that the O_2 level was above ambient, meaning that the guy was using less oxygen than normal. That's the guy who's sleeping!

Now where was the other one? Just outside the JPM, standing guard? That's where she would be, in case she tried to escape. But these guys by their very nature wouldn't think that a woman would have the guts to go after them, so the other one was probably somewhere else in the station. But where?

Just in case, Kimberly pushed off to the JPM viewport. She looked into Node 2 and the adjoining Columbus module from as many angles as she could, and she didn't see any sign of either one of them. So where was the SOB if not in Node 2 or Columbus? Node 3? The U.S. lab?

She floated back to the laptop and studied the CO_2 and O_2 levels again. She couldn't find any obvious signs of where he might be, so she called up an electrical power system diagram of the ISS circuitry. Aha! The EPS showed there was electrical activity in Node 3, the Tranquility module. In the zero-gee toilet. One of them was using the bathroom!

Her heart started to race. If she moved quickly enough she'd have a chance to leave the JPM and surprise him.

And introduce him to Shep's incredibly sharp knife. Fatally.

Murphy's Law, Kimberly thought. If anything can go wrong with my plan, it *will* go wrong. And there was too much at stake for her to screw up. The other terrorist might awake from his nap unexpectedly. Or the one using the toilet might be in there just to make her think he's indisposed. A dozen other things could go wrong.

But she had to do *something*. She couldn't sit here in the JPM like a frightened baby. Sooner or later they would figure out how to regain control of the thrusters. Sooner or later they'd force the ISS into a fatal plunge down to Earth.

Sooner, not later, Kimberly knew.

She needed another weapon, in addition to Shep's knife. She'd have to bring a backup, something that could incapacitate them until she could either restrain them or kill them. What could she use?

The Russian flashlamp had worked well enough, but it was now somewhere back in one of the Russian modules. And in any case it would have to be recharged, and she certainly didn't have the time for that. Whatever her choice was, it had to be something here in the JPM, something she could use, or jury-rig, and quickly.

She glanced around the module. There were still bags of equipment attached to the walls, but she didn't have the time to rummage through them. Looking back at the electrical activity in the Node 3 toilet, she saw that it had gone up again. He was probably trying to acquaint himself with how to use the john.

Kimberly looked frantically down the JPM axis. What could she use? Her eyes lit on the experiment table. Anything there? She had put the data stream from the Air Force Academy's crystal growth experiment on a repeating loop after embedding her steganographic message for help, and the rest of the equipment was now dormant—

Of course! The 98 GHz traveling wave tube that excited the crystal's molecular resonances! She pushed rapidly to the table, put out a hand to stop her motion through the air, and grabbed the portable source. She turned back to the laptop. She'd recharged the miniaturized millimeter-wave device while breaking down the experiment, so she could send her plea for help over the data stream to PAYCOM. With the traveling wave tube now fully charged she'd have juice enough to get off several shots.

Kimberly remembered the searing heat she'd felt when her arm caught the sub-terahertz beam. Must be what it's like to be cooked in a microwave oven, she thought. Only worse. Scott had made fun of her when she'd told him about the experiment, teasing that she'd be the first to deploy a directed energy gun in orbit, and if the United Nations ever learned about it, the U.S. could be accused of breaking the international treaty prohibiting the deployment of weapons in space. Their argument over that had foreshadowed their divorce.

Reaching the PCS laptop, Kimberly quickly ran through the graphical interface and closed the valve from the JPM to the outside vacuum. Then she physically disconnected the metal VAJ tube from the vestibule separating the JPM from Node 2 and allowed air to flow back into the vestibule, releasing the enormous force that had held the JPM and Node 2 hatches closed.

She felt her face growing warm as she steeled herself for battle. Quietly, she opened the JPM hatch and waited for a moment as she peered into Node 2. No one was in there. She opened the connecting hatch as silently as she could.

Holding Shep's knife in one hand and the millimeter-wave source in the other, she quickly pushed into Node 2, then turned for the U.S. lab as she headed for Node 3, ready to take out the killer. First she'd incapacitate him by blasting him with the pain-inducing sub-terahertz beam, and while he was stunned, either confine him or slit his throat.

And then she'd go after the one who was sleeping.

Kimberly shot down the Node 2 axis and entered the U.S. lab. She'd seen no one in the Columbus module and her focus was on getting to Node 3 and the zero-gee toilet as quickly as she could.

She could almost feel the adrenaline pumping through her veins. She'd have only one chance at this and if she failed she'd be signing a death warrant not only for herself but for an uncountable number of people when the ISS impacted the Earth.

And in the back of her mind she realized that she'd also be putting an end to the human exploration of space.

She floated through the U.S. lab, her hands getting slick with sweat. There wasn't any doubt in her mind that she'd be able to use the 98 GHz source to incapacitate the first terrorist; that could be accomplished at a distance, she wouldn't even have to be close, in case he tried to stop her. All she needed was a line-of-sight and she'd be able to bathe him with a nonstop agony of incredibly hot pain.

But would she be able to kill him with Shep's knife when she was up close and personal, and do it before he regained his senses? Would she be able to follow through and actually kill him?

Kimberly steeled herself as she approached the hatch to Node 1, getting ready to kick off from its metal side and spring into Node 3 and surprise the terrorist.

With any luck, he'd still be sitting on the can and this would be a quick, but potentially messy, end for him.

Breathing hard, she entered the Node 1 hatch, powered up the 98 GHz source, and started to kick into the module.

Farid floated down into Node 1 as he exited headfirst from Node 3. His eyes bulged wide as he spotted Kimberly.

"Zhalep!"

Kimberly kicked out to change her momentum as Farid twisted in midair, reaching out to grab her. He caught her elbow and she twirled. She brought the millimeter wave source up and pressed as hard as she could on its activating switch while sweeping the beam toward Farid.

"Sheshen sigiyin!" he screamed. He started writhing in the air, bucking his torso back and forth as he desperately tried to get away from the hellish pain of the heat-inducing beam.

Turning in the air, Kimberly tried to keep the beam trained on him, but she hit the module wall and bounced away at an angle.

Momentarily free from the beam's painful power, Farid yelled hoarsely as he whipped his arms and legs around. He tried to move through the air so that he could find a place to push off and reach her.

Kimberly swung around and held her thumb on the activating switch, coolly bringing up the device once again and bathing him in the invisible beam.

Farid screamed and started bucking back and forth in the air, trying to flee, but Kimberly kept the beam steadily on him. Her foot hit the side of the module but she immediately compensated, pushing herself toward Farid while keeping the invisible millimeter radiation waves on him.

The module rang with his cries, but Kimberly tuned them out. She brought up Shep's knife in her other hand and, keeping the beam steady, bore in on Farid's neck, intent on his jugular—

Something hard and painful struck her foot. She cried out and started spinning, taking the 98 GHz beam off Farid.

Yelling erupted behind her, and as she continued to spin around she saw that Bakhet held the titanium Russian prybar in both hands as he drove toward her.

Kimberly instantly saw that Bakhet wasn't going to risk throwing the prybar at her, as he'd done earlier. Instead he charged at her, intending to take her out with a swing to the head. Kimberly brought up the millimeter-wave weapon.

She pressed the activator switch and Bakhet pulled up, a look of astonishment on his face. But it quickly passed; he hovered before her, looking puzzled.

He'd felt only a brief pulse of the heat beam, Kimberly realized. She pressed the switch again, as hard as she could. Nothing happened.

It's out of power, she realized. Without thinking she threw the little cylindrical device at Bakhet. It hit the side of his face, making him yowl with pain as he let go of the titanium prybar.

Reacting to the throw, Kimberly spun in the air. Her foot hurt like hell from the hit she'd received a moment before. She kicked out with her other foot as Farid drove toward her, having regained his wits now that he was no longer being roasted.

Kimberly ducked beneath his outstretched arms and shot back into the U.S. lab. She flew down its axis to Node 2, turned the corner by kicking against the wall, and finally reached the JPM, with Farid and Bakhet roaring gutturally as they came after her.

She quickly dived into the JPM and closed the Node 2 hatch, then hastily duplicated the procedure she'd used to evacuate the air in the vestibule connecting the two modules.

Within seconds the air gushed out of the small compartment and vacuum filled the two-foot space. Once again tons of air pressure kept both hatches tightly sealed.

Kimberly turned away from the hatch, gasping for breath. She didn't bother to peer at what the terrorists might be doing in Node 2. Her foot throbbed painfully and her hip was still sore from being sliced by the prybar yesterday.

Trying to ignore the pain, Kimberly focused her thoughts on what she might do to stop the terrorists from deorbiting the station. They'd shown that they were human and not infallible. Damned smart, she admitted ruefully. But not infallible.

Kimberly told herself that if she put her mind to it, she would discover something she could do to stop those two SOBs, with or without NASA's help.

PAYLOAD OPERATIONS CENTER, MARSHALL SPACE FLIGHT CENTER, HUNTSVILLE, ALABAMA

Every person but one in the air-conditioned operations center had their eyes riveted to the largest monitor in the big room, or was searching the Internet on his or her own console, watching as many news streams as they could, all trying to glean any new information that might help keep the ISS from deorbiting.

The big wall monitor was split into myriad windows, displaying feeds ranging from Fox News and CNN, to MSNBC, Bloomberg, CNBC, BBC, Telemundo, and Al Jazeera, while the individuals scanned space blogs and tried to chase down rumors online: international news sites, social media and user forums, trying to dig up anything that might be used to keep the ISS alive.

On the newscasts, news pundits hosted a wide range of "experts" who speculated and pontificated about the Vasilev's murder that had been broadcast over NASA TV before the feed had been cut. The video loops were replayed over and over, as psychiatrists analyzed the possible motives of the two killers. Rogue cosmonauts? Misguided extremists? Freedom fighters? Warped. Duped. Zealots. Terrorists.

Other experts analyzed the International Space Station's orbit, which had not deviated at all from NASA's published orbital predictions, released a few days before the killings. Still others speculated about NASA's silence, the agency's refusal to answer any and all queries about what had happened, how it could have happened, or if there had been additional deaths aboard the ISS. Was there even anyone left alive up there?

The news media—and the public who watched their TV broadcasts—widely believed that after killing all the astronauts and cosmonauts who had been aboard the station, the two terrorists had committed suicide, mirroring worldwide terrorist behavior from the past. Previous terrorists on the ground had often killed themselves—and others—with explosives they carried on their bodies. Could these terrorists have done the same thing, possibly by venting all the station's air to space? And if they did, what was their motive? No one knew, and NASA wasn't talking. Neither was the rest of the U.S. government, nor Russia, nor any of the other international partners.

No contact had been made with the station after the broadcast of the first two killings had been shut off. The Russian Space Agency, Roscosmos; the European Space Agency; the Japanese and Canadian space agencies all confirmed their own communications blackouts.

The rumor grew that NASA was heroically attempting to control the ISS from the ground, so that it could continue the so-called housekeeping functions and keep its orbit stable, and not allow it to decay because of atmospheric friction. Space experts noted that the station normally lost about a hundred meters of altitude per day, and had to periodically engage its thrusters to boost to a higher orbit, going back up as much as three kilometers in altitude every three weeks to prevent the ISS from deorbiting. That would explain NASA's reluctance in releasing any additional information. But while NASA, the U.S. government, and other space agencies remained quiet, other more nefarious rumors rocketed through the media and over the Internet.

The professionals at Marshall were well aware of the threat that had been broadcast by the terrorists to deorbit the ISS over New York City, so in addition to assisting Johnson Space Center and NASA Headquarters to brainstorm ways of regaining control of the station, all the pros avidly scanned the news reports for any iota of data that could help.

That is, all but one.

Old Joe Krantz, the point-of-contact at Marshall's Payload Operations Center, the person in charge of archiving data, was widely regarded as an oddball. Balding, paunchy, just a few weeks away from retirement, he had a reputation for doing things his way and letting the chips fall where they may. Early in his career he had frequently been called onto the carpet to justify his nonconformist behaviors. He had walked away triumphantly so often that his superiors eventually gave up and admitted that Old Joe had a special talent for being right.

He decided to review the information that was still being transmitted from the station over an open data link. Strangely, there was only one experiment still transmitting files. Even more curious, the streams themselves seemed to be oddly modified, spiking the link's intensity levels in a weird manner, as though they were being sent in a pattern. At first Joe suspected that the ISS transmitter was starting to conk out without anyone aboard to fix it.

But curiosity is a powerful force. Whatever the reason for the anomaly, he decided to at least check it out.

He accessed the last transmission and saw that the file descriptor was from an Air Force Academy experiment designed to accelerate crystal growth through the excitation of molecular resonances by irradiating the crystal with sub-terahertz radiation. He fully expected the files to be empty of any information, since the experiment should have long run its course. But when he pulled up the folder he found that it was full of data. Overflowing with data, in fact.

Joe frowned. That's strange, he thought. The sensors generating the data should have stopped working; he also knew the ISS's handheld 98 GHz radiation source should have run out of power if it had been left on continuously. And since no other communication had been received from the ISS since that crazy terrorist threat, why would this link still be transmitting data? And with modulated power intensities?

He scanned the file. The header said it was a compressed digital image, probably a picture of the crystal taken through a microscope. Okay, nothing unusual there. The station frequently compressed large files to cut back on bandwidth.

Clicking on the icon, he fully expected to see an innocuous picture of some boring type of crystal lattice structure, or something just as elementary. After all, the experiment had originated at an undergraduate military college, not some high-powered research university. He opened the photo on his high-resolution screen—

And fell backward in his chair, crashing onto the floor.

He picked himself up and stared at the screen.

Instead of a six-sided cubic structure, the screen showed a terse handwritten order. From astronaut Kimberly Hadid-Robinson.

She was directing NASA to contact the Japanese Aerospace Exploration Agency and have them immediately voice-enable the JAXA Ka-band link in the JPM module, and to re-vector it through NASA's Tracking and Data Relay satellite network so she could communicate with the ground. She also ordered them to enable the two JPM cameras so they could have visual contact, and use the cameras as backup in case the voice link failed.

He felt a stabbing pain in his chest. His left arm ached and his breath gusted in short burning spasms.

But he didn't have time for a heart attack. At least one astronaut on the ISS was still alive!

OLD EXECUTIVE OFFICE BUILDING, NATIONAL SECURITY COUNCIL, WASHINGTON, D.C.

Scott Robinson parallel-processed while sitting rigidly behind his desk, looking through his first-floor window for the NASA Administrator to leave the White House and her meeting with the President.

Kimberly's message had rocketed straight to NASA Headquarters. Administrator Patricia Simone assumed it would be hard to keep quiet, so she'd ordered the revelation to be tightly controlled.

Scott simultaneously cradled the old, black landline phone with his left shoulder while scrolling through his NASA-issued smartphone's e-mail. He also tapped on the flight iPad on his desk, which contained the Dragon capsule's emergency procedures. All while keeping an eye on the cable news channels, as he waited with mounting impatience for Simone to finish briefing the President about Kimberly and the rescue mission.

Beyond the door to this office Scott had been loaned, the NSC staff was in a frenzy of excitement. The furor out in those halls reminded Scott of video clips he'd seen of government agencies preparing to go to war, rather than just getting ready for another launch from Kennedy Space Center. But he knew that this wasn't simply another mission to resupply the ISS. Kimberly was alive on the station! She'd barricaded herself from the terrorists in the JPM. The crisis had taken on a new urgency.

And now, instead of the accelerated launch having the goal of bringing back the bodies of the murdered crew members, it was a true rescue mission, rescue of both Kimberly and the space station itself. And because the mission had changed to storming the station—an inherent military operation requiring Title 10 authority to conduct Operations of War—the necessary approval had escalated from the Administrator of NASA to the President himself.

Scott assumed that Patricia Simone should have received the President's go-ahead for launching the rescue mission by now, and he was more than ready to be on that flight to the ISS himself. As he reviewed the Dragon capsule's emergency procedures, he mentally ran through the rationale for him to be manifested on the launch.

He was confident that he'd be chosen for the mission; the only question was whether Simone would agree to put him in command. With his T-38 jet still parked at Andrews Air Force Base, just fifteen miles away from this NSC office, he could be down at Cape Canaveral within a few hours, prepping for the flight.

Out of the corner of his eye, Scott caught a glimpse of movement on the street below. It was Patricia walking briskly next to a tall woman wearing sunglasses, a dark skirted suit, a small coiled wire in her ear: Simone's Secret Service escort, bringing her back from the West Wing to the NSC offices.

Although still on hold with Kennedy Space Center, Scott slammed the landline phone onto its cradle and minimized the screens on both his smartphone and the iPad. On second thought, it wouldn't hurt to have Simone see that he was already reviewing the Dragon's emergency procedures: that just might tip the scales in favor of his being appointed to command. He realized that she normally wouldn't inject herself into the selection procedures, and would defer to both George Abbey and the head astronaut for that decision, but this was an extraordinary situation and he knew it called for extraordinary measures.

And extraordinary people, such as himself.

Scott got to his feet and headed out the office door, walking briskly across the black limestone and white marble floor that had been inlayed in the 1870s. Turning a corner in the high-ceilinged corridor, he tapped down the steps and arrived at the entrance just as Simone stepped through the massive archway. The Secret Service agent stayed with her instead of returning to her White House post, which meant that Patricia was probably going to be escorted back to the President.

Simone's face looked drawn. "Has JSC achieved communication with Kimberly?"

Walking with the Administrator toward the office NSC had loaned him, Scott replied, "No, ma'am, not yet. They're working with the Japanese to enable the two video cameras in the JPM. As soon as they're up, they'll start scanning the module. They're also bringing up a voice link over the Ka-band, per Kimberly's instructions. Johnson is expecting to make contact with her any minute now. They're just having some hiccups in the Ka-band handoff from the JAXA people, and patching it through the TDRSS satellites."

Reaching his temporary office, Scott opened the door and motioned for Simone to take one of the two overstuffed chairs along the wall next to the couch and coffee table. The Secret Service agent stayed in the hallway.

As Scott closed the door he asked, "How did the meeting with the President go? Did he approve the mission?"

"Yes," said Patricia, quickly adding, "but there are caveats, some pretty serious ones, and it's important that I speak with Kimberly once the links are up. I need to pass this information to her myself."

"You can spend as much time here as you need to," Scott assured her. In the back of his mind he was planning to head down to Kennedy Space Center to prep for the launch. "This is really your office, not mine."

Simone shook her head. "I've got to get back to the West Wing. The President has called in the principals of the National Security Council, and I'll be sitting in as soon as they get here. This is serious, Basher."

"Yes, ma'am, I understand." He wheeled his desk chair close to the Administrator's. "And with your permission I'd like to go ahead and fly down to KSC—"

"Excuse me?"

Scott continued hurriedly, "You know that I have the most experience on the station, and with that last flight I have more zero-gee time than anyone in the astronaut corps. As an active duty officer, I don't need a Presidential finding to participate in Title 10 war operations. And I probably have more combat time than anyone in the astronaut corps. In addition, I've launched on the Dragon and I just helped put together a training class on the Boeing CST-100 capsule before rotating in as CAPCOM three days ago, so I'm qualified on every platform that we have. So I thought that with all my experience . . ."

Simone frowned. "What exactly are you asking, Basher?"

Scott felt his cheeks go warm. He'd thought for sure she'd be the first to grasp that he'd be perfect for the flight. It was so obvious! "I know it's out of place for you to intervene in the selection process, but I thought that with my background and experience I'd be your top choice as the mission commander."

Simone stared at him, her face radiating disbelief. She drew in a breath, then spoke in a low tone. "You know the selection process is out of my hands, Basher. And although I appreciate your enthusiasm I can assure you that every astronaut on the roster is jumping at the chance to fly this mission and do whatever they can to help both Kimberly and the station survive. And as far as you being an active duty officer, you of all people know that the selection process was set up for a purpose, to reduce risk and assure mission success. Just like it is in the military, NASA makes these decisions, not individuals. Astronauts are too close to the activity and can't distance themselves from the needs."

"But that's the only reason I mentioned this, ma'am, the need to assure mission success."

Coldly, Simone said, "You speak to George Abbey and Chief Astronaut Tarantino about that. But in my eyes, you're not only trying to jump the chain of command, you're also putting the mission and the entire nation at risk!"

Scott sat up straighter. "I beg your pardon?"

"Your ex-wife, Kimberly, is on board, Basher. *Your ex-wife!* Although I don't doubt your intentions, NASA cannot and will not risk you making a decision on orbit that might endanger Kimberly, the other astronauts, or the ISS. We don't know the situation up there, but if there is even the slightest chance that you might hesitate or make the wrong call because of Kimberly, I can't afford to allow you on this flight."

"But—"

"Because if this mission fails and the ISS deorbits, then the panic and rioting the President is worried about just may happen.

And that's why I need to return to the NSC meeting once the principals arrive. It's that serious."

Scott felt his jaws clenching. With an effort to control his growing anger, he said as mildly as he could manage, "But if the selection process plays out and I'm manifested on the flight, then—"

"Then I'd overturn Tarantino's decision in a hot second. Period. You will *not* be on that flight. Understand?"

Scott felt as though he'd just failed the most critical check ride of his career and was being forced to retire, sent out to pasture. A sick, sour feeling rose from the pit of his stomach.

"Basher, do you copy?" Patricia demanded.

Scott mutely nodded over the sound of blood pulsing in his ears. He disagreed with her, but he also understood that it wouldn't help to push her—or anyone else in NASA, apparently—any further. Even George Abbey. It was a losing battle, and he needed to cut his losses. "Yes, ma'am. I . . . I understand."

"Good." Simone settled back in her chair. "If it makes any difference, I've been in contact with the Secretary of Defense." She glanced at her wristwatch. "She was on the line when the President approved the rescue mission, and her department has already come up with a short list of active duty officers currently in the astronaut corps: two Army Special Forces, a Navy SEAL, and an Air Force MD. They're all experienced in hand-to-hand combat and tactics, and they don't have the emotional ties that you have. I've already passed their names to JSC, so this conversation is OBE. Copy?"

"Copy." Scott realized that his efforts really had been overwhelmed by events.

"Good. Now that that's behind us, I absolutely need to speak to Kimberly as soon as the voice link is up. I need to pass along some information that's going to be hard for her to take, and she needs to know about it as soon as—"

A rapid knock on the door interrupted her.

Simone looked up and called, "Yes?"

The door inched open and the Secret Service agent stuck her face into the office. "Sorry to disturb you, ma'am, but the last NSC principal just drove through the White House gate. The Director of National Intelligence will be entering the West Wing shortly and your presence is needed."

"Thank you." Simone stood up and smoothed her skirt. "Basher, get on the horn to CAPCOM and let me know the instant they make contact with Kimberly. If you can't pull me out of the meeting . . ." She hesitated. ". . . then you've got to tell her about the antisatellite option."

Scott got to his feet as she headed for the door. "Do you think that's wise, letting her know that her own country might choose to shoot down the ISS?"

"The President says he won't do it if the station stays in a stable orbit and doesn't descend. But the Aegis cruisers are deploying, and once they reach their positions, if the ISS starts to deorbit I don't have any doubt in my mind that the President will give the order for them to employ their ASAT weapons. And the ISS will be destroyed—even if Kimberly is still alive and the Dragon rescue mission makes it on board. The President has stated that he cannot allow the nation to unravel. Period. The lives of five astronauts are expendable."

"But—"

"We can't keep Kimberly in the dark about this. Chief Astronaut Tarantino will brief the Dragon crew, and she deserves to know as well that she *will* die if the ISS begins to lose altitude, even if the terrorists are no longer alive. So if Tarantino doesn't tell her, then you must."

"Yes, ma'am."

"And finally, be sure to tell her about the rescue mission. We need to keep her hopes up, so save that for last. But first, she has to know who she's dealing with up there." She hesitated, then narrowed her eyes. "What I'm going to tell you is code word, from the CIA's most sensitive human intelligence source, and can't be discussed with anyone but Kimberly." She quickly filled him in with the latest information she'd just received from the White House Situation Room. "Make sure she understands. Copy?"

Scott felt nauseous. "Copy. I understand perfectly well."

JAPANESE MODULE (JPM)

Kimberly focused on slowing her breathing. She was safe for the moment, barricaded in the JPM. Farid and Bakhet were unable to reach her. Be calm, she told herself. Concentrate on what you need to do.

Survival was her number one priority, of course. But right alongside it was a powerful urge to defeat the two terrorists, to kill them if she could.

Does that make me as bad as they are? Does that make me a murderer? Maybe, she realized. But they've killed six men and want to kill millions more. I'm not a murderer, she told herself. I'm an exterminator, an agent of retaliation, a sword of justice.

Almost, she laughed at herself. Don't get so pompous, she thought. You just do what you have to do and hope you live through it. If not . . .

She shoved that thought out of her mind. Stop the bullcrap, she warned herself. Get on with the job.

Pushing to one side of the module, she opened the Velcro seal on one of the blue ESA bags secured there and pulled out a water pouch. She drained it and reached for another, surprised at how thirsty she was, and realized that she was ravenous.

She rummaged deeper into the bag and found one of the meals the guys had squirreled away when they'd temporarily used the JPM for short-term storage while unloading the last Progress resupply vessel. Kimberly remembered she'd been miffed that they'd been so cavalier about where they were dumping the supplies, and she'd fully intended to come back later and straighten things up. But because of the enormous demands on her time, she'd forgotten about her intent to store the supplies in a more proper place.

Good thing, she admitted to herself, as she started wolfing down the food. Got to keep my body fueled and hydrated; otherwise the next time I tangle with those two bastards they might win because I've become exhausted.

As she ate she ran over in her mind the options she had on hand to overpower the two. If she could regain administrative control of the ISS's systems she'd be able to turn off their power. They wouldn't be able to access the thrusters and would be virtually trapped until the next manned ship could reach the station. Or better yet, maybe she could somehow surprise them. Without power they'd be without any light. She felt sure that even though he'd been aboard the ISS three years ago, Farid wouldn't be able to find his way around in the dark. He couldn't stop me from attacking them again.

Could I isolate them from the rest of the station? she wondered. Maybe trap them in one of the modules, much like she'd barricaded herself in the JPM, and seal them off from the rest of the ISS? She wasn't sure she could pull that off remotely, but if she left the JPM again she might be able to lure them into one of the airlocks, or maybe even the inflatable Bigelow module, and seal off their hatch.

Kimberly knew it would really help if she had the folks on the ground working with her to brainstorm these options. They were the best of the best, but they were certainly no use unless she could communicate with them. Which meant she had to try another mode of communication other than embedding steganographic messages in the experimental data streams.

Still munching on her food, she turned to the laptop and pulled up the ISS orbital nodes. The station was just about to hit a descending orbit, and in fifteen minutes they would be over the coast of California. Time to try the ham radio again. And she wouldn't be shy about transmitting her situation and asking that somebody patch her through to JSC.

She was about to take a last sip of water when she was struck by a sudden thought.

She froze and nearly choked on her swallow. She felt an icy chill race through her, making her shiver. Did her message on the experimental data link get through, or could the terrorists somehow have intercepted her efforts? Had they gained access to the Japanese link and somehow overridden it? If so, were they watching her now?

She really thought that her message should have gotten through and that the MCC in Huntsville would have either tried the voice link over the Ka-band or activated the video cameras. So why haven't they? From what she'd seen of Farid's competence with computers, she wouldn't put it past him that he'd taken over control of the cameras.

The wide-angle cameras were fixed in their mounting, giving a view of the entire module. Their foldout LED screens showed what the ground should see. Kimberly quickly kicked away from the laptop and pushed off across the compartment, fully intending to blank the lens by attaching pieces of cardboard to them—

Suddenly, an urgent voice came through the tiny speaker next to the Ka-band setup. "Kimberly! This is CAPCOM. We can see you. Can you hear me?"

CAPCOM! Johnson Space Center! I've made contact! Kimberly twirled in midair, overjoyed, triumphant.

She recognized the voice: Fred Tarantino, chief of the astronaut office. Where's Scott? she wondered. He's supposed to be CAPCOM.

She pulled up and rotated in midair, just missing the video camera and instead careening into the module's metal frame, hitting her injured hip. Grimacing, she bounced back into the center of the JPM. It felt as if her wound had reopened, but instead of crying out in pain, Kimberly felt elated, exalted, her face warm, her pulse thundering.

We've made contact! She wanted to do flying loops through the module. Someone on the ground must have seen her embedded message, and now NASA was using the voice link transmitted over the Japanese Ka-band!

Kimberly felt as if the U.S. Cavalry had just thundered aboard the ISS, bugles sounding the charge. She wasn't rescued, of course. She wasn't yet safe. But she was no longer alone.

She grabbed the experimental table to stop her wild gyration and stabilized herself. Now she had the wizards on the ground who would give her the edge she needed to defeat those two SOBs.

And most important, to save the ISS.

Kimberly quickly brought CAPCOM up to speed, detailing the murders of Al, Robert, and the Russians as unemotionally as she could, in cold clinical terms, even though something inside her wanted to scream for vengeance. She knew that her passions might suddenly well up unless she kept them under strict control;

it took every ounce of her astronaut training to remain sternly professional. She was *not* going to put on a display in front of Tarantino and the rest of NASA—and who knew how many more people throughout the government would eventually watch her report?

But where was Scott? Where was the one person she wanted to speak to, to release her emotions, to ease the ache that gnawed at her innards?

As she spoke to CAPCOM, Kimberly told herself that someday she'd have time to grieve for her murdered crewmates. But not now. Now was the time to focus her inner rage toward defeating the two terrorists.

Don't get mad, get even.

She assumed that this interchange with CAPCOM was not being transmitted to the public, but in the back of her mind she knew that no matter how this ordeal turned out, eventually her words and demeanor would be aired all across the globe, eventually they would be dissected for all the world to see.

She pushed those thoughts out of her head—almost. She concentrated on explaining how she had barricaded herself in the JPM and what moves and countermoves she'd tried toward regaining control of the ISS.

At last she asked the only question that really mattered: "So what can you do to help me stop these two bastards and save the ISS?"

JOHNSON SPACE CENTER: ISS CONTROL CENTER, HOUSTON, TEXAS

Chief Astronaut Tarantino didn't pull any punches about Washington's overriding concern that the ISS's possible impact and radioactive contamination would cause nationwide panic.

"They're afraid of rioting and civil unrest that would tear the country apart, Kimberly," he said, his voice getting edgy despite his attempt to control it.

"You're our first line of defense," Tarantino continued. "We'll do everything we can to support you, but if push comes to shove, the President's going to order those Aegis ships to shoot down the station."

Kimberly nodded solemnly, thinking, I'd rather go down with the station than let those two murdering bastards win.

Tarantino warned her not to use the ham radio or any other means of communication that might be intercepted by the terrorists. Their one advantage now was that the intruders didn't know she could communicate with Earth. They thought she was cut off from any help or advice.

Kimberly listened to his assessment, but she thought that she didn't need a pep talk; what she needed was something that the terrorists wouldn't expect, a bolt out of the blue.

She knew the dangers of spaceflight, and didn't kid herself about the possibilities of dying. She'd known since she'd first started the astronaut training program that if she was ever lucky enough to be assigned a flight, that there was a finite probability that she might never return to Earth. The launcher could explode, or the reentry might go bad, or there might be a disaster in flight. If she'd wanted to stay safe and avoid danger she would have remained at Princeton and followed the academic track, where she'd probably still be an assistant professor, perhaps teaching PhD students who themselves would aspire to nothing more than a life in academia. It would have been a nice safe life.

And it would have bored her to tears.

So she looked at the situation she was now in as she would look at any problem: the biggest problem of her life, perhaps, but still as a problem that had a logical solution that she would eventually discover.

Still, she couldn't help thinking that the most logical solution was being killed when those ASAT missiles destroyed the ISS.

CAPCOM normally sounded matter-of-fact when he spoke. It was part of Tarantino's nature as an ex-military officer. Nothing seemed to rattle him. Yet today Kimberly detected a hint of urgency in his voice as he briefed her.

"Kimberly," he said in a low, measured tone, "you should know that the Administrator assigned Basher as her liaison to the National Security Council. The President has directed that all government agencies support NASA during this crisis, and to go through Basher for everything dealing with NASA."

"Good for Scott," she replied. "He deserves it." Despite their rocky relationship, she knew that appointing Scott as Administrator Simone's point man made all the sense in the world. He could make things happen, and since the NSC staff resided in the Old Executive Office Building, across the street from the White House, he'd be right in the middle of the action. Right where his fighter-pilot heritage would want to be. And his overinflated ego.

Tarantino hesitated. Then, "There's one more thing. Patricia needs to pass something critically important to you, ASAP. She'd speak to you herself, but she's currently in with the President."

Kimberly drew in a breath. What was so urgent that CAPCOM couldn't relay it himself? Why all the secrecy? "Can't you tell me?"

"I don't know what it is," Tarantino replied, his voice edging up a notch. "I just wanted to give you a heads-up that you'll be transferring lines. Are you ready?"

"I suppose I don't have any choice."

"Stand by one."

Before Kimberly could say anything more the voice link went silent, and then suddenly came back, but without any of the background noise typically present at the mission control center.

"Kimberly . . ." Scott's voice! But he sounded pained, stressed.

"I'm running out of time, Scott," she said. "What do you have for me?"

"I'm so sorry—"

"CAPCOM said it was urgent. If this is about the Aegis anti-satellite weapons, Tarantino already told me. So out with it, what do you have?"

She heard a scraping sound, as if Scott was straightening his chair. Then his voice, troubled, distressed, "I'll get to that in a minute. But first, Administrator Simone wants me to pass along some classified information at the SCIF level: Sensitive Compartmented Information. I wouldn't normally use an open channel like this, but you need to know who you're dealing with."

Kimberly wanted to scream. Instead, she said merely, "Then go ahead."

"The CIA discovered that Farid was recruited for this attack soon after returning from his last flight to the ISS. He was recruited by Bakhet, who really isn't from Qatar; he's also a Kazakhstani and had met Farid at the Al-Farabi Kazakh National University, while they were both majoring in computer engineering. Bakhet amassed his fortune through the software world, while Farid followed his dream of going into space.

"Bakhet was introduced to Anwar Awlaki, the imam who had preached to three of the 9/11 hijackers, years ago during a trip to Yemen. Awlaki's admiration of Mohamed Atta, an engineer and one of the 9/11 ringleaders, inspired Bakhet to use his wealth to devise a scheme that would dwarf the 9/11 disaster: he wants to wipe out the center of the financial world and topple the U.S., by not only destroying NYC, but by paralyzing the entire nation with fear."

"How long has the CIA known about this? Why wasn't I told sooner?"

"I told you, this is code word information—meaning very few people even knew of its existence, and there was a delay—"

"They could have been taken off the launch!"

"They're doing their best," Scott said. "Patricia told me the information was literally relayed by people riding donkeys, and the original carrier of the info had been killed—his son completed the mission, and at first he had not been believed by the CIA station chief . . . and when the information was finally relayed through classified channels, the Soyuz had already been launched to the ISS."

"Dammed government bureaucracy," Kimberly muttered.

"They've both been training for more than two years, refining not only their network and computer skills, but immersing themselves in Krav Maga, a lethal martial arts system developed by the Israeli Defense Force. This style of fighting isn't for sport: it gives no quarter and its only purpose is to kill."

"Thanks for the news flash," Kimberly said dryly. "I've already seen what those two can do."

"You stay away from them," Scott insisted.

"Look," Kimberly replied, "what I *really* need is access to the station's 1553 system. Either Farid or Bakhet have locked me out of the computer below the Linux level. Unless I can regain administrative control they'll eventually discover how I've stopped the engine fuel line. Once they unravel that they'll be able to engage the thrusters and start the deorbit."

"Copy. I'll get the Flight Director to throw our people on it. And don't worry, the NSA can help—"

"NSA?" Kimberly yelped. "What are the spooks doing on this?"

That was out of left field, she thought. What's an intelligence agency doing meddling in NASA? Scott had also mentioned that the information on Farid's and Bakhet's backgrounds came from classified CIA assessment. Just what else was going on down there? Had Scott already been co-opted by the Washington intel crowd?

"What's this got to do with the National Security Agency?" she demanded. "They don't know NASA and they certainly don't have any business—"

"Kim, their *business* is to live in our adversaries' computers. They've got thousands more people than we do that they can throw into this, to help us solve this problem. Your two terrorist friends—"

"They're *not* my friends!" Hotly.

"—would now be saturating the social media with worldwide propaganda and causing riots all over the place if it wasn't for your so-called spooks. NSA started jamming Farid's communications attempts through the TDRSS satellites once they threatened to deorbit the ISS, and they're still keeping Farid from contacting anyone on Earth."

Kimberly drew back, stunned. The station's S-and Ka-bands were transmitted through the Air Force's Tracking and Data Relay Satellite System, and because those links weren't now active, she couldn't communicate with the ground.

"But I thought Farid killed that downlink to Earth," she said slowly.

"He took down the direct link, so any ISS survivors couldn't use it; NSA killed the TDRSS cross link later, after he'd made the threat over NASA TV. He and his pal Bakhet tried to transmit more propaganda, worldwide over other links, but the NSA stopped them as well. The Kazakhstanis now only control your ISS internal comm. They must not have known about PAYCOM's Wallops or Glenn data links to the ground, or even the Japanese Ka-band. Otherwise we would never have found your messages embedded in the experiment data files. So you can thank the good guys for keeping this whole debacle out of the public's eye. If the NSA hadn't moved so quickly we'd already have rioting in the streets."

Kimberly shook her head. "I . . . I didn't know."

"It gets worse. NSA also traced Bakhet's sixty-million-dollar tourist fee being held in escrow at Sberbank, Russia's largest bank. The money didn't originate from his personal account in Qatar, or even Kazakhstan. It's from a series of international accounts, all tied to nations unfriendly to the U.S. Which means this isn't just a run-of-the-mill terrorist plot. It's got nation-state implications. The spooks are pulling on that string now, trying to find out just who's implicated. But that's not the point. We'll get you whatever software patch you need to regain control; just don't worry how we get it. *Your* business is to survive—"

"And to stop those bastards," Kimberly finished, feeling embarrassed at her old prejudice against the very agency that was now trying to save her life.

"Roger that." Scott fell silent for a moment. Then, "Listen, I thought Patricia would be back by now, but do you have anything else for me, before I tell you what else she wanted me to pass along?"

"Just feed me creative ideas on what I can do to stop them, throw a wrench in the works. I won't stay holed up in the JPM and play computer hacker."

"You stay clear of them!" Scott snapped, his voice urgent, fearful.

But Kimberly replied, "I'll never be able to stop them if I just go at them with a laptop; these guys are too good with their computers for me to go head-to-head with them."

"Not so," Scott insisted. "Remember, we've got the Pros from Dover on our side. NSA is second to none. And everyone in the government is working on what *you* can do to stop them. So don't try anything risky. Stay safe."

Safe, Kimberly thought. Like where I am is safe. She and Scott had been divorced for nearly eighteen months now and he was still trying to play the knight in shining armor.

Instead of arguing with him, she asked, "So what else did Patricia want me to know?"

"First, an unmanned Dragon capsule is on the pad. It was originally manifested for a Falcon 9 resupply mission but it's being modified for a rescue attempt. Launch in three days. Just hold out for a little while longer and you'll have help on the station."

"I may not be able to make it that long without leaving the

JPM," Kimberly said. "Anything KSC can do to accelerate the launch, get it here faster than five days?"

"Kennedy's already pulling out all the stops. And they'll be there in three days, not five. They're shooting for a ten-second launch window and a direct ascent rendezvous."

"Ten seconds! They've never done that before. Can they pull it off?"

"They'll have to. So once they lift off you'll need to control the robotic arm and pull them into one of Node 2's berthing ports. They'll be there pretty damned fast after liftoff, a few hours at most."

"Copy," Kimberly said. "I just hope they make the launch window."

"So does everybody else." Scott hesitated a moment, then asked, "Now are you sure you don't have anything else?"

Kimberly shook her head. "No, not now."

"Okay. Hang in there. Like I said, you've got the whole government behind you and we're doing everything we can to help. Patricia's sending up our best." He hesitated again, then added, "And one more time: we're keeping the whole fact that we're in communication with you strictly private from the public, in case Farid and his pal discover this link and somehow shut it down. Do you have a problem with that?"

Kimberly shook her head. "Glad not to talk to the media. The less distraction the better. Gives me more time to focus on stopping these bastards."

Scott was silent for a moment. "I certainly don't have to tell *you* what you have to do. Just remember, hang in there for three more days. Stay safe. And when we get that software patch you won't have to worry about them engaging the thrusters to deorbit the station. I guarantee it."

It sounded as if he was walking around the desk with his phone.

"One more thing. This is coming straight from me. I . . . I might as well tell you something I've realized for a while, but haven't told you . . . ."

"What is it, Scott?"

"Kimberly . . ." He sounded choked up. "I . . . I . . ."

Kimberly felt her face grow warm and started to speak, but she sensed a slight, sudden vibration in the ISS. She barely floated toward the JPM wall, drifting incredibly slowly, but moving nonetheless.

"Kimberly! What's going on? You're moving out of video range."

That's strange, Kimberly thought. She couldn't feel any increase in air flow through the module, but if she was being carried along by moving air, then of course she wouldn't feel any current. It would be like not being able to feel the presence of wind when you're in a hot air balloon. She'd be carried along with the flow . . .

She heard a low thrum. She realized she wasn't floating inside the module, but rather the JPM was moving, slowly rotating around.

In fact, it wasn't just the JPM. The entire ISS was moving.

She twisted in the air and swam over to the laptop. Quickly she pulled up the graphical interface.

Her pulse thudding in her ears, Kimberly saw that the state for the helium pressure valve had just been switched from OFF to ON. The hypergolic propellants were pressurized and fueling the thrusters.

The ISS was rotating around, and in ten minutes when its engines were facing in the direction of motion, it would soon start its fall to Earth.

MAUI SPACE SURVEILLANCE SITE, MOUNT HALEAKALA, HAWAII

Second Lieutenant Chip Johnson struggled to stay awake in the small vault while sitting watch at the classified communications console. Three cans of Bang energy drink lay crumpled in the trash can at his feet, almost a thousand milligrams of caffeine. It was enough jolt to revive the dead, but his head kept lolling forward, a casualty of surfing Maui's north shore earlier in the day.

The twenty-three-year-old Auburn engineer had been on active duty for only six months and considered himself lucky to have been assigned to the Air Force Research Laboratory's Maui site, based in the small town of Kihei near AFRL's Maui supercomputer.

But tonight, instead of being down at sea level, as the junior officer in the small military detachment overseeing the contractor staff that ran the seventy-five-ton Advanced Electro-Optical

System telescope's massive twelve-foot mirror, he'd been assigned the graveyard shift at the observatory atop Haleakala's 10,033-foot peak.

Viewing operations didn't normally demand the presence of military personnel; the private contractor personnel operating the Air Force's space surveillance site handled the telescope and its equipment with professional competence. But with classified activities sucking up all the AEOS's telescope time, the reason for Lieutenant Johnson's presence was to ensure a continuous Title 10 chain-of-custody for the viewing data gathered by the state-of-the-art surveillance system.

When he'd first arrived at Maui six months earlier, with a newly minted bachelor's degree in mechanical engineering, Johnson had thought he'd be performing cutting-edge research or solving some high-tech problem, such as working on the lasers or the deformable telescope mirror that took the twinkle out of the stars and gave the system as clear a view of the skies as a 'scope in orbital space. But he quickly discovered that the long-term, experienced contractor people did all the fun stuff like conducting research, and his role was to serve as oversight to whatever activities they were engaged in.

But for the past two days the facility had been tasked with a highly classified Title 10 Operations of War, and the Maui site needed an active duty Air Force officer to pass the telescope's detailed viewing data through a classified link to Space Command's JSPOC, the Joint Space Operations Center at Vandenberg Air Force Base.

So now, Second Lieutenant Chip Johnson found himself not merely overseeing routine contractor operations, but being squarely in the middle of certifying tightly classified information from the AEOS's twelve-foot, adaptive optics system that could reveal details on satellites down to a resolution of less than a foot.

He wasn't sure what the information was being used for, but it seemed strange to be observing the International Space Station every time it passed overhead. Rumors buzzing through the Haleakala facility claimed that the real target was some other satellite that would be observed at a later date, and what they were doing now was just some sort of exercise. In any case, Chip was excited to be finally at the center of the action, and not just sitting on the sidelines monitoring contractors.

So when his nodding head almost slumped onto the communications console, Chip reached for another can of Bang and prepared for another 300-milligram jolt to his nervous system.

"Lieutenant?"

Chip swiveled in his chair while still holding the unopened can. "Yeah?"

Standing at the door to the communications center was Dr. Young, a thin multiracial woman with pale freckles sprinkled across her face.

"Could you take a look at this?" she asked.

"Sure." Chip turned back to his console. The data links were all working; there was no indication that the AEOS had taken in any information that he needed to pass on to JSPOC.

"What's going on?" he asked, over his shoulder.

"I'm not sure," Young replied. Frowning, she stepped up to the console, holding a thin sheet of paper. The comm center, barely big enough for two people, was electronically shielded as a Faraday cage so that its classified communications gear could not be tapped.

"There's no change in the ISS imagery," Dr. Young said, sounding slightly uncertain, puzzled. "Since we had time on our hands, we decided to use the overflow crew to calibrate the ISAL against the space station, instead of sitting around, doing nothing. And the ISAL discovered a change in its orbital elements."

"Excuse me?"

"ISAL: the inverse synthetic aperture laser experiment we're bringing online to image satellites in geosynchronous orbits."

"Okay, go ahead."

"The ISS uses solar panels similar to the communications satellites in geosynchronous orbit," Dr. Young explained, "so by imaging the space station's arrays with ISAL, we can compare that imagery to other satellite arrays located at GEO, twenty-two thousand miles higher up. That way we can take into account any difference in what we see at low Earth orbit, where the ISS is, and GEO satellites."

Chip shrugged. "Sounds like a good use of the crew's time. But what's going on with ISAL?"

"Here. Look what happened when we tried to calibrate the laser with a distance measurement." Dr. Young handed him the paper. Chip saw it was a computer-generated plot of altitude with respect to time. The line was nearly straight, showing a near-constant altitude of the ISS. At first there was a barely perceptible decrease, then suddenly, just a few minutes ago, the station's altitude precipitously fell. Instead of its normal slow edging lower in altitude due to atmospheric drag, it looked to Chip as though the International Space Station was taking a nosedive, and rapidly falling to Earth.

Chip frowned. "The station's altitude is decreasing. Is something wrong with the laser?"

Dr. Young shook her head. "Don't know. We'll have to take additional measurements. But if this trend continues the rate will increase as the station gets closer to Earth. As it falls deeper into the atmosphere, the air gets thicker, which means more atmospheric drag, and it will drop even faster. Depends on a lot of things, but from this drop rate I give it two, maybe three more days at the most before it hits."

"Wow. That's weird." Handing the paper back to her, Chip mused aloud, "It's not part of our tasking, but since they've been so anal about imaging the station I'd better send this on to JSPOC."

Dr. Young pulled a flash drive from a pocket in her slacks. It had UNCLASSIFIED/FOR OFFICIAL USE ONLY stamped on its side in small print. "Downloaded this after I printed out that graph. Thought you might need it."

"Thanks. Is the drive clean?"

She nodded. "Scanned it before I used it."

"Good." Chip took the flash dive, wrote TS/SCI over its side with a felt-tip pen, then turned back to his console. Inserting the drive into the classified computer, he rapidly typed a header explaining the diagram, then shot it over to JWICS, the Joint Worldwide Intelligence Communications System of JSPOC.

"Hope you don't need the drive anymore," he said to Dr. Young. "You know that the second you brought it here into the vault it became classified at the SCI level. Now it's here to stay."

Dr. Young smiled at him. "That's okay, Lieutenant. Like I said, I thought it was more important for you to have it. We can always buy more."

JOINT SPACE OPERATIONS CENTER (JSPOC), VANDENBERG AIR FORCE BASE, CALIFORNIA

"Admiral, could you take a look at this, sir? It just arrived from Maui over JWICS."

Watch commander Rear Admiral Harrison looked up from his desk. The Joint Space Operations Center was the hub for space situational awareness, keeping track of over twenty-two thousand objects in Earth orbit, from items as small as two inches across to the massive International Space Station. JSPOC tracked objects ranging from the most highly classified spy satellites to pieces of space debris created by the occasional collisions between satellites.

Maui was one of the two unclassified sources that provided highly detailed visual imagery of the International Space Station, which the JSPOC now forwarded to PACOM for up-to-date targeting if the order was ever given to shoot down the station.

Stretching from the west coast of the U.S. to the west coast of India, and ranging from the Arctic to Antarctica, the United States Pacific Command was headquartered just outside of Honolulu. It was responsible for conducting military operations over an area of more than one hundred million square miles, nearly 52 percent of the Earth's surface. PACOM's Aegis antisatellite weapons were so accurate that individual modules of the ISS could be targeted separately to ensure that the entire station would fall harmlessly into the vast Pacific Ocean. The high-resolution imagery from Maui was the key to both choosing a spot to hit the station, as well as detecting if the ISS deviated from its prescribed orbit.

The core of the Space Operations Center was a large room, bustling with activity. Navy, Army, Air Force, and Marine personnel worked at their consoles side by side with a smattering of civilians. Sections of the room were partitioned off by blue cloth-covered foam rectangles with gleaming metal siding. Stenciled signs hung over each functional area, from J2: INTELLIGENCE, and J3: OPERATIONS to J6: COMMAND, CONTROL, COMMUNICATIONS, AND COMPUTER/CYBER.

Admiral Harrison was a compactly built officer with a graying crewcut and steely blue-gray eyes. The officers under him sometimes ran betting pools on when the Admiral would smile again. The Chief Master Sergeant standing before his desk was a new man, blond and youthful, but almost as stern as the Admiral himself. They got along well.

"What've you got, Chief? Any change in the imagery?"

"No, sir. But it's bad news."

The Admiral glanced at the red-bordered sheet that the young

Chief slid across his desk. Marked TS/SCI on both the top and bottom of the sheet, instead of showing a highly detailed image of the International Space Station, it bore a single, decreasing line on a two-dimensional plot of altitude versus time.

Harrison frowned. "You've only plotted two points on this graph."

"Yes, sir, but it clearly shows the station's descending."

"Two points don't show a trend; this is a hiccup." Harrison looked up, frowning at the younger man. "Any verification on this?"

"No, sir, not yet. The ISS is due to come in range of the Space Fence in fifteen minutes, and we'll have more points for the graph, to see if this is real or just an artifact from the Maui site. We'll also get dual confirmation at that time, as well as a rough estimate of a time and location of impact. Spacetrack sensors update every four hours and we'll be able to verify it then as well, with the other sensors. MIT's Haystack radar and our Ground-Based Electro-Optical Deep Space Surveillance telescopes will be able to provide more detail by its next orbit."

"Okay," said the Admiral. "Go ahead and shoot this stuff over to the Joint Staff as well as PACOM. But tell them we won't have verifications for another quarter hour. Still, the JCS will want to forward this to the National Security Council as soon as possible, I imagine. And immediately after you send it, copy 14th Air Force as well as the other service space elements through JWICS's special access channels as a heads-up; and inform NASA liaison. In the meantime, work on confirming the data. We've got to keep PACOM in the loop on this, real-time."

"Yes, sir." The Chief hesitated. "But what if the astronauts are still alive? Do you really think PACOM will shoot down the station, Admiral?"

"They will if given the order," Harrison said. "Right now the President has a choice to either let a few astronauts die—if they're even alive up there—or risk the lives of thousands, probably more, if the public learns that the ISS will crash and may hit them. But the Aegis cruisers won't even be in position to take down the station for another three days or more, so it may turn out that the station crashes anyway."

"Isn't there anything else we can do?"

"Classify the orbital elements so the public won't have access. That'll keep it out of the unclassified Spacetrack."

The Chief was silent for a moment. "Then we'll have to take down the entire Spacetrack database, sir. We can't just go in and remove or change the data, especially if the public has unfettered access."

"Okay, then take down the whole damned Spacetrack website before the next sensor update, ASAP if not sooner. We can't afford to let this go public."

"But sir . . . that will take some time, and since the data is updated automatically, we may not be able to prevent the station's orbital elements from being entered. It'd be like waving a red flag in front of a bull. The press is already looking for anything unusual happening with the space station, and this will only start more rumors flying."

"Just do it!" Admiral Harrison snapped. "If the ISS is really coming down, we can't afford to be feeding the media an update every four hours on how fast the station's deorbiting. They'll just bring in their own experts and start making forecasts of where and when it will hit, and that'll stoke the flames even higher. And don't give 'em any lame excuse, like the site's down for maintenance. They'll see right through that. Just take the damned thing off-line!"

"Yes, sir. Anything else, Admiral?"

"Yeah." Harrison handed the sheet back. "Pray for a miracle to happen, Chief."

JAPANESE
MODULE (JPM)

"Kimberly!" Scott yelped, alarmed. "What's going on?"

Kimberly ran her fingers over the laptop's keyboard. "Something tells me we don't have three days for the Dragon to get here. At the rate those yahoos are pushing the thrusters, the ISS is decelerating a lot faster than they threatened. Can you get CAPCOM to come up with an estimate of how long I have?"

The voice link bleeped, and suddenly it sounded as if the transmission was coming from a large room filled with people.

"Kimberly, CAPCOM." Tarantino's reedy voice. "We broke your link with Basher and now you're broadcasting over the MCC. Do you read?"

"Rog."

"ADCO reports you're dropping in altitude, and TOPO estimates station at entry interface in less than seventy-two hours. Our liaison with JSPOC and 14th Air Force at Space Command confirms the orbital elements. Can you engage your fore thrusters to raise your altitude?"

Kimberly stared intently at the laptop's display screen, her mind racing. *At entry interface*, she echoed: NASA gobbledygook for fully hitting the atmosphere, moments before impact.

She mentally raced through a dozen options, trying to find a way to stop the flow of hypergolic propellants and cut the aft thrusters, or at least rotate the ISS back 180 degrees so that the thrusters would then reverse the deorbit. But nothing worked; she was locked out and couldn't access any of the controls.

Her jaw tightening, she replied, "Negative, CAPCOM. I need to regain control. I think they've locked me out of the system at the 1533 level. Scott said he'd have the Flight Director expedite a fix. How long will it take to get a software patch?"

"Stand by one." The link to the mission control center fell silent for a moment. Then, "We're working on it. You'll have the patch within thirty-six hours—"

"Wrong answer!" Kimberly interrupted. "You've got to do better than that. Thirty-six hours will put the ISS too deep down in the atmosphere to recover. I'll be pushing up against the entry interface. We wouldn't have enough fuel on board to boost back up, even if we tapped the FGB reserve and the fuel on both Soyuzes."

"That's the best estimate I'm getting," Tarantino said. "MCC's thrown everybody on it. It's our top priority—thirty-six hours."

"What about those Pros from Dover that Scott was touting? They're supposed to be software wizards!"

The link went quiet for a moment. "The pros from . . . *where*?"

"Dover. It's an old expression for expert, outside consultants. NSA—the spooks!"

"Oh, right. Stand by one." Silence. Then CAPCOM came back curtly. "Revised estimate is less than twelve hours. The patch will be transmitted over the Ka data link. We'll alert you before it's broadcasted, and will be continuously looped so we can be sure there's been a valid transmission. Recommend you go ahead and set up an interface to accept the patch so you'll be able to directly insert it into the 1553 system. You'll need some kind of large storage capacity as it's going to be a big one. Copy?"

"Copy," said Kimberly. She left the laptop and pushed off for the crystal growth experiment table, intending to cannibalize its data acquisition system and connect it to the JPM data uplink so she could store the software patch when it came up from the ground. She felt grateful that the Air Force Academy experiment used solid-state storage instead of the older and cheaper rotating hard discs. The time difference in buffering alone would expedite the insertion of the software.

Now that the ISS was decreasing in altitude her old worry about where the software patch might originate from evaporated into thin air. Getting the fix and regaining control of the ISS was now top priority. She just hoped that whoever jury-rigged the patch would at least test it on the virtual software platform NASA used to simulate the ISS's operating system. She didn't want to have any bugs in the patch show up that would make matters worse. She didn't think she'd get a second chance to try it again.

She knew there was still an open mike to the MCC, and she'd never say it out loud, but if the station really did deorbit and she wasn't shot down, Kimberly knew she'd burn up from the heat during reentry. Either option was a hell of a way to go, literally.

The next seventy-two hours might be her last.

Instead of moping about it and wringing her hands, though, the thought made her even more determined to stop the SOBs who were threatening the lives of thousands, if not millions of people.

Including her own.

FLASHBACK: KIMBERLY AND SCOTT

With nothing to do except wait for the software patch from the ground to reach her, Kimberly gave in to the need for sleep that was overwhelming her. Her entire body ached, the wound on her hip throbbed sullenly, and her eyes felt heavier with each passing moment.

Get a few minutes of sleep, she told herself. You don't want to screw up everything by making a mistake because you're sleep-deprived.

She didn't feel altogether secure in the JPM. The hatch that led to the vestibule was firmly held in place by tons of air pressure, she knew, but still the thought of the two murderous terrorists on the loose in the ISS made her jittery.

Reluctantly, she wriggled against the bags of supplies and equipment held against the module's wall by the webbing of bungee cords. But it wasn't the terrorists that she thought of. It was Scott, and the last night of their marriage . . . .

Kimberly remembered lying on her side of the bed, warm and

sticky after their bout of lovemaking. Despite his massive ego and macho attitudes, Scott was a passionate, attentive lover.

He had turned over on his side of the bed and murmured drowsily, "G'night, Kim."

"Kimberly," she'd said. Was he doing this on purpose? He didn't respect her as a scientist and certainly not as a fellow astronaut. And just because it was announced she'd be the new ISS commander—a position he'd recently filled—didn't give him the right to take it out on her.

"Huh?"

"My name is Kimberly. I don't like being called Kim. You know that."

Turning back toward her, he said, "Kim, Kimberly, Kablooey. What's the difference?"

She propped herself up on an elbow. "I want to be called by my correct name. Kimberly."

She heard him puff out a weary sigh. "G'night. Kim."

"Kimberly!"

"Aw, don't make such a big deal about it."

Anger rising inside her, she asked, "How would you like being called Scotty?"

"I've been called worse."

"Beam me up, Scotty. Captain Kirk's looking for you."

"You're being ridiculous."

"No, *you* are. I want to be called by my proper name. Is that too much to ask?"

"I like Kim. It's cuter."

"I don't like it. I don't want to be reduced to a Kewpie doll."

"Kewpie doll? Good lord!" In the darkened bedroom, she heard the irritation in Scott's voice. "Just go to sleep, will you? I've got a big day tomorrow."

"And I don't?" she snapped.

"Come off it, for chrissakes."

"You're an insensitive macho gorilla."

"And you've been reading too much feminist crap."

"I have a right to be called by my correct name!"

"You're a spoiled brat. What you need is a good spanking."

Kimberly threw the covers off her naked body and got out of bed. It was the last straw; the jerk's ego was so big he couldn't think of anyone but himself. He couldn't stand to know that his wife—a *scientist* of all people, and not even a pilot—was just as competent as he was, and was commanding the ISS. But he'd never admit it.

"Scott, if you can't call me by my real name, if it's too much to ask you to come down from that high-and-mighty throne you're always perched on . . ." She hesitated, and then plowed ahead, "We might as well put an end to this right here and now."

With that, Kimberly marched to the bathroom, flicked on the lights, and began pulling her cosmetics from the drawers . . . .

Half-asleep in the bungee-cord jail of the JPM, she told herself, *That was stupid. You overreacted.* But then she thought, *What's done is done. You can't undo it.*

That didn't make her feel any better.

International Space Station

International Docking Adapter
(IDA)

Inflatable
Module

Cupola

Fuel Access Panel

Node 3

PMM

Zenith Berthing Port

Experimental Airlock

JLP

JPM

←aft

Service Module (SM)

MRM 2

DC-1

FGB

MRM 1

Node 1

Joint Airlock

U.S. Lab

Node 2

Nadir Berthing Port

COLUMBUS

Russian ПpK (Peh-err-ka)
"transfer chamber"

Flattened "Roadkill" view — does not reflect
modules extending into/out of page

DAY THREE

NASA HEADQUARTERS, WASHINGTON, D.C.

Scott Robinson walked briskly down the carpeted hallway and turned into the Administrator's suite. The Chief of Staff's door was open and Scott headed for Mini's office when Simone's Executive Assistant stood up and hurried to the Administrator's door.

"They're all in here."

"Thanks." Scott veered toward the frosted door that had an old blue NASA meatball emblem painted on it. "Who else is in there with them?"

As he opened the door, the Executive Assistant half-whispered, "Public Affairs, Legislative Liaison—and they've flown in Sophia Flores, the acting PAO from Johnson, to make sure we're all on the same page."

Scott grunted as the man held the door open for him. A long-time NASA employee, Patricia's EA seemed to know everyone in the Headquarters building, as well as any arcane facet about the nation's space program, both the manned spaceflight side and the science programs.

As the EA closed the door behind him Patricia motioned for Scott to join the four others seated around her table. He lifted an eyebrow as he recognized Sophia, the acting PAO from JSC—it was the "Voice of NASA" who narrated the Soyuz docking. At first he'd thought she'd deserted her post, but he'd later learned that, lucky for the senior PAO, the quick-thinking young lady had saved the man's life.

Mini nodded toward the large TV monitor on the opposite side of the room. It showed a CNN reporter standing with other newscasters outside the Johnson Space Center, in Texas's baking heat. Nearby, a crowd of people milled around disconsolately, carrying signs protesting the lack of information about the ISS and demanding that NASA release details about the astronauts.

A stream of text flowed beneath the picture, identifying the spokesperson being interviewed as the webmaster for Heavens -above.com, an amateur website dedicated to providing customized predictions of satellite locations and other astronomical data.

"They've discovered the station is descending." Simone kept her eyes on the TV screen as she spoke. "What's the status of that software patch?"

"The NSA's thrown everything they have on it," Scott said as he slid onto an empty chair. "Our Failure Investigation Team at Johnson has given them a copy of the ISS software operating system and you'll be the first to know when they have the update."

Simone swung her amber eyes to Scott. "I want to be the second to know. Kimberly's the first. She should get access to the patch as soon as it's complete."

"Copy that," said Scott.

"Good. We've generated a news release to try to quell these protests—"

"Is that a good idea?" Scott asked. "The White House is pretty hard-over about not releasing any information."

"And they're also pretty hard-over about killing our astronauts," Patricia snapped. "The public now knows the station is descending at a much higher rate than you'd expect from atmospheric drag. The media is also rebroadcasting last month's Russian launch of those RTGs to the station—and what could happen if the plutonium is released. We've got to do something; otherwise we'll come across as the gang that couldn't shoot straight."

"Yes, ma'am. I understand. But you know the President is well aware of the consequences if the station continues to deorbit. I don't agree either about having a total news blackout. We need to throw the public a bone, quiet things down before they get hysterical about impact. The Dragon mission may be our best chance to keep the nation from panicking."

Scott sensed his pulse rate rising. He knew that he should bite his tongue and not say anything about Simone refusing to put him on the Dragon mission. That would be the best course of action. But he kept hearing his own motto: *Never give up, never give in.* And he knew he wasn't about to start backing down now.

Simone asked, "Did you tell Kimberly what the President is considering? That he may take preemptive action and shoot down the ISS?"

"Chief Astronaut Tarantino told her before I could. But I think she'd already figured that out for herself," Scott replied. "She's no fool."

Simone nodded and said, "I want to talk to her personally, whether or not that patch arrives in time. She deserves to know that it wasn't an easy decision that her own nation may take out the ISS, much less there's a very good chance that she's going to die. I don't want her hearing any wild rumors secondhand from her ham radio."

"She can handle it," Scott said. "She knows the risks. This isn't some research job here on the ground."

The head of Public Affairs cleared his throat. "This is probably a stupid question, but there are all these movies where astronauts are in danger and they end up surviving in their spacesuits, even making it to the ground—"

"That *is* a stupid question," Mini growled, his face flushed. "You'd better know how to answer it, too, with a roomful of cameras on you. You'll be asked it if it ever gets out that Kimberly's still alive."

"You mean *when* it gets out," Scott said softly. He didn't want to further embarrass the Public Affairs man from Headquarters; they were all on the same team, after all.

Sophia leaned over and said quietly to the man, "The EVA suits only carry enough oxygen for about eight and a half hours. And even if astronaut Hadid-Robinson did manage to get into one of the suits, the Dragon capsule couldn't bring her inside. It doesn't open up to vacuum; it needs to mate with a berthing port on the station. So an EVA suit wouldn't help; *no* suit would help, much less survive reentry. Plus, she doesn't have access to either a spacesuit or an airlock; she's holed up in the JPM."

Scott stared at Sophia. She's good. What was her name? Sophia Flowers . . . Flores?

The young woman reddened. "My father worked at Johnson all my life."

"I couldn't have explained it better myself." Scott thought for a moment. "Kimberly does have access to one of the second-generation suits we squirreled away in the JPM, but it doesn't have its own air supply, it needs a hose to provide oxygen, so that's useless as well."

"Thanks," the PA man said. "I . . . I guess I suspected as much."

Simone turned to the head of Public Affairs. "Okay. Now what about the news release? What do you have?"

Seemingly glad to have attention moved away from his EVA

question, the man slid a paper from a stack in front of each person at the table. "Per your direction, we wrote a press statement, but we kept our communications link to the ISS secret, so the terrorists don't discover it exists. In addition, we recommend not revealing that Astronaut Hadid-Robinson is still alive and has barricaded herself away from the terrorists—"

"Excuse me." The Legislative Liaison man held up a finger. "You don't think that news would rally people around the astronaut, and NASA, as well? This could really have a positive impact for the station if we played this well, especially now that it's out that the station is descending."

"And it would give the terrorists a heads-up that she's in contact with us," Mini countered. "They'd cut the Japanese Ka-band in a New York second and we'd be out of contact."

"Yes, but—"

"Mini's right," Simone said flatly. "And we'd also be risking the only way of getting that software patch to her." Turning to Public Affairs, she continued, "No mention of Kimberly. The release should be short and sweet: NASA doesn't know what has happened, and we're doing everything we can to raise the station to its proper altitude. That gives us, and the President, as much wiggle room as possible for keeping the rescue mission quiet, as well as ensuring that the link stays alive." She nodded at Sophia. "Get back to Houston, as fast as you can." She looked around the room. "And change of plans: All announcements will be done at JSC. They've got one hell of an acting PAO. Got it?"

"Yes, ma'am," said the PA man, a bit sullenly, as he gathered up the sheets of the draft news release.

Simone turned to Scott. "Next topic. How much time do we have before the President executes Burnt Haunt?"

"The Aegis cruisers need to be in position, and they're under sail, top speed. They left Pearl Harbor twelve hours after the

President authorized the Joint Chiefs to pre-position the ships. I checked with the JCS just before heading over here and they estimate the cruisers will be in optimum range in three days."

Simone looked back at the TV screen. It showed a heavyset man shaking a fist at the camera as a young woman tried to cover a sign that read: KILL NASA NOT ASTRONAUTS! THE TRUTH IS OUT THERE!

Shaking her head mournfully, Simone said, "We're in a race against time. Burnt Haunt, the software patch for Kimberly to take back control of the ISS, and the rescue mission are all running on the same time scale. But which one gets in position first?" She turned back to the conference table, pulled in a breath, then went on, "Okay. Continue with the rescue mission until Burnt Haunt is executed. And in the meantime go ahead with that news release, generic as it is. At least the public should know that NASA is doing everything we can to reestablish communication with the station."

"And hopefully keep them from panicking," Scott said. "So we won't force the President's hand on Burnt Haunt."

"Unless the press finds out that the station is descending and forces him to do it. He may decide to cut his losses and take out the ISS early, before the panic gets really out of hand. So we go on the assumption that once those Aegis cruisers are in place, the ISS is dead meat."

"As well as Kimberly and the rest of the space program," Scott muttered.

JAPANESE MODULE (JPM)

For what seemed like the hundredth time, Kimberly checked the solid-state data acquisition system, worrying that the mission control center had either forgotten to alert her that the software patch had come through, or that something had happened to the voice link and MCC couldn't alert her that it had arrived.

The light on the solid-state hard drive gleamed a steady red, showing no activity. Frustrated, Kimberly once again pushed back to the middle of the JPM, trying to control her fear that the ISS was plunging to Earth.

Patience is a virtue, she told herself. And quickly added, Yeah, but I'm going to be tearing my hair out in another five minutes.

Get your mind off it, she thought. Focus on something else until the mother-loving patch comes through.

She looked over the bags stowed on the JPM walls in their various bungee-cord prisons, but nothing jumped out at her as a weapon she might use against the two terrorists. She mentally kicked herself for missing her chance when Farid had been using the toilet and Bakhet had been asleep.

By monitoring the electrical activity and nontraditional sensors located throughout the ISS she could tell that the two now seemed to be nearly inseparable, most likely having learned their lesson that if they were isolated she would pounce. So before she could engage them again, she had to figure out a way to separate them, move them apart so that she could take them out one by one.

So much for the Israeli Defense Force's Krav Maga and the CIA's assessment of how dangerous those guys were. The nonsport martial art was probably deadly enough in a normal Earth environment, but here on the ISS—where they had nowhere as much experience moving around in zero-gee as she did—their refined, lethal moves were of no use as long as she was barricaded safely inside the JPM, separated by the twelve tons of force tightly sealing her hatch.

But if the software patch didn't arrive soon she knew she wouldn't have the patience to stay holed up in the JPM while the station continued to descend in altitude. The sooner she could engage the forward thrusters to boost the ISS into a higher orbit, the better. She didn't want to wait too much longer before she reacted.

She floated across to one of the bungee-cord prisons and started rummaging through the supplies cached inside it one more time. She'd already searched through everything in the module, but she had a nagging feeling that she might have overlooked something she could use to overpower the two.

MCC continued to offer suggestions over the voice link, and they certainly had some good ideas, but since they didn't have real-time knowledge of exactly where everything was located in the ISS, their recommendations were useless. She would have been able to whip up three or four MacGyver-type devices to take out the terrorists if she only had access to the entire station. But for years the station's astronauts and cosmonauts had been continuously moving supplies around and not relaying down to

Earth what they'd done or where they'd stashed the equipment. Kimberly simply didn't have access to the things she needed to construct a single, credible weapon. The bungee-corded bags and food pouches in the JPM were all that were available.

Be that as it may, she knew she still needed something to fight with. Even if the software patch came through right away, Kimberly knew she would eventually have to move out of the JPM. Even if NASA successfully launched the reconfigured Dragon with a few astronauts in it, when they got to the ISS she'd have to pull them in to a berthing port, using the robotic arm. She'd have to control it from the U.S. lab, since the cargo vessels couldn't dock themselves automatically.

Then, after they'd docked, she'd somehow have to get to Node 2, where the port for berthing with an unmanned commercial spacecraft was located, and let the astronauts into the station— all while making sure that Farid and Bakhet were kept at bay, so the "rescuing" astronauts could come aboard. Otherwise, what could they do if they couldn't get into one of the berthing ports? Ram the ISS?

That wouldn't do any good.

And the astronauts in the modified Dragon capsule couldn't leave their vehicle and spacewalk to the station. The Dragon wasn't like one of the old Gemini or Apollo capsules, where the astronauts wore spacesuits into orbit and could open their hatch to the vacuum of space, exit their spacecraft, and perform an EVA. The new commercial capsules were designed solely to dock with the station and not open directly to vacuum. The astronauts had to enter the ISS through a berthing port if they wanted to get on board.

So in any case, Kimberly figured she'd eventually have to confront the two terrorists face-to-face. And if MCC couldn't brainstorm a weapon for her to use, then she'd have to whip one up herself, either now or later.

She pushed away from the bags and stopped her momentum by grasping the frame that anchored the data acquisition equipment. She peered at the storage device. Still nothing. Her feet rotated up and she felt her heart thumping with frustration. *Come on, guys! Where's the patch?*

So what would she do if she left the safety of the JPM? First she'd have to separate the two, perhaps by making a feint and tricking them into thinking she was somewhere else after she'd left the JPM. And just like her original plan to ambush them after they'd passed through one of the modules, she'd have to quickly surprise and disable the first one, then somehow overpower the second. It was a gamble, but with her speed and ability to maneuver in zero-gee, Kimberly thought she could pull it off.

And with what little time she had left, she knew she'd have to.

But what would she do even if she did manage to overpower them?

One of them, probably Farid, had gotten into the ISS system and was preventing her from rotating the station by 180 degrees and turning the deorbit into a re-boost. That was a software problem, not hardware. Since all the station functions were controlled through the graphical interface, it wasn't as though there was a physical knob she could turn, or a valve like she'd find back on Earth to twist. There was simply nothing physical she could do to solve the problem.

She raced through different scenarios in her head, following various logic trees and coming up with possible outcomes, and she didn't like any of the answers.

What if the MCC didn't come up with a usable patch, or what if they needed to have direct access to the station's 1533 system in order for her to regain control?

Or what if their patch simply didn't work?

She couldn't just sit around and wait for the U.S. Cavalry to ride up and rescue her. If it turned out that the software patch didn't work after she'd installed it, and the entire twelve hours had already passed, then it would be that much harder for her to boost the ISS back up to a stable orbit. Maybe impossible.

Then a flash of memory reminded her of a motto from the military construction battalions of World War II: *The impossible we do right away; the miraculous takes a little time.*

I'll have to do the impossible, Kimberly said to herself. And do it right away.

She wondered how much of the thrusters' propellants those guys had used. She knew she could always tap into an emergency propellant reserve by shunting propellants from the two docked Soyuz capsules. She wouldn't have any propellants left to return to Earth at that point, but it really wouldn't matter if her other option was doing nothing and allowing the ISS to deorbit and crash. And if she waited too long to act, the station would be at such a low altitude that all the propellant on board wouldn't be enough to boost it back up to a stable orbit.

Kimberly glided over to the PCS laptop and pulled up a schematic of the nontraditional sensors. It looked as though the two were in Central Post, at the other end of the station. They must be satisfied that they'd engaged the thrusters, and that she remained holed up in the JPM, too terrified to put up a fight.

Grimly, she pushed over to the hatch and grabbed Shep's knife from where she'd stored it after reentering the JPM. She peered out the viewport while tightly grasping the ultrasharp tool. The data acquisition system remained silent.

She couldn't do anything physically to stop the ISS from deorbiting; she was wholly dependent on a software solution. And that had to come from the patch transmitted by MCC to regain access to the thrusters—unless she could force one of the terrorists to do it.

She was convinced it was Farid who'd locked her out of the station's controls; if he'd taken away her access, maybe with the right motivation he might give it back to her.

She'd first have to take out Bakhet, then turn her attention to Farid, keeping him lucid enough to . . . *encourage* him to remove the block he'd placed on her access.

Encourage him with Shep's knife. It wouldn't be pretty, and just the thought of what she might have to do made her feel nauseous.

Unbidden, a memory of something her father had told her long ago surfaced in her mind: *The essence of evil is that it leads good people to perform evil deeds.* Could I really carve up Farid to save the station? To save millions who might be slaughtered? To save my own life?

Kimberly nodded bleakly. I'll have to, she told herself. There won't be any other way.

Time was running out. And although the two of them had supposedly been trained in the Israeli Defense Force's Krav Maga, Kimberly told herself that she could outmaneuver them.

If she didn't, the station would continue to fall Earthward. And if it crashed that would not only be the end of the International Space Station, but it would also be the kiss of death for America's space program.

And her death, as well.

She couldn't wait any longer for MCC or anyone else to solve her problem.

Time for a showdown.

NASA HEADQUARTERS, WASHINGTON, D.C.

Scott hung around the Administrator's office as Patricia Simone signed off on the freshly typed news release. He waited until the last person headed for the door, and closed it softly when only the Administrator and her Chief of Staff, his friend Mini Mott, remained.

Simone went to her desk as she said to Mini, "Patch me in to the ISS over the Ka-band voice link. I need to explain to Kimberly everything that's going down here."

"Again, do you think that's wise?" The diminutive Marine shot a glance at Scott. "She's likely to try to take matters into her own hands and not wait for the software fix."

Simone drew herself to her full height, several inches taller than Mini. "She's one of our top people in the astronaut corps. She won't go rogue."

"She took the initiative to barricade herself in the JPM," Mini replied. "That was out of the box."

"That was plain survival. Her life was at stake, for God's sake.

If she'd done anything else she'd be dead now." Simone shook her head as she sat at her desk. "She won't go off script."

"I'm . . . not so sure about that," Scott said slowly.

"What?"

Scott glanced at Mini, who gave him a *go-ahead* nod.

"She's my ex-wife, remember?" Scott asserted. "I know her better than anybody else, even the shrinks. She's driven for success, and she'd do almost anything to get her way."

"Of course I know that," Simone snapped. "She's an astronaut, not only a scientist."

"She's *both*. And that's what makes her dangerous to the terrorists." Scott hesitated briefly. "Do you know that if her last extended interview with NASA's psychologist had gone any longer than two hours she would have probably gone off script and said something that would've flunked her out of the application process?"

Simone stared at him. "What are you talking about?"

"Just that she's incredibly bright, extremely competent, and can only contain herself for a limited amount of time when she's dealing with stupid rules, stupid interviewers, or someone who's trying to stop her from reaching one of her goals. The NASA psychologist tried to trip her up—like he tried to trip up *all* the astronaut applicants—to see if she'd do something out of the ordinary. Of course, she didn't. But she would have if he had kept her cooped up in that room for another half hour.

"You think *I'm* spontaneous? She's not an ex–fighter pilot, or a SEAL who would never go off script and deviate from the mission. But after a certain amount of time, if she'd tried all the approved procedures that she'd needed to survive, she'd figure out something new and come out on top. She'd reinvent the rules. And win."

Simone was silent for a moment. Then, "So she won't sit still and wait for that software patch to arrive, even though CAPCOM ordered her to stay put."

"No she won't." Scott shook his head. "I'd give her another couple of hours at the most. Then she's going to go after the terrorists and get herself killed."

Dead silence. Until Mini spoke up. "So what do we do? The rescue mission launches in two days, but if Kimberly doesn't wait for that patch and tries to take out the terrorists on her own—"

"They'll kill her," said Scott.

"We can't be sure of that," Simone said, drumming her fingers on her desk.

"The hell you can't," Scott growled.

"Whatever you do," Mini said to Simone, "don't remind her about the Burnt Haunt option. Net yet."

"I told you she already knows," Scott said. "She's not stupid. And it's probably at the top of her mind, driving everything she does."

"But maybe . . ."

Scott's chin went up a notch. "Madam Administrator—"

Simone focused on him. "What is it, Basher? You've never called me that before—at least, not in private."

Scott pressed on. "I didn't make a fuss about not being manifested on the Dragon crew."

Simone rolled her eyes and Mini suppressed a snort.

"Well . . . not much of a fuss," Scott continued. "Especially since everyone knows I'm the best qualified to command the rescue mission."

"We've been over this before, Basher. You just said she's your ex-wife, remember? You reminded us about that with your little story of how she beat the psychological exam. So what is it?"

Taking a step toward Simone's desk, Scott answered, "And I respect your decision to not send me on that flight. But look, there's a Boeing CST-100 Starliner capsule on Pad 39B down at the Cape. It's scheduled to launch next month, carrying fuel and other supplies to the ISS . . . ."

"We can't have another launch trying to meet a ten-second window, Basher," Simone said firmly. "And not with that booster. If we lose one rocket, no way am I going to authorize another one—"

"I'm not talking about a ten-second window, Patricia. I'm talking about a normal, NASA risk-averse launch using a two-hour window. Look." Scott turned and pointed to a small, scale model of the International Space Station that hung from the ceiling by the TV set. "If the Dragon reaches the ISS—no, *when* it reaches the station—Kimberly will have already taken control of the ISS and used all its reserve propellants to boost it back up to altitude, or the Dragon's crew will use all the station's reserve propellant after they board."

"What are you getting at?" Simone asked.

"In both cases the ISS will be out of propellants, and not have any left for normal station housekeeping. Not have enough to use the Soyuz or the Dragon for an emergency egress, much less the old Soyuz we're keeping as an escape vehicle. And certainly not enough fuel to boost up in another few weeks to counter atmospheric drag."

Mini objected, "But the two Soyuz capsules already have their own propellants. That's why they're set aside as emergency vehicles for a return to Earth."

"No, they won't," Scott insisted. Turning back to Simone, he went on, "Kimberly's going to use all the propellants on the station, every last drop, to re-boost the ISS back to altitude after what the terrorists have already done. And it doesn't matter if Kimberly gets the best of the terrorists or if the Dragon team overpowers them. If she uses all the reserve propellant, including what's in the two Soyuzes and the Dragon capsule, then the station is eventually going to deorbit from atmospheric drag and not because of the terrorists. Kimberly won't even have enough fuel left to boost the ISS to counter atmospheric drag. And that needs to be done within a few weeks, at best. Right?"

Simone nodded reluctantly. "You're . . . right. Much as I hate to say it, we'll have to accelerate the Boeing launch anyway, in order to resupply the ISS with propellant. The Russians aren't due to launch another Progress resupply vessel for another eight weeks. That's much too long."

Scott pushed ahead. "The CST-100 won't need a ten-second launch window, and you know I'm the best qualified to command that mission. I helped Boeing establish the two-week training course for their Starliner, and just taught the first course. If I can launch after the Dragon, I can get there as soon as a half day after the rescue mission and be able to resupply the ISS with more than enough propellants. I'll give the station the ability to boost to a higher, stable orbit."

Mini objected, "The CST hasn't been approved to carry people yet, Basher. Just fuel. We'd have to certify it for human use, and that would take weeks, way beyond our timetable for saving the ISS." He shook his head. "So don't go there, Basher. It was hard enough certifying the Dragon."

Before Scott could reply, Mini went on, "Besides, like you said, the CST is on Pad 39B, mated with the NASA Space Launch System booster. Which is only a little over a mile and a half from the Falcon 9 carrying the Dragon on Pad 39A. If the Falcon 9 blows up on launch it could take out the Starliner with it. Then we'll lose the ISS for sure, even if Kimberly takes out the two SOBs, because we won't have any boosters left to launch."

Simone nodded, tight-lipped. "So we'll have to send the CST unmanned."

Glaring at her, Scott argued, "You mean you'd risk not being able to dock the CST to the station if the terrorists have screwed with the IDA port, or a hundred other things?" His voice edgier, he went on, "Look, the Starliner is rated for humans; it was designed that way. It just hasn't been certified. And you have the authority to put me on board. All it takes is a waiver, since that capsule hasn't been scheduled for a manned mission. This is an emergency, dammit! Are you going to help save the ISS by putting me on that launch, or are you going to let some bureaucratic bullshit kill the ISS? And Kimberly?"

Simone seemed to be gazing beyond him, staring into space. Scott imagined her mind whirling through all the pros and cons of approving another launch, to resupply the ISS with propellants. And rescue the station by boosting it back up to a stable orbit.

More softly, Scott added, "If you're going to give Kimberly a pep talk, then speak to her about your confidence in the rescue mission succeeding. And tell her that NASA is launching the CST-100 to ensure that the station has enough propellant to goose it up to a stable orbit and keep it there for months to come. *That's* the right talk to have with her. Give her hope that the Dragon mission will succeed and you're already looking past that to stabilize the ISS in orbit. Not remind her that her President is planning to shoot her down."

Patricia Simone refocused her gaze on Scott, but spoke to her Chief of Staff, Mini Mott. "Do it."

JAPANESE MODULE (JPM)

Still clutching Shep's knife, Kimberly pushed away from the hatch and floated to the PCS laptop. She felt her heart thumping beneath her ribs as she once again ran through the graphical interface and prepared to close the valve to the vacuum access port.

She'd run through her plan of action so many times that she thought she could do it in her sleep. Once she'd filled the vestibule connecting the JPM to Node 2 with air she'd quickly open the two hatches, then race through the U.S. lab and Node 1 into Node 3. Once there, she'd perform a feint by screaming like a banshee, then ducking into the PMM module. After the terrorists passed, she'd surprise them from the rear by quickly taking out Bakhet, who would most likely be lagging behind, and then disabling Farid.

Good plan, she thought. But will it work? It's easy to imagine disabling Farid, but can I actually nail the bastard?

She sucked in several deep breaths, preparing for battle.

A faint ding rang from the data acquisition hardware, just as a voice came over the Ka-band link. "Kimberly, we're ready with the patch. You need to move fast. We've got people here who will walk you through the upload. And the Administrator needs to talk to you after you're finished."

She stopped in midair, her heart pounding wildly as she tried to bring herself down from the adrenaline high of anticipating going after the terrorists. She glanced back at the hatch. It would be easy to continue, surprise them when they least expected her to leave the safety of the JPM. Then she'd be able to engage the thrusters and be rid of all her problems.

Again she pulled in deep breaths and tried to refocus. She knew that eventually she'd have to confront the two when the Dragon capsule arrived, but compared to the urgency of stopping the ISS from deorbiting, that task was now an infinite time in the future. She first had to take back control of the station.

Her heart rate started to slow as she pushed away from the laptop and floated to the data storage connected to the Ka-link. Her priorities now pivoted from exiting the JPM and engaging the two terrorists to making sure that the software patch was successfully installed. Her hands felt clammy as she slid Shep's knife into a trousers pocket.

After connecting the solid-state disc to the laptop, the MCC experts first verified that the patch had arrived uncorrupted, and that no bits had somehow changed while being transmitted to the ISS. Then they walked Kimberly through the installation procedure, carefully going over each control to gain access to the vehicle 1553 system.

Once she'd completed the final step Kimberly floated in front of the PCS laptop. "Nothing's happened," she said. "How do we know it worked?"

"Can you rotate the station to re-boost?" the disembodied voice from MCC came over the link. "The patch was inserted covertly below the Linux level. We needed the extra time getting the software to you to ensure that the ISS system wouldn't reboot while installing and tip the bad guys off. You should now have regained control and have user authority, locking them out."

Kimberly ran her fingers over the graphical interface. "I'm in!" She tuned out the muted sound of applause that came over the voice link. She pulled up the control functions. Good. It appeared that the terrorists hadn't put in any physical roadblocks, such as disconnecting any data channels.

Working rapidly, she slowly yawed the ISS, causing it to rotate 180 degrees. She kept the aft thrusters going, turning the station so slowly that she couldn't detect the motion. The acceleration from the thrusters was only 100 micro-gees; the only way the terrorists would be able to detect the motion would be if they were to look out a hatch and see the Earth moving. Within ten minutes Kimberly rotated the ISS and now, instead of losing altitude, the station was boosting up to a higher orbit.

A thrill ran through her. But she wasn't finished yet.

Farid had used most of the station's reserve propellants in his deorbit burn. Kimberly needed to ensure that she'd not only have enough fuel available to raise the ISS to a stable altitude, but have enough of the hypergolic propellants left over for station-keeping: to periodically re-boost the ISS to counter atmospheric drag.

Her time horizon instantly expanded, and now that the station was rising like a Phoenix, she started planning how to keep it alive and kicking for the long haul. Still at her laptop, her fingers flew through various options as she methodically opened a pathway from the docked Soyuz vehicles to the propellant tanks, diverting their propellants for later use by the station.

But although she'd won this match, Kimberly knew she wasn't out of the woods yet.

She started to switch over to her "intelligence" schematic of nontraditional sensors in the ISS to see if Farid and Bakhet had moved since she'd started the forward thrusters. On a whim, she opened a window on the laptop and accessed the web cameras in

Central Post, normally used for private conversations with families back on Earth. She also tied in their microphones.

Her laptop screen showed the ISS command center. The feed was from one of the first sensors that Farid had cut after they'd killed Ivan Vasilev and Al . . . .

In the webcast's small window she saw the two terrorists storming around the module, frenziedly attempting to access several of the Russian and Ops laptops all at once. They must have detected the rotation, Kimberly guessed, and her actions had obviously infuriated the Kazakhstanis. It appeared that they were trying every conceivable countermove they could think of to take back control of the station.

His face radiating fury, Farid moved from keyboard to keyboard while Bakhet slammed a hand against the metal frame. The movement sent him flying upward and he twirled slowly to the center of the module, spittle oozing from his mouth.

Kimberly drew back from the laptop and felt a satisfied sense of calm roll over her. For the first time since the two intruders had come aboard, she felt she might finally have a chance to survive. She'd always known she wouldn't give up without a fight, but there was always the inescapable fear in the back of her mind that things wouldn't work out. It wasn't that she doubted herself, but rather it was the knowledge that she knew her limits, and there were always the unknown unknowns that might somehow rear up and defeat her.

That still might happen, she knew, but seeing the two frustrated terrorists flailing helplessly around the Russian module at least gave her a renewed sense of hope.

"Kimberly, CAPCOM," the voice came over the link. "ADCO reports your altitude has stopped decreasing. What's your situation?"

Without taking her eyes off the frustrated terrorists, Kimberly replied, "The patch worked. Please forward my thanks to everyone who had a hand in helping."

"Copy. We'll be keeping the Ka open as a backup, and in the meantime you should have access to all your down and cross links. And the Kazakhstanis have been locked out of all system control. Once you bring up the video we'll patch you in to the Administrator. Patricia Simone has some good news for you about the Dragon and its backup."

"Rog," Kimberly replied.

Now that the ISS wasn't losing altitude she thought she should set about reestablishing contact with her other links. But she hesitated and instead resumed watching the two terrorists flailing about the Command Center.

She briefly thought about taunting the bastards, rubbing it in that she'd won, but she realized that such an action would infuriate them even more and make them redouble their efforts to circumvent what she'd done. They certainly had shown what they're capable of doing; if she hadn't had immense resources on the ground backing her up, the situation might well have been reversed, and it might well be them watching her fight for her life.

At least everything was in the clear for the moment. CAPCOM had confirmed that she now controlled the ISS systems and the terrorists had been locked out, unable to change the situation. She didn't have to worry about the terrorists reengaging the thrusters.

But she also knew that within a few days the Dragon would arrive and she'd still have the problem of dealing with Farid and Bakhet face-to-face. And although she controlled the ISS systems now, she was alarmingly low on propellants.

So she'd still have to confront the murderers if she was going to use the robotic arm to pull in the Dragon and then assure that one of the Node 2 berthing ports was available and working.

And once again that meant intelligent preparation of the battlefield.

She knew that if Scott were getting ready for battle the first thing he'd do would be to ensure that he had the upper hand. That implied making certain that the terrorists were in no shape to fight. Which in turn meant wearing them down physically.

She had two days. The easiest way of wearing them down was to take away their air and let the SOBs suffocate. But if she tried to vent the air in the ISS there was nowhere near enough reserve to fill the station back up again. The ISS's 33,000 cubic feet of pressurized volume would require several resupply flights just to replenish its air; it would overwhelm the Oxygen Generation System's meager five to twenty pounds produced in a day. The total mass of all the air in the station weighed more than a ton.

Scratch that, Kimberly thought. It would be tough to gain the upper hand by doing something to the ISS that wouldn't affect her.

Maybe she could do something that would affect them psychologically, mess with their minds.

She called up the master function for the station's lighting systems. She clicked the boxes next to all the modules except the JPM, then set the control state to OFF. Glancing at the webcast, she saw the view from Central Post had plunged into darkness. Except for the faint glows coming from the laptops in the modules, she saw nothing but blurs crossing the screen as Farid and Bakhet stumbled in the shadows.

They were screaming so loud that she turned the volume down on the audio. She could make out garbled curses, but could barely understand what they were shouting:

> . . . *a Middle Eastern whore is stopping us!*
> . . . *an affront and a dishonor to our culture!*

Smiling, Kimberly switched off the monitor and tried to think of what else she could do. She had only two more days to prepare the battlefield before the Dragon arrived.

International Space Station

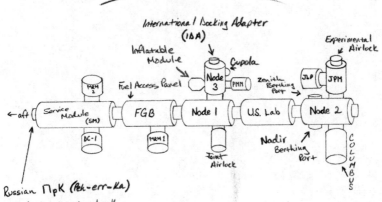

Flattened "Roadkill" view — does not reflect
modules extending into/out of page

TWO DAYS LATER

DAY FIVE

KENNEDY
SPACE CENTER,
CAPE CANAVERAL,
FLORIDA

Scott Robinson lay on his back in the acceleration couch of the CST-100 Starliner's crew module atop NASA's Space Launch System booster rocket, his booted feet elevated, waiting for the launch.

Unlike his three previous Soyuz flights from the Baikonur launch center in Kazakhstan, where he'd had to wear the Russian-designed Sokol-KV2 spacesuit, he felt quite comfortable in the so-called "Boeing Blue" spacesuit, manufactured exclusively for the Starliner with its touch-screen-sensitive gloves, flexible material, and soft helmet.

Over the continuing chatter from the launch team he could hear the muted sounds of the rocket coming alive: creaking and groaning as the liquid oxygen and hydrogen propellants were pumped into their tanks, the background hum of electrical connections, the pops and sighs of metal expanding and contracting throughout the incredibly sophisticated assembly.

The CST-100 was like a vast, voluminous cavern compared to what Scott had experienced in the cramped Soyuz launches. But to be fair, he told himself, Boeing's Starliner was the new kid on the block; the Soyuz had direct lineage from the 1960s Cold War days, the brainchild of the Soviet Union's renowned Korolev Design Bureau.

The Starliner carried no other supplies except enough hypergolic propellants to fill the reserve tankage of the ISS.

Scott had complete faith in both the Dragon launch and his own, despite there being less than nine thousand feet separation between the two rockets. He knew that Mini Mott fretted over the risk that a catastrophe with the Dragon on Pad 39A could very likely engulf the Starliner and make it explode, too. But life was a risk, Scott thought. So he was sitting at the top of a massive Roman candle, 322 feet above the ground, ready to be hurled skyward by 5.5 million pounds of thrust from two solid rocket boosters and four RS-25 liquid fuel engines. And even that was *nothing* compared to what Kimberly was going through.

He flicked his eyes over the control board's readouts while half listening to the ongoing countdown for the Falcon 9 booster and its Dragon capsule on the next pad. Those guys have a much tighter launch schedule, and even if they make their ten-second window, they'll still have nearly four hours of flight time before reaching the ISS and trying to carry out a rescue.

The last he'd heard, while he was suiting up and getting ready to head for the launch pad, was that Kimberly had agreed to stay in the JPM and not get involved in a face-to-face confrontation with the two terrorists.

Right.

He didn't believe that for a nanosecond.

He just hoped that she hadn't heard about the massive protests that had broken out when the public learned that the ISS had started coming down. The Heavens-above.com amateur satellite-tracking website had released the government's latest Spacetrack database just before mysteriously going off-line. Their analysis showed clearly that the space station was descending. Now, without access to more current data, the public didn't have any confirmation other than NASA's assurance that the ISS's orbital elements showed that the station was *not* descending.

Which hardly anybody believed. Traffic jams started to clog the arteries of New York, Los Angeles, and many cities in between. People were marching in the streets, demanding to know what the government was hiding. Vacations for local police throughout the country were canceled in anticipation of the growing protests, and eleven state governments had called up the National Guard as a precaution.

Scott knew that behind the government's silence a fierce power struggle between different factions was raging. The military wanted to keep the ISS's orbital data secret and out of the public's knowledge, since it would probably be used as targeting information for the Aegis antisatellite weapons. NASA wanted complete transparency, to quell the public's fears. But the National Security Council and the President had the upper hand and refused to allow the release of more data, because if the ISS started descending again, knowledge of the station's rate of fall would generate only more panic.

Scott pushed the whole brouhaha out of his mind. He knew that university telescopes and amateur laser enthusiasts were now focusing their instruments on the station and producing their own altitude measurements—and releasing their dubious results to the news media—while the government tried to stuff the proverbial information genie back into its bottle.

Bullshit, he thought. The only thing that counts is getting to the ISS and stopping those two madmen before they destroy the station and kill maybe a couple million people on the ground.

And Kimberly.

He felt a sudden rumble and the CST capsule swayed slightly. They've launched the Dragon! he realized. Because of his distance from Pad 39A it took a little over eight seconds for the sound to reach his own launch pad.

The Falcon 9 pad was enveloped in smoke, and a fiery trail of rocket exhaust climbed into the sky. Scott's capsule quivered with the thunderous vibration of the Falcon's launch. The rocket appeared to be well on its way.

Scott renewed his focus on the words coming over his headset. His own countdown was continuing on schedule. I'm next up, he knew, as the low sound of "Standing on Higher Ground" came over his headphones; the old Alan Parsons Project song was Kimberly's favorite, and he'd chosen it for her when mission control had asked him what he'd like to hear in the minutes before launch.

Unconsciously he licked his lips. Okay, he thought, kick the tires and light the fire, igniting the rockets. Half a day from now I'll join Kimberly and the four-man rescue team with a full load of propellants.

But if the rescue mission wasn't successful, even if he was present the ISS would deorbit and crash.

With Kimberly aboard.

Scott suddenly realized that he might very well be the last American ever to rocket into space.

JOHNSON SPACE CENTER, BUILDING 2: PUBLIC AFFAIRS FACILITY, HOUSTON, TEXAS

The NASA auditorium was full of reporters and media pundits, anticipating an update on the International Space Station. Standing in the wings just out of sight from the unruly crowd, Sophia Flores smoothed her skirt before entering the room. But her focus was not on waiting press—it was riveted on a TV screen above the entrance to the auditorium that showed live coverage of the protests in New York City.

It looked like the entire population had taken to the streets. People chanted and held signs, accusing NASA of covering up the danger from the space station. One sign linked the ISS to the aliens held in Area 51.

The picture switched to an airborne view high above the city. The camera panned the distance, showing backups on the interstates, parkways, and side streets leading out of the city.

She'd seen enough.

Sophia drew in a deep breath and briskly walked into the main auditorium as if going into battle. She knew her briefing would be carried live over all the networks, the Internet, and foreign channels, so every detail was important: her poise, her explanations, and her diction were needed to quell the rising panic.

The briefing room overflowed with reporters. It was standing room only as people lined the wall. She was nearly overwhelmed by the bright lights and sudden rise in chaotic noise. People clamored for her attention.

Stepping behind a podium, she drew in a breath and smelled the pungent smell of too many bodies packed into an overheated room. "Ladies and gentlemen, may I have your attention please. I'm Sophia Flores—"

"Ms. Flores! Is anyone still alive on the station?"

"How many astronauts are on the Falcon 9? Are there any cosmonauts on board?"

"Why are you launching the CST-100?"

Sophia held up a hand to quiet the crowd. She remained stoic, her face a mask. She wasn't baited by the questions, no matter how outlandish. Moments passed and Sophia remained stone-faced.

Slowly the volume decreased as the crowd realized that she would not speak until she was given control of the floor. When the noise abated to hoarse whispers Sophia put down her hand and spoke into the microphone.

"I have a short, prepared statement detailing the latest events surrounding the International Space Station—"

"Cut to the chase and just tell us when will it hit New York!"

A reporter standing next to the man gave him an elbow. "Quiet!"

Sophia waited a moment before continuing. "As I was saying, after my statement I will take questions from the audience."

She glanced down at her notes. "NASA has convened a FIT—a Failure Investigation Team—comprised of experts throughout government and industry. They're going over all details of the incident, and you'll be hearing from them at a later date.

"However, they wanted me to relay that the height of the Earth's atmosphere fluctuates by up to thirty kilometers a day, purely due to natural causes such as solar activity and upper atmospheric air currents. Because of this, the air friction slowing the ISS and causing it to drop in altitude also fluctuates, sometimes by as much as a factor of a hundred. This affects both the speed of the station as well as its altitude. Therefore, no one knows with any certainty the trajectory of the ISS and if—or even where—it might enter the lower atmosphere.

"As such, there is an extremely low probability that the ISS will impact the Earth and hit NYC, much less the eastern seaboard—or even the U.S. If the ISS lands anywhere, it will probably splash down harmlessly in the ocean, as water covers seventy-one percent of the earth's surface. So it is very likely that no one will get hurt." She looked up. "Are there any questions?"

"Ms. Flores! What about the terrorists steering the station down and hitting New York, like astronauts used to fly the Space Shuttle—"

Sophia tried not to roll her eyes as she patiently began to explain the difference between the old Space Shuttle and the unpowered mass of the ISS . . . .

JAPANESE MODULE (JPM)

"Kimberly, CAPCOM," came the disembodied voice over the speaker. It sounded as if Tarantino had returned to the CAPCOM chair. Which made sense to Kimberly: he was NASA's Chief Astronaut. It had been two long days since he'd last served in that position—and all the while she'd been holed up in the JPM as the tension mounted.

Kimberly turned in midair to face the video camera as it focused its lens with a tiny whirring sound. She steeled herself. *What now? Bad news or worse?*

"Yes?"

"Good news, Kimberly. The Dragon achieved second-stage separation, with an ETA of a little less than three hours. Are you able to monitor the location of the two bandits?"

Kimberly flicked a glance at the laptop where she'd previously put up a schematic of both the electrical activity and the O_2/CO_2 sensors, so she could get a rough estimate of where Farid and Bakhet were located.

The two had shrouded the webcams she'd been using to visually keep track of what they were doing: they'd figured out that she could watch them using their video feeds. A day earlier Kimberly had taped over all the sensors in the JPM except for the JAXA video cameras in case somehow they were able to turn the tables and spy on her.

"That's a rog," she said. "I'm not a hundred percent sure, but it appears they haven't moved from Central Post."

"Can you tell what they're up to?"

Shaking her head, she replied, "No. But I bet they're still trying to access the ISS system and regain control of the thrusters."

"That's what we think, too. We'll keep the comm to a minimum so they won't tumble onto the fact that you've opened up communications with the ground. We want them to stay in Central Post as long as possible, doing whatever the hell they're doing, just as long as they can't get the thrusters started up again. Our best scenario is for them to stay so busy they won't detect the Dragon during its approach. Can you tell if they know it's approaching?"

Kimberly turned back to the laptop and traced a finger across the computerized schematic. "I can't tell what specific equipment they've powered up, but they don't seem to be doing anything unusual, other than trying like crazy to hack into the system. I don't know of any reason why they would suspect the Dragon will be on approach."

"Again, that's exactly what we want," Tarantino said. Kimberly thought he sounded tired, his voice a bit scratchy. But he went on, "The Dragon will attempt to reach the Node 2 zenith berthing port by coming in from above, so they won't be seen if one of the two happens to look out a viewport. But *you* should be able to spot them since Node 2 is next to your location in the JPM."

Kimberly nodded.

Tarantino went on, "The Dragon will be expending more propellant than usual so they can approach from the zenith, but it's critical that they reach the port undetected."

Kimberly closed her eyes briefly, her mind racing through what she'd need to do to help them aboard. "Okay, but I'll need a diversion, something to give me enough time to get to the U.S. lab and access the robotic arm. It'll take several minutes to capture the Dragon with the arm and pull it in and dock it manually."

"We're working on that. And we're reopening some of the links to engage the terrorists in psych warfare while you're making your move."

Kimberly felt a huge weight lifting off her shoulders. "Right." So far, so good.

His voice edging slightly higher, Tarantino went on, "Finally, after you pull in the Dragon, we'll need you to access all the ISS systems and interfaces during their engagement. So you scoot back to the JPM and stay there after they dock. It's going to get pretty bloody when our team exits the Dragon, and you need to stay out of the way. Understand?"

Kimberly shook her head. "I don't think that's a good idea."

"Kimberly, listen to me—"

"No, *you* listen. All the terrorists have to do is to surprise the Dragon team as they come through the berthing port. I've seen what they can do with that prybar. And then what happens?"

"Do you think they suspect something's up?"

"No, and there's no reason why they should. But still, if they do spot the Dragon approaching it'll be pretty easy for them to kill the team while they're coming through the hatch, one by one."

"That's even more reason for you to go back to the JPM!"

"But you can't guarantee they won't get lucky. Until I installed that patch from the NSA, they've been one step ahead of us the whole time. It'll be much easier for me to sidetrack them after the team is docked than for the guys to be slaughtered when they disembark."

"Kimberly!"

She pressed on. "I'll create a diversion and make sure they're away from the Node 2 berthing port."

"Do *not* leave that module! That's a direct—"

The lights in the JPM blinked out. In the sudden darkness Kimberly heard the air blowers sigh to a stop. The module went dead quiet. The only light came from the viewport and the laptop screen, now running on battery.

They've cut the power! They've done to me exactly what I did to them. Somehow they've gotten past the firewalls I've erected around the controls.

Her eyes rapidly adjusted to the faint light as she pushed off to open the window shutters, allowing sunlight to come through. Fifty minutes of sunshine to each orbit, Kimberly reminded herself.

She kicked off to the laptop. Grabbing the metal frame that held the computer, she rotated around and pulled herself close to the screen. The screen icon showed there was slightly more than two hours left on the battery's charge. She was still tied in to the ISS system and was still able to access everything she'd controlled before.

They hadn't yet cut the lines that carried the signals, but there was no doubt in her mind that they would go there next. They'd obviously been able to hack into the system and get around the firewall while their own power was cut. Kimberly saw light streaming from Node 2, just outside the JPM. They'd successfully brought their lights up while taking hers down. They might also physically unplug the power and data cables that ran through the vestibule region from Node 2 to the JPM, but since there were redundant cables, she didn't think they'd even bother to try.

But the big difference was that now the Ka-band link to the ground was down, and she wouldn't know when the Dragon would be making its final approach to the station. She still had access to her laptop, though, and she could probably still try to hack back in and turn on her power. But if she did, it would tip off Farid and Bakhet, and they'd probably physically disconnect her cables. Then she'd really be up a creek, trapped in the JPM.

She glanced at the time display at the upper right corner of the laptop screen. CAPCOM had told her that the Dragon would be on station in a little less than three hours. With the time that already had elapsed since then, Kimberly figured their ETA was now somewhere around two and a half hours.

The laptop's battery must be draining like crazy now that its external power source was cut off; and if the guys hadn't moved the other three laptops normally stored in the JPM, she could have switched out their batteries.

She doubted that the Dragon would arrive any sooner than the time CAPCOM had given her; astrodynamics was astrodynamics, and when not under thrust the vessel obeyed the physical laws that dictated orbital elements. So the laptop power would run out before they arrived, meaning she would be deaf, dumb, and blind: unable to monitor the Dragon's approach or the ISS's internal systems.

Which meant that she couldn't rule out either Farid or Bakhet somehow getting lucky and detecting the Dragon capsule before it arrived. And then they'd do everything in their power to stop the rescue team.

The most straightforward and easiest thing to do was simply to deny them access to the berthing port. Very simple. And very effective. Putting the robotic arm out of commission would ensure the fiery deaths of both the rescue capsule and the hundred-and-fifty-billion-dollar space station.

So, in all reality, Kimberly knew there was little chance that the SpaceX Dragon capsule would be able to reach the ISS in time to save it. And with her power cut off, she couldn't stop the terrorists from rotating the ISS again and renewing its death plunge.

So what can I do? she asked herself.

She was alone again, cut off from the rest of the world. But she knew she wasn't going to roll over and play dead. Not by a long shot. The two terrorists had managed to hack back into the ISS system and overcome seemingly insurmountable odds. So she'd have to go them one better.

Kimberly pulled in a breath and tried to think. Time to solve another problem.

SOUTH PACIFIC OCEAN, NORTHWEST OF THE SOLOMON ISLANDS

The weather wasn't cooperating.

The three Aegis cruisers moved farther apart as they plowed through heaving seas toward their predetermined launch position. The sea was getting rougher by the minute, driven by a gale that exceeded Force 9 on the Beaufort scale. Green water was crashing over their prows with each heaving wave as the cruisers—USS *Lake Erie*, USS *Decatur*, and USS *Russell*—battened down to ride out the storm.

The order to fire their antisatellite missiles would be given by PACOM Headquarters outside Honolulu, once the President made his decision.

The challenge was to shoot down the ISS so it would crash somewhere over the open Pacific Ocean, which would minimize the effect of any plutonium or debris that might survive the searing heat generated by the station's 17,500-mile-an-hour plunge into the thickest layers of the atmosphere. The Aegis ASAT missiles were equipped with onboard terminal guidance radars, with the capability of updating their positions up until the last few miles of intercept, when the projectiles would continue to their target on a ballistic trajectory.

The tactic for shooting down the ISS is for multiple ASATs to target the largest and most massive modules of the station, and not be erroneously guided to other objects such as the conspicuously large arrays of solar panels. If that happened the Aegis missile warheads would splash on through the thin, lightweight objects without preventing the main body of the station from continuing to deorbit.

The military's entire space situational awareness assets were focused on supporting the shoot-down. Space Command's Space-Based Surveillance System, ground-based radars, Ground-Based Electro-Optical Deep Space Surveillance optical tracking, and observatories in Maui and Kirtland Air Force Base at Albuquerque, New Mexico, were assigned to closely watch the ISS and to immediately forward any change in configuration or altitude to PACOM and the National Security Council.

Earlier in the day, before the three Aegis cruisers reached their storm-battered positions, the President announced to the NSC meeting that he would only order the ISS shot down if it started to descend again. He was willing to give the station—and NASA's efforts to save it—the benefit of the doubt.

But after the meeting he privately told the NASA Administrator that he was considering going ahead and shooting down the station because of the growing public panic.

"It's for the greater good of the people," he said.

Patricia Simone felt angry enough to spit at him, but she nodded silently and kept her fury to herself.

JAPANESE MODULE (JPM)

Kimberly floated in the dark at the far end of the JPM, the opposite side from the vestibule leading to Node 2. She peered out the two large windows, looking for the approaching Dragon rescue capsule.

She wasn't sure how much time had passed since she'd turned off the laptop, but she knew she needed to conserve as much of its battery power as she could. She needed that small computer to close the vent to the outside and allow the VAJ to reintroduce air into the vestibule. Otherwise, if the laptop's battery died she'd never be able to get around the force of the air pressure holding the hatch tightly closed. She'd be stuck in the JPM—*for the rest of my life!* she realized, with a pang of fright that edged close to panic.

The capsule was due to arrive soon, and right before it docked she planned to ensure that the mating mechanism in the Node 2 berthing port worked. But her power and lights were still out, and with her laptop off she didn't have a clue as to where the two terrorists were located, or even what time it was.

She'd followed Farid and Bakhet's movements immediately

after they'd cut the JPM's lights, while she simultaneously tried to hack into the ISS's controls. She didn't have any luck getting in, but she could watch the various sensors that showed the pair moving down to the JPM and then back to Central Post. Since then, she could tell they remained in the Russian module until she turned off her laptop.

She assumed that the two of them were now methodically trying to remove the blocks she had set up on starting the thrusters, and with what she'd seen them accomplish, she had no doubt that they would eventually succeed. It would just depend on how much time they needed to do it.

Wherever the two had received their training, they were definitely part of the A-Team. And from what Scott had passed on about what the intelligence services had discovered, they weren't just a pair of homegrown terrorists: they'd had to be trained by a sophisticated, nation-state agent.

Still looking outside the station, she scanned the blackness, looking for any light the Dragon might be emitting. Now that the sun was on the opposite side of the Earth, she assumed she wouldn't be able to see the capsule unless she spotted emissions from inside the Dragon itself. She knew that the rescue team wanted to approach the station as stealthily as possible, but that would make it tougher for her to spot them. She also knew that she'd have to rapidly leave the safety of the JPM to help them dock, so she had to keep searching.

She could feel tension tightening its grip on her as she moved around to different angles, peering through the large windows, desperately searching for anything out of the ordinary, any dim light or glint of reflection that might catch her eye—

There! Just beyond the nearest solar array. She strained to look in the zenith direction. Hopefully as the capsule grew closer she could keep track of its approach.

The barely visible object was moving slowly, about one foot per second, she judged, as it inched toward Node 2's zenith berthing port. The Node 2 port, specifically designed for unmanned U.S. commercial spacecraft such as this Dragon, provided a common, universal mechanism for docking. Kimberly hoped the terrorists hadn't spotted the arriving vessel. She knew the Dragon would stop about ten feet from the dock and wait for the robotic arm to reach out and pull the capsule in.

Trembling with anticipation, Kimberly briefly closed her eyes and mentally rehearsed what she needed to do: let them know I'm here, then leave the JPM and engage the arm's controls.

She pushed off for the laptop and started it up, then quickly disengaged it from its mooring and carried it with her back to the window. The screen lit up, illuminating the darkened module with diffuse light. She waved it back and forth across the viewport, hoping to catch the rescue team's attention.

The capsule continued to edge slowly toward the berthing port, looking like a snail heading toward a wall, moving just as maddeningly slow. There was no sign from the Dragon that they'd seen her.

Her breath quickening, Kimberly waved the laptop up and down, then sideways across the narrow viewport. Here, over here! *Look! for goodness' sake.*

Suddenly a muted light flicked on and off from the Dragon's front viewport, once, twice, then went dark. They've seen me! Kimberly exulted. They knew that she was still alive. Now she had to do everything in her power to make sure they docked successfully.

Seeing the U.S. capsule and knowing that her fellow astronauts were just minutes away infused her with a renewed sense of hope and elation. She almost couldn't contain her excitement.

Almost.

Steadying herself, Kimberly knew she had a huge job ahead of her. She turned from the window, glided back to the laptop's console, and strapped the computer back into place. Pecking at its keyboard, she pulled up the ISS controls. Although power to the JPM was still cut, the station's redundant cables allowed her access to the system. As long as the laptop stayed alive she'd be able to close the valve to outside and repressurize the vestibule. Then she could leave the Japanese module and go to help dock the Dragon.

She mentally ran through the sequence and was about to set the vacuum control state from OPEN to CLOSED when it hit her that there was a better than fair chance that the terrorists would discover what she was doing. She needed a way to fight them off.

Swinging her glance around the darkened JPM, she tried to find something that she might use as a long distance weapon, rather than getting in close with Shep's knife. The Air Force Academy's traveling wave tube wasn't in the module any longer, and the laser flashlamp was not available, either. There wasn't anything like the titanium prybar she could use, and the module was even void of the basic tools she had grabbed earlier. Nothing here but bungee cords and food pouches. What could she use?

She pushed over to the MO bags and started to go through them once again, hoping desperately that there might be something in them that she'd overlooked before. But all they contained were clothing, spare parts, and some food.

She pulled out a plastic bottle of Sriracha sauce; the astronauts called it Rooster sauce because of the rooster depicted on the bottle's label. Her eyes widened at the discovery. She remembered that one of the visiting astronauts, a biochemist, had told her that the hot sauce pegged at a sizzling 2500 to 8000 Scoville heat units: if it hadn't been labeled a food product for the ISS, its pH level was low enough that NASA would have banned it as a caustic acid.

She'd rather have a can of Mace to incapacitate the terrorists, but she didn't have any other choice or much time, so Rooster sauce would have to do. She grabbed the bottle and kicked back to the laptop.

Kimberly pressurized the vestibule and removed the VAJ. Taking a deep breath, and stuffing the bottle of Sriracha sauce and Shep's knife into her coverall pockets, she pulled the hatch open and prepared to leave the JPM so she could engage the robotic arm and help the waiting rescue team to turn the tables on those two murdering SOBs and regain control of the ISS.

ISS U.S. LAB, ROBOTIC ARM CONTROLS

Kimberly floated out of the JPM as quietly as she could, taking care not to bang the hatch against the vestibule siding. She glided through the cool, fresh air that spilled into the Japanese module, relieving the stuffiness that had grown in there since the power had been cut.

Once in Node 2 she changed her direction by grabbing the hatchway's inner handrail, changing her linear momentum to angular. She couldn't see any sign of the terrorists while she flew down the module's axis. She prayed they were still in Central Post. If they've spotted the incoming Dragon, she reasoned, maybe they'll think it's a regularly scheduled unmanned commercial resupply vessel. She hoped so.

In a few seconds she was through Node 2, and as she entered the U.S. lab she once again changed her momentum and headed straight for the robotic arm controls. She pulled the Rooster sauce from her pocket with her right hand. Reaching out with her left, she grabbed the control panel and spun around, stopping herself in front of the panel's screen.

Her heart was thumping hard from the exertion and the adrenaline roaring through her system. She consciously slowed her breathing as she positioned the screen to give her a view of anyone approaching from Node 1 while she started working the controls. No sign of the terrorists; she'd made it without being detected, she thought.

Kimberly ensured that MCC had powered up the arm, while the outside camera showed the Dragon capsule, floating motionless just a few yards in front of Node 2's zenith berthing port. The Dragon's velocity was so precisely matched to the station's that it appeared to be hanging in space, not moving as it waited to be pulled in for berthing. She knew it was actually hurtling through space at exactly the same 17,500 miles an hour as the ISS, but the absence of relative motion gave the illusion that it was suspended stationary just outside the station.

Since the capsule was not moving relative to the ISS, in effect it was hidden in plain sight. Now for the tough part, Kimberly said to herself. She knew that it was one thing for the Dragon to have approached the ISS without being detected by the terrorists, but the instant she started moving the robotic arm they would be alarmed and alerted.

A series of numbers ran across the bottom of the screen and a green light began blinking. The software checks were complete. She drew in a breath and slowly, slowly moved the controls, not bothering to go through the normal safety and checkout procedures to test the arm's response.

She kept glancing at the hatch leading from Node 2 to the U.S. lab, expecting the terrorists to appear at any second. But she saw no motion, heard no sound from outside the module.

On the screen the long, hinged robotic arm slowly unfolded

and stretched out toward the waiting Dragon. It looked as if a giant skeletal hand was reaching out to grasp the snub-nosed metal vessel, extending inch by inch toward it.

Its slow motion started to grate on Kimberly's nerves. Part of her forced her movements to be methodical, precise, calculated; but another part screamed inside her head to hurry and quickly pull the damned thing into the docking port! She felt her cheeks flushing, the tension escalating as the arm slowly crept toward the capsule, like an arthritic old man.

Out of the corner of her eye she caught a flicker of something just inside Node 1, near the hatch.

The blood thundered in her ears. Should I continue working the damned arm or get ready for an attack? Taking her eyes off the screen, she peered toward the hatch. Nothing moving. Had one of the terrorists merely gone to the zero-gee toilet in Node 3 again, or were they systematically checking all the modules before moving to the JPM to see if she had left her sanctuary?

She turned her attention back to the robotic arm. It was almost there, mere centimeters until contact. Slowly she opened the robot's metal hand—three snare wires, arranged in a triangle that closed like an iris diaphragm around the capsule's grapple pin—wanting to make certain that she could firmly grasp the Dragon. Only seconds away, she'd have the vessel safely under control and start pulling it to the Node 2 zenith berth . . . .

She flinched as she spotted Farid entering the U.S. lab. He floated above her, traveling slowly down the axis of the module. If she'd kept still he might have missed her entirely.

But his eyes widened with disbelief and he opened his mouth, obviously shocked at seeing her in the module. He started to shout as Kimberly whirled and flicked open the top of the bottle of caustic Rooster sauce.

She thrust her arm at Farid and squeezed the plastic bottle as

hard as she could. A stream of red liquid spurted from the nozzle, quickly breaking into a cloud of pulsing globules that hurtled
toward the terrorist. Kimberly rotated her hand in a small circle
and the onslaught of acidic liquid spewed out in a swirling, expanding cone.

Screaming, Farid arched his back and tried to duck out of the
way. He started flailing his hands as if to wave off the engulfing
red cloud. His torso began to rotate in midair. The Rooster sauce
splashed against his hands and face, breaking into still-smaller
globs of searing liquid that ricocheted randomly through the
module, spinning away in every direction.

"Kugan, suka!" he roared, twirling, kicking, pulling his hands
up to his face, trying to do anything to get away from the blinding,
burning pain.

Kimberly coolly turned back to the control panel. The robotic
arm was still hanging just over the Dragon. She ignored Farid's
anguished cries and slowly moved the controls to engage the vessel and start pulling it in. Now that she'd been discovered she
knew that she'd have only a few more seconds until Bakhet would
appear. Once she made contact she'd hurry the berthing process;
it would take only scant moments until the Dragon was docked
and the guys could take over. They would access the module and
storm the station—

There. She started to close the arm when something else hurtled into the module. Bakhet. His eyes wild, he held the titanium
prybar and headed straight for her.

Crap! She turned from the screen, pulling Shep's knife out of
her pocket as she ducked and kicked away, flying through the air.

Bakhet threw the prybar at her. It flew past her and hit the
robotic arm's control screen, which shattered, spewing pieces of
debris around her as she moved from the carnage.

Farid kept yowling with pain, still tumbling weightlessly in the module until he smacked into the opposite side. Bakhet tried to stop his own momentum, but without any footing he smashed against the forward wall of the U.S. lab and bounced away from her.

Kimberly ducked away from them and, kicking out, shot toward the hatch back into Node 2 and the sanctuary of the JPM. She flew just under Bakhet, who reached out to grab her by the arm, yelling wildly. As she passed she swiveled and lashed out with Shep's knife, slashing his arm.

He howled as globules of red spurted from his arm like a fire hose of blood spewing through the module. The two of them bounced against the insulation and the metal frame of the hatch as thousands of tiny spinning spheres of blood mixed with the Rooster sauce in a cloud of liquid asteroids.

Kimberly pulled loose of Bakhet's grip and flew into Node 2, leaving the yelling cacophony behind her. Reaching the module's far side, she used the inner handrail to change her direction and sailed into the darkened JPM. Once inside she turned, closed the hatch covers, and evacuated the air in the vestibule between the two modules, once again sealing both hatches with vacuum.

JAPANESE MODULE (JPM)

Only when the JPM's air pressure tightly sealed the hatch with tons of force did Kimberly slow down to take a deep breath. She felt her heart rate start to slow, but the blood still pounded in her ears from the exertion.

Once again she'd escaped from harm by barricading herself in the module. But this time, instead of peering out the hatch into Node 2 and sneering at the terrorists she turned her focus to the large JPM windows at the far end of the module and craned her neck, trying to catch a view of the waiting Dragon.

She spotted the snub-nosed capsule, still floating just a few yards from the Node 2 berthing port. She felt a depressing pang of disappointment. The Dragon was so close, but also incredibly far away. The robotic arm was positioned just centimeters above the vessel, frozen in place, not moving.

If she'd had only another half minute, she thought. Only a few seconds. She could have brought the Dragon in and positioned it right at the Common Berthing Mechanism, allowing it access to the station. And if that had happened, she wouldn't be staring at the rescue vessel from the darkened JPM: her fellow astronauts would have overpowered Farid and Bakhet, ending this insane nightmare. They'd have wrestled control of the ISS away from the terrorists, and perhaps even could have transferred some fuel through an EVA fuel-line connect from their capsule to the station's tanks, so they could have re-boosted the ISS to a higher, safer altitude.

As she watched through the small window, the Dragon slowly backed away from Node 2, leaving the station and the dangling robotic arm. It crept away slowly, only centimeters per second. But it was leaving the ISS, Kimberly knew.

She felt like a shipwrecked sailor, marooned on a desert island. With cannibals stalking after her.

Minutes dragged by as the Dragon pulled away, moving at a slight angle instead of heading straight back. Using the capsule's small thrusters, the vessel started to circle slowly around the ISS, swinging in an arc that brought it around until it was directly in front of the JPM experimental hatch.

At first Kimberly thought the guys might somehow be planning to use the cramped airlock. But the 1.5-meter-diameter, two-meter-long chamber was big enough for only small experiments to be ejected from the pressurized volume of the JPM into the harsh environment of orbital space. Besides, the guys didn't have any spacesuits with them.

Briefly she thought that they might try to rapidly decompress the air in their Dragon capsule and attempt to reach the JPM's experimental airlock where she might be able to pull them in, one by one. But the airlock could only be opened from the inside control panel, and without wearing spacesuits they wouldn't have a chance.

It was an insane idea. It would never work. How long could a human body survive in vacuum at more than 400 degrees below zero? Twenty or thirty seconds at most, before their eyeballs burst, their eardrums ruptured, their lungs exploded.

But these weren't normal people in that Dragon trying to rescue her. They were astronauts, Navy SEALS, and Army Rangers in top-notch condition, supremely competent and incredibly confident—if not a touch crazy.

But no one could survive the passage from the Dragon to the small JPM hatch without a suit, even these guys, good as they were. That was the stuff of bad sci-fi movies, not the real world. She just hoped they weren't so overconfident that they would try it anyway, and depend on her to pull them in.

She glanced at the second-generation spacesuit stored next to the hatch. It could barely fit in the airlock itself, and it wouldn't be of any help to the guys anyway. There was no way to get it to them, and they'd have to open their own hatch to reach it. And even if they could access it, the suit needed a long, insulated hose to provide its air supply.

Kimberly felt a sense of relief as the Dragon glided past the JPM airlock and continued in a long arc around the station. It started to move out of her sight as it headed toward the station's nadir, or Earth-facing side. It finally hit her that they may be trying to conduct a 360-degree inspection of the ISS. Or maybe they were approaching Node 2 from the nadir in an attempt to berth at the module's nadir port.

But why would they do that? she wondered. She couldn't access the robot arm, and since their ship was a resupply version of the Dragon it didn't have the ability to approach any closer. So what are they trying to do?

She watched the capsule slowly move around the station until it passed beyond her sight. Now she couldn't see the Dragon from the hatch or from any of the outside feeds. Kimberly could do nothing but wait, wondering what would happen next.

She decided that she had to go out of the JPM again, and this time make it a do-or-die effort.

It was obvious that the Dragon would never be able to berth without her help. And since the terrorists had destroyed the robotic arm's controls in the U.S. lab, that left her only hope to dock the Dragon up to the arm's primary controls in the Cupola. Could she get there? She had to somehow find something else in the JPM to overpower the terrorists and regain control of the robotic arm.

But how? What could she use?

Feeling more than a little desperate, she turned to rummage once again through the MO bags. In the darkened module she pulled aside the bungee-cord netting and groped through bag after bag, fumbling through the objects in them, squinting in the dim light filtering in through the hatch. I'll have to jury-rig something, she thought, something deadly that will stop them cold, not just a half-assed contraption like the Rooster sauce. Digging through bag after bag, she felt her frustration mount.

The sun peeped over the curving horizon as Kimberly turned from the bungee-cord jail to the small experimental hatch. She spotted the Dragon, sunlight glinting off its curving flank. It was moving away from the station. They've probably hit bingo fuel, she realized. It grew smaller against the backdrop of the now-glowing Earth.

The guys had spent the best part of an hour trying to approach the ISS stealthily, and then trying to berth. All for naught. Kimberly watched her hopes drifting away from her.

She imagined the guys aboard the Dragon were deeply disappointed, but she also understood that there was nothing they could do. They were just as constrained by the laws of physics and the implacably hard facts of the situation as she herself was. The terrorists had the upper hand.

Things would have been different if it had been a manned Dragon capsule instead of a jury-rigged, unmanned supply version.

A manned capsule was designed to be able to dock at one of the station's numerous IDA, or International Docking Adapter ports on its own and wouldn't need the robotic arm to pull it in.

Kimberly fought down an urge to cry. If only, she kept telling herself, if only. Those guys had volunteered to fly in the jury-rigged capsule. They'd flirted with incredible danger on the pad to launch in that ten-second window. Just a few years earlier a SpaceX launch pushed the envelope trying to make that window and exploded on launch. Those four astronauts could have met a fiery death on the pad.

And although Scott's Boeing Starliner launch had been successful, he was in a different predicament than the four now returning to Earth: he'd be able to dock at the Node 3 IDA, but the International Docking Adapter didn't have the ability to transfer fuel—she'd have to go EVA and connect a fuel transfer hose. Which meant somehow getting down to the Joint Airlock, donning an EVA suit, and exiting the station, all while keeping away from the terrorists.

Kimberly shook her head, trying to clear her thoughts. Scott won't be here for several more hours, she knew. What she didn't know was whether she'd be able to survive that long. She still had to leave the safety of the JPM, somehow overpower Farid and Bakhet, and go EVA to transfer Scott's fuel.

If she failed, the station might not even survive for a few more days. And she would die with it.

As she watched the Dragon capsule dwindle from her sight, Kimberly felt anger simmering inside her, anger that she hadn't been sharp enough, resourceful enough, to thwart the two terrorists.

What else could I have done? she asked herself. What can I do now? She knew she had to do *something*. She couldn't roll over and play dead.

As she turned back in exasperation to the bungee-cord jail she felt a barely perceptible vibration shudder through the module. If the module still had power she probably wouldn't have noticed it at all. There. Again. The faintest movement of air, but not from the ventilating system coming back to life. Kimberly recognized that it was caused by the station's minute deceleration.

The thrusters.

Farid and Bakhet had at last circumvented her lockout of the hypergolic propellants and regained control of the station's thrusters.

She realized that the ISS was slowly rotating, revolving, so that it could start to deorbit once again. It would take ten minutes to turn 180 degrees.

She had only a few hours left to live.

CLAY CENTER OBSERVATORY, BROOKLINE, MASSACHUSETTS

The eastern sky was just beginning to turn a pearly pink. Early morning was clear and crisp, perfect for observing, the first good viewing window in more than a week. A thin layer of clouds had blown away with the cold front that had passed two hours earlier, allowing Alicia O'Sullivan an opportunity to grab some footage of the International Space Station before full daylight hit.

The station would be in view for an unusually long period—five full minutes—over the greater Boston area. If the adaptive optics that allowed the telescope to cancel out the blurring effects of the atmosphere's roiling motions was up and running, she'd be able to record some spectacular material.

Like everyone else, Alicia was curious about what had happened aboard the station. She'd seen the video of the Russian cosmonaut's brutal death, heard rumors that there were no survivors on the ISS. NASA's news blackout only fueled speculation, and although the Internet was wild with crazy conjectures, no one had actually seen recent pictures of the space station; at least, NASA and the rest of the government hadn't released any new footage. Whatever NASA had, they were keeping it from the public. That was pretty evident from the lack of information given during NASA's recent press briefing.

Since Alicia ran one of the most versatile telescopes in the world, she wanted to see the station for herself. So she downloaded the projected position of the ISS and loaded the software instructions to swing the observatory's twenty-five-inch reflecting telescope to the spot where it should come up over the horizon. The station should reach a maximum height of 77 degrees. Just before the sun came up it would be the third brightest object in the Massachusetts sky: a great way for her to end her shift.

The center's Ritchey-Chrétien reflector was one of the few civilian telescopes that could traverse fast enough, and with the proper accuracy, to resolve the ISS. Other, larger telescopes spent hours focused on a single object in the sky, slowly resolving the image by following the Earth's rotation. Her telescope could whip from horizon to horizon and even follow the fastest, lowest-flying satellite. So the reflector was used both for research and education.

Alicia had a fair amount of freedom for scheduling viewing on her own; that is why after completing her master's degree in astronomy at MIT she was content to stay in the Boston area running the Clay Center 'scopes, unlike her classmates who'd been thrown into the dog-eat-dog environment of publish-or-perish university research.

Alicia scanned the telescope's controls as she sat back and waited for the station to come into view. Minutes passed until finally she heard the rumble of the telescope starting to slew from west-southwest to northeast, tracking the ISS. Everything was automated, allowing her to watch the screen as the station's wobbling image came into view. Within seconds the image sharpened as the adaptive optics system resolved the view, revealing incredibly sharp, small detail. The station appeared to be slowly rotating as it orbited, but Alicia knew it was simply an artifact caused by the station's orientation.

She squinted at the screen. *That's odd.* Something was sitting just outside the ISS, at the zenith position, above the middle of the station.

Stunned, Alicia leaned forward in her chair. A blunt-nosed space capsule was hovering close to the station. And from one of the station's modules a long, thin-hinged arm was unfolding toward the capsule, as if trying to grasp it in its extended fingers. Then the arm stopped short, just before it touched.

Alicia gaped at the screen. What was going on?

She watched, frozen and wide-eyed, as the capsule started to move away from the ISS. Suddenly the image went dark. The station's orbit must have taken it out of view.

Alicia didn't hesitate. She quickly saved the file and tapped out a short summary of what she'd seen, then posted the footage to as many Internet sites as she could think of.

Within five minutes her footage was the fastest trending topic in Internet history.

JAPANESE MODULE (JPM)

In the darkened JPM Kimberly pushed over to the laptop. She punched at the keyboard but she couldn't get a response from the portable computer. She leaned on the power button, and when nothing happened she tried unplugging and then plugging the laptop into one of the other outlets. No go. The controller would not boot up.

She smacked the laptop's restraint in frustration, and as her legs swung back she pushed toward the small experimental airlock. The terrorists had cut the power to the module, and now, with the laptop's battery dead, she had no way to access the station's controls and try to countermand the ISS's rotation.

Within minutes the station would be in position for them to reengage the main thrusters, and with the forward part of the ISS now facing aft, they'd be able to slow the station's speed and cause it to drop to a lower altitude. Facing increasing atmospheric drag, the station would start rapidly deorbiting—until it impacted on Earth.

Desperately, she tried to think of what she could do. She might be able to slow them up if she once again left the JPM and confronted them. But without the guys in the Dragon to back her up, or even divert the terrorists' attention, there was a good probability that she'd lose the fight. Then she'd be dead and the station would crash, spewing radioactivity in the atmosphere while the debris might kill countless numbers of innocent people. She wasn't even sure that the U.S. antisatellite weapons were in position to take the station down.

What could she possibly do?

Her pulse rate steadily rising, Kimberly tried to keep her cool by running through emergency checklists in her head, going over each procedure: what to do in case of a power outage, a loss of communications, hoping that somewhere, somehow she'd stumble across something that she hadn't thought of before.

How could she stop the thrusters? She didn't have physical or electronic access to the ISS state controls, so what else could she try?

With the laptop out of the picture, she couldn't stop the flow of the fuel and oxidizer tanks. Was there another way to shut down those valves? They weren't even accessible from the JPM, and the hypergolic propellant tanks themselves weren't accessible from anywhere inside the station, much less the JPM.

She stopped, her eyes wide. But the propellant line *was* accessible *outside* the station, under a panel on the surface of the FGB, about halfway between the JPM and the far Russian SM module.

Her heart started to race again.

All she had to do, she told herself, to stop the flow of propellants was to crimp the fuel line: a narrow metal tube only a few millimeters in diameter. She could get to it by going outside the station, performing an Extra-Vehicular Activity.

Meaning she'd need access to one of the EVA suits—a nearly impossible task, since she'd have to get to the bulky suit by leaving the JPM again, travel to the Joint Airlock, suit up, and then exit the space station, all without drawing attention to herself.

And, oh yes, she'd have to spend an hour pre-breathing the low-nitrogen, enriched-oxygen air the suits used if she wanted to avoid getting the bends.

She couldn't move the robotic arm without them discovering her presence, so how could she ever get all the way to the Joint Airlock and suit up without being detected?

Bleakly, she turned and looked at the JPM airlock, thinking that only moments before she had seriously thought the guys in the Dragon capsule might risk exposing themselves to the frigid vacuum of space in order to shoot across the distance from their vessel to the JPM's undersized airlock.

What else can I use to survive outside the station, long enough to stop the flow of propellant to the thrusters?

And there it was, staring her in the face: the second-generation suit dangling in a bundle of bungee cords next to the airlock.

For once Kimberly was happy about her petite stature. She could squirm into the suit and squeeze through the experimental airlock, even in the suit. She was sure of it.

But the compact spacesuit didn't have its own oxygen supply. It relied on a long insulated hose, an umbilical cord that provided life-giving air. By using it an astronaut could work outside the station indefinitely.

Her heart sank as she realized that the umbilical cord wasn't nearly long enough to reach the fuel line's access panel. This new experimental suit was meant to be used only near a hatch, not to traverse across the entire length of the station.

Okay, she thought. That's just another problem, another bump in the road compared to everything else she'd encountered. And it wouldn't be the last, she knew. Like, she'd also have to modify the small airlock to be operated from inside the module, rather than outside, as it was designed. To Kimberly these were merely engineering roadblocks, not physical impossibilities like trying to exceed the speed of light.

Okay, how can I do this? She raced through the logic. She could ditch using the umbilical cord and instead jury-rig the suit with one of the emergency oxygen bottles. She could fill the suit with oxygen before she exited the JPM through the experimental airlock, and then quickly attach another oxygen bottle. That way she'd have fifteen or twenty minutes of oxygen—more than that, really, as that length of time was calculated for much larger male astronauts.

Plenty of time to crimp the line, no problem. But she'd be going from air at a normal 14.7 psi to pure oxygen at a much lower pressure. She didn't have time to pre-breathe; she just hoped that she wouldn't get the bends. She felt an urge to cross her fingers.

She quickly began to take down the suit from its mooring by untying the bungee cords holding it to the insulated wall. As she unfolded the suit she found that it was bigger than she'd thought. She'd have to really squeeze through the small airlock. And since she'd have to get to the opposite side of the station with so little air, after she'd stopped the flow of fuel by crimping the line, she'd have to reenter the ISS using the Russian ПрК, or *Peherr-ka* transfer chamber, at the far aft SM module.

And she'd have only twenty minutes of oxygen in the suit, tops, to accomplish all that she had to do. Plus, if she didn't prebreathe, then with all the exertion she'd have to go through, she was sure to get the bends, making things even worse. She recalled an in-suit exercise that dropped the oxygen pre-breathing time from three hours to as low as fifteen minutes in order to purge the nitrogen from her bloodstream, but she didn't have even that much leeway.

Yet there was no other way. She *had to* stop the station from deorbiting.

Kimberly quickly shucked off her outer clothes and, stabilizing the suit on a fitting bar, she started pulling on the second-generation spacesuit.

As she worked her arms into the suit's torso, out the small airlock viewport she saw stars streaming across her field of view. The station was still rotating into position to engage the main thrusters and begin its plunge to Earth.

She didn't have much time.

INTERSECTION OF NASA CAUSEWAY AND HIGHWAY 1, CAPE CANAVERAL, FLORIDA

A growing crowd of people milled outside the barricades set up on the road, several miles from the main entrance to Kennedy Space Center. Barricades blocked the highways, with signs proclaiming road closures and that the Visitor Complex was temporarily shut down. A half dozen people carried hand-lettered protest signs demanding information about the rumors that NASA was conducting a secret military rescue mission. Family groups, couples, and elderly visitors strained to see past the barricades, tourists upset by the center's closure, ruining their vacations.

TV news vans from local stations and national networks were parked by the side of the road, their satellite dishes pointing at an angle toward the southern sky. A young female reporter, stylishly blonde and wearing a formfitting red jacket, stood next to a middle-aged man as she began a live interview.

"Good afternoon, ladies and gentlemen. This is Janie Baldwin reporting live from outside Kennedy Space Center. This morning's stunning release of footage by the Clay Center for Science and Technology has electrified the world. It shows in remarkable detail the International Space Station's robotic arm extending out, but failing to latch on to a co-orbiting SpaceX Dragon resupply capsule. NASA has refused to make a statement other than that the supply ship has failed to berth with the space station."

Turning toward the man beside her, Janie Baldwin continued, "I have with me Lawrence Torres from the online publication Space.com with some breaking news." Raising her microphone to Torres's chin, she said, "Mr. Torres, tell us what happened in this latest footage."

"Thank you, Janie," Torres said, in a slightly rasping voice. "First, NASA refused to confirm or deny that there were any astronauts aboard the Dragon—but I can tell you for a fact that it's impossible for anyone to be on board that space capsule, because that version of the capsule is used only for unmanned resupply missions. It simply can't carry humans. And since the unmanned capsule can only berth when pulled in, someone was inside the ISS, controlling the robot arm."

"NASA couldn't control the arm from the ground?"

"Yes, they can—but not for cargo vehicles. It takes too long for their commands to reach the station. The time lag between what they're seeing and their remote controls is too large."

"So that proves there are survivors aboard the space station?"

"Yes, it does." Torres cleared his throat, then went on, "In fact, Space.com has sources in the NASA contractor community that have confirmed that there are three people still alive on board the ISS—"

"Three people!" The reporter shoved her microphone even closer to Torres's lips.

"That's correct. The American astronaut Kimberly Hadid-Robinson, and the two cosmonauts who flew up on the last Soyuz, Farid Hazood and Adama Bakhet, who tried to take over the station. Our source has been helping NASA communicate with Kimberly through her ex-husband, astronaut Lieutenant Colonel Scott Robinson."

Her eyes widening, Janie asked, "Why hasn't NASA released this information?"

"You'll have to ask the government about that. But our source tells us that the cosmonauts are trying to deorbit the space station and cause it to crash down to Earth. Their target is New York City, where the impact could cause an explosion more powerful than the atomic bomb that destroyed Hiroshima. Even worse, the station has over three hundred and sixty pounds of deadly plutonium stored in RTGs, compact nuclear power sources carried up by the Russians, making the ISS the world's largest radioactive dirty bomb. A highly radioactive cloud will be released as the space station burns up in the atmosphere, contaminating thousands of square miles along its trajectory. And with the uncertainty of the point of impact, everyone on the east coast from Miami to Boston is at risk."

"I . . . I . . ." Janie swallowed visibly and pulled herself together. "And Kimberly? How is she? Is she all right?"

Grimly, Torres replied, "Our sources say that astronaut Kimberly Hadid-Robinson is doing everything possible to stay alive. As I understand it, she is the only thing standing between the space station remaining in orbit and a catastrophic crash that will cause perhaps millions of American deaths."

JAPANESE MODULE (JPM)

Her hands shaking slightly, Kimberly pulled up the last zipper and folded over the seal, enclosing herself in the second-generation spacesuit. She pushed away from the stabilizing stand and secured the oxygen bottle to the front of her suit by twisting the bottle's open flange onto the helical nipple, which had been originally designed to clamp the long oxygen-supplying umbilical cord. She pulled on the helmet, locked it to the neck ring, and started the oxygen. After filling the suit she planned to quickly substitute another bottle to give her the maximum time to work outside the station.

She drew in deep breaths of pure O_2 while vigorously moving her shoulders and arms, trying to increase her heart rate to 80 percent max; there'd be no time to pre-breathe, but she needed to flush as much nitrogen as possible from her bloodstream, giving her as much time outside as she could. EVAs were rarely routine, and she knew from experience that if anything could go wrong, it would. Best to be prepared for almost anything out there—especially with no one around to back her up.

The suit slowly ballooned out, filling with life-giving oxygen. She started to reach for the extra bottle when she noticed

movement on the other side of the vestibule hatch window leading from the JPM to Node 2. It looked as though one, or maybe
even both, of the terrorists were trying to peer into her module.

Were they trying to see if she was still alive? Why would they
care? They knew they could keep her trapped inside the module
until the station deorbited. Perhaps they thought that with the
resiliency she'd already shown she might very well be hacking
into the station's controls, trying to set up a digital roadblock to
prevent them from engaging the main thrusters.

As far as Kimberly could tell, they didn't know that she'd been
clandestinely communicating with the ground, or that it had been the
NSA's software, not hers, that had allowed her to temporarily regain
control of the ISS. So maybe they wanted to ensure that she wouldn't
be able to throw a software wrench into their plans once again.

Grinning to herself from inside the spacesuit helmet, Kimberly thought that they were going to get the surprise of their
lives once she stopped the flow of the thrusters' propellants. She
hoped they'd never suspect that she was going to do that from
outside the ISS. So let them try to guess what she was up to. They
couldn't see much inside the JPM because they'd shut off the
power; at least that would work in her favor.

And if they camped outside the JPM, instead of staying at the
far end near Central Post where the Russian ПрК transfer chamber was located, then they wouldn't be able to get to her when she
reentered the ISS—if she could reenter. She needed the ПрК's
inner hatch to be closed so she could open the transfer chamber's outer hatch. But she'd worry about that later, since there was
nothing she could do about it now.

She groped a gloved hand inside the equipment pouch on
her suit's leg, to make sure the compound pliers was there: the
EVA-modified vice grip that she would use to crimp the fuel line.
There it was, along with Shep's knife. Okay, she thought. All set.

Suddenly the module shuddered. Looking back at the vestibule hatch window, she saw one of the terrorists swing something at the Node 2 window. She couldn't hear anything through her helmet and the vacuum outside the vestibule, but the module shook again. They were swinging the titanium prybar at the window! The fools were trying to smash their way into the JPM!

She felt a chill run down her back. If they somehow managed to break the Node 2 window, it was possible that they'd quickly transit the depressurized vestibule. But they'd also lose all the air in the ISS, killing themselves as well as her. She had to hurry and quickly modify the experimental airlock so she could get outside the station. The controls were on the outside of the airlock, so she'd have to work fast.

Flying through the darkened module, she pulled Shep's knife from her equipment pouch as she dashed toward the experimental lock. She opened the inner hatch, reached in and cut the cable mechanism that controlled the outer hatch. She took a deep breath and steeled herself, knowing that as soon as she took the next step, all the module's air would rush out through the airlock like a miniature hurricane.

Careful now, she told herself as she opened the airlock depressurization valve halfway. Instantly she felt the force of air pushing her into the airlock. She went in headfirst. Small ice crystals from what little humidity had been in the module sparkled over the lock's metal surfaces as the temperature plummeted. Even with her helmet on Kimberly heard a shrill whistling as the air rushed through the airlock.

Wriggling forward in the cramped space, she contorted her body and reached between her legs for the hatch handle, now behind her. She pulled the inner hatch closed. It slammed shut, helped by the rush of the evacuating air. She was instantly plunged into silence.

Panting with exertion and excitement, Kimberly waited a

moment for whatever air remained in the lock to leak off into space, then used the vice grip to turn the long screw that fully opened the outer hatch. It took several eons-long moments, but at last she stared down at a clear, unobstructed view of Earth.

The entire procedure had taken only a few seconds, so with any luck the station depressurization alarm hadn't sounded and the two terrorists didn't realize that she had exited the module.

The air still left inside the JPM kept the inner hatch sealed behind her. She wouldn't be able to reenter the station from here, but she should have enough air to complete her task and then get to the ПрK transfer chamber at the far end of the Russian service module.

She hoped.

She imagined the terrorists on the other side of the vestibule momentarily stopping their hammering on the hatch window, probably wondering what she was doing in the JPM, but she didn't stick around to see what they'd do next. She had to crimp that fuel line and stop the propellants from getting to the thrusters.

She pulled herself forward, out through the narrow lock. Originally designed to extract experiments from outside the ISS, the airlock was never meant to support EVAs, but Kimberly had changed that now. She was outside the station.

Without the suit's umbilical cord she could move unhindered around the station—for the few minutes her bottled oxygen supply lasted. Can't afford to dawdle, she knew.

The view outside was spectacular. The station's metal surface gleamed in the sunlight with an almost unreal, razor-sharp clarity, with the Earth slowly rotating below, belying any feeling that the station was moving. Any other time she'd performed an EVA she had taken a few minutes to enjoy the sights, but she had to keep moving and conserve her air—

Damn! She realized she hadn't replaced her oxygen bottle; the spare canister was still inside the JPM, impossible to get now. She had less time than she'd thought.

She wanted to kick herself for forgetting something so important. You can't afford to screw up any more, she scolded herself. It's not just your life you're messing with, thousands or more could die if the station crashes.

Kimberly forced herself to draw in slow breaths, trying to slow her metabolism and focus back on the task she'd set herself. Keeping one gloved hand on the station at all times, she pulled herself fully outside the airlock and down the outside of the JPM. Grabbing metal interfaces, handrails, struts, and other extrusions on the station's skin, she pulled herself hand over hand down the module until she was just above Node 2.

Somewhere inside were the terrorists, hopefully not gaining any headway on breaking the node's window. If they were successful it would solve her problem of having to face them again: The station's air would blow out into space and they'd be quickly, painfully dead. On the other hand, she'd die soon after them if the station's air blew away.

She tried to push that possibility out of her mind as she laboriously continued her hand-over-hand trek across the ISS's exterior. Knowing that her oxygen supply was dwindling and the station descending, she quickened her pace across Node 2 toward the U.S. lab. With both her mike and the suit speaker off all she could hear in her helmet was her own labored breathing. Again she concentrated on slowing her breath, trying to conserve precious oxygen as she continued her crossing to the FGB.

In less than a minute Kimberly reached the junction between the station's U.S. and Russian segments. The modules here were not as closely spaced, but a Kevlar strap crossed the five-foot separation, serving as a gap spanner. Previous crews had installed the strap, and Kimberly wordlessly thanked them for making her journey easier.

Grasping the gap spanner, she pulled herself over and reached the Russian FGB module. Now to locate the fuel line.

Moving hand over hand, hanging on to the railings studding the station's skin, she moved to where an access panel was embedded in the FGB's outer skin. The Earth rotated slowly below; gleaming metal rose on either side around her, contrasting sharply against the utter darkness of space while brilliant pinpricks of stars glowed steadily against the void, without the twinkling caused by atmospheric aberrations.

Kimberly knew the thin fuel line ran down the length of the station, and this should be where it came closest to the outside. Wrapping her feet around an angled metal strut that stabilized one of the solar arrays, she fumbled in her equipment pouch and withdrew a utility wrench, then quickly pulled open the panel cover. Then she tucked the wrench back in her pouch and took out the vice grip, which had a short line secured to its end. She looped the end of the cord to her wrist so the compound wrench couldn't inadvertently float away.

She squinted into the panel. A jumble of wiring, fiber-optics lines, and insulation covered the millimeter-thick tube, just visible under the other stuff. Slowly, she wormed the pliers into the access port, gently pushing aside the insulation until she grasped the fuel line. Squeezing lightly, careful not to tear the metal or rip the thin tubing open, she slowly crimped the line . . . .

As she worked, doubts swirled through her mind. Was she applying too much pressure? Or not enough? Would the fuel keep flowing? What would she do if this didn't work?

She felt resistance. There. Fuel could no longer flow through the line, no longer get to the thrusters.

Almost immediately, out of the corner of her eye Kimberly saw a flash of light burst from the thruster. And she sensed that the station had ceased vibrating.

The thrusters must have stopped, she realized. They're not getting any propellants! Inside, the terrorists may have heard the thrust end with a small explosion as the hypergolic propellants were cut off, like a gasoline engine backfiring. But to Kimberly the event was soundless.

A surge of excitement raced through her. She'd stopped the station from deorbiting, but she knew her victory was only momentary. Unless she could get back inside and somehow neutralize the terrorists, she wouldn't be able to re-boost the station to a higher, safer altitude.

Which meant that sooner or later she'd have to come back out here and de-crimp the fuel line. And then rotate the station and re-boost it. Otherwise the station would continue to deorbit, much more slowly, but atmospheric friction would inevitably drag the ISS down to its doom.

First things first, Kimberly told herself. I've got deal with the terrorists . . . somehow.

With her feet still wrapped around the strut, she pushed back from the access panel and slipped the vice grip back into her equipment pouch. She felt slightly giddy; she couldn't tell if it was from her success at stopping the thrusters or because her oxygen supply was starting to run out.

Keeping her breathing slow and steady, she unwrapped her legs and pulled herself along the outside of the FGB toward the service module, at the far end of the station. She hoped the terrorists were still down by the JPM, since she'd have to enter the ISS through the Russian ПрК, the transfer chamber used by the Progress and Soyuz space capsules when they docked with the station.

But if she could get back inside without being detected, she'd be able to surprise them from behind and maybe do away with those two slimeballs—this time permanently.

She moved carefully across the station's outer skin, focusing on firmly grasping a pipe, a metal ridge, and handrails that ran along the FGB as she made her way to the ПрК.

It was time to confront the terrorists.

HADID HOME, VIENNA, VIRGINIA

The two-story house sat at the end of a cul-de-sac. The house was ideally located, half a mile up the street from the last stop on Washington D.C.'s Metro Orange line. White windowsills accentuated the blue paneled siding. A wide porch ran across the front and red maple trees covered the yard. An elementary school stood two blocks away, the community swimming pool was across the street, and the normally quiet neighborhood was home to well-to-do, two-income families who mostly worked for the federal government.

But this day was different. The streets leading to the circle of houses were packed with crowds of people, honking cars, armadas of police officers, and a line of TV news vans with satellite dishes on their roofs. Helicopters thrummed overhead.

Adding to the chaos, traffic was backed up throughout the neighborhood, all the way out to I-66, a half mile to the east, and extended from downtown D.C. to past West Virginia. Cars clogged the interstate systems throughout the east coast, all trying to head west, away from the cities, but mired in the traffic and making no headway.

The evacuation that had started only hours earlier with the startling revelation of the space station's impending crash now paralyzed the transportation infrastructure. Air terminals, bus and train stations were packed with frightened, panicked people. Rental car lots up and down the east coast were stripped bare, emptied in scant minutes. The number of people abandoning the east coast dwarfed the outflow of people after the terrorist attacks of 9/11.

Newscasters stood on the street just outside the lawn of the Hadid family home. Every so often their cameras caught a glimpse of someone peeking through the drawn curtains. More and more details were leaking out about the young American woman astronaut aboard the ISS as Kimberly Hadid-Robinson's childhood home became a magnet, a storm center, a focus of attraction for the curious, the fearful, and the news media.

Kimberly's picture, along with photos of Kazakhstani cosmonaut Farid Hazood and Qatari tourist Adama Bakhet were splashed in news venues across the whole world.

Despite the press encampment outside the Hadid home in Virginia, NASA maintained a stony silence about the whereabouts of her ex-husband, astronaut Scott Robinson, or what he was doing.

Even worse, because of Kimberly's Arab American background and her darkish Middle Eastern features, rumors were swirling that she might actually be in cahoots with the terrorists. But most of the American public was sympathetic toward the photogenic young astronaut—when they were not in a panic about being hit by a million pounds of radioactive space station debris.

Inside the Hadid home, Kimberly's father sat alongside his wife on the living room sofa, his eyes fixed on the family's high-definition TV screen. The same scenes, the same suppositions, the same wild guesses from self-anointed "experts."

And it all amounted to the same thing: No one knew what

was happening on the International Space Station. No one really knew if Kimberly was dead or alive.

Kimberly's mother could not stand watching the so-called news broadcasts. Her head rested on her husband's shoulder as she quietly sobbed. Her father wished he could cry, too, but the tears would not come. He sat like a statue, waiting, hoping, silently praying to the God of the universes that his daughter would live through this terrible day.

NEW YORK, NEW YORK

The streets surrounding Grand Central Station were mobbed with people, overflowing into an area of over five million square feet reaching from East Thirty-Ninth to East Forty-Sixth Street and from Fifth to Second Avenue. An ocean of people pushed to the station as they fought to catch nonexistent trains out of the city. Screams mixed with crying, sobs, and angry shouting. People gagged at the stench of unwashed bodies and vomit. The less fortunate were trampled as the crowd surged over them.

The parkways were congested. Smoke rose from stalled cars and buses, unable to move in the largest traffic jam in the world. People scrambled over smaller vehicles, struggling their way to bridges that were just as packed as the streets. The roads were so packed that bicycles were unable to make their way through the throng.

LaGuardia and JFK International were closed, the last planes having long deserted the area, but people still jammed the terminals, overwhelming the few TSA employees trying to keep people away. Fathers helped boost their families over the fences surrounding the airport, and soon the tarmac and runways were covered with people desperately searching the skies for incoming planes.

Lines into liquor stores snaked around the block as people stockpiled anything containing alcohol. Wine stores were over-run as rumors spread about a limit on purchases.

Groceries and convenience marts were filled with people making a run on canned goods, dried food, and bottled water. Signs at the front of the stores prominently announced that credit and debit cards would not be accepted; transactions were on a cash only basis. Most of the ATMs were empty, and some had their fronts defaced by frustrated customers. Banks and the financial district closed early; the only people not hoarding, seeking shelter, or trying to evacuate stood around ragtag preachers on street corners proselytizing the crowd.

In Central Park robed druids danced around a bonfire made from fallen trees and trash laid out in a giant X, marking a projected impact point like a bull's-eye for the incoming space station. Across the park, wiccans led their acolytes in chants, putting a hex on the station to miss the city. Elsewhere throughout the city, mainstream churches were packed in prayer meetings.

A majority of people barricaded themselves in high-rises, apartments, townhomes, and condominiums, unconvinced that the station would hit the city—but seeking shelter from the mayhem generated by the fraction of eight million residents that seemed to have completely lost their minds.

RUSSIAN SERVICE MODULE (SM)

Gasping for breath, Kimberly reached the end of the Russian Service Module, ready to enter the ПρК's cramped docking port. She hoped desperately that the inner hatch to the port was closed; otherwise she'd have to vent air from the entire station through a small valve to get in, and that would take hours.

But she didn't have hours, she knew. Maybe minutes. Maybe less.

Floating outside the airlock, she felt as if she were groping through a fog as she started depressurizing the ПρК's small volume. She recognized the symptoms of oxygen deprivation, yet knew she couldn't afford to rush and make a mistake. Moments dragged by as the air vented from the transfer chamber.

She shook her head, momentarily at a loss as to what she needed to do next. Then she fumbled in her utility pouch and pulled out a ⅜-inch square ratchet. Holding it firmly in her gloved hand she giggled as she thought, *A square peg in a hex hole.* Then she wondered why that was funny.

Carefully, she inserted the ratchet in the recessed hexagonal opening, and then turned it to open the hatch. The circular metal hatch swung open. Kimberly felt a gust of relief: the inner hatch had been closed. Thank God.

She clambered inside and blinked, trying to clear her mind as she tugged at the outer ПρК hatch to close it. It shouldn't be this hard, she thought. She wasn't yet gasping for air, but she knew her oxygen was almost gone: her indecision and slow judgment were signs of central hypoxia, but she couldn't seem to do anything about it. Struggling, she pulled at the hatch again.

The hatch swung shut. She suddenly felt claustrophobic, trapped, and unable to get into the station while her air was running out. The terrorists wouldn't even bother to overpower her; they'd just let her suffocate out here in this old Russian transfer chamber while they rained death on millions of guiltless Americans.

She needed oxygen.

With a shake of her head she quickly debated opening the re-pressurization valves located on the inner hatch. No, she told herself. The terrorists could detect even small pressure changes in the ISS, and she wasn't in any shape to fight them if they stormed the service module when she entered it. Instead, she opted to re-pressurize the chamber with the Russian *bea-em-pea* high-pressure tanks attached to the transfer chamber's side.

She stared at the tanks, trying to remember what she had to do. She knew that somehow she had to get back to basics, to be practical, positive, and not a victim. She was better than this: she was an astronaut.

Through the fog that was enveloping her mind, she reminded herself that the terrorists couldn't stop her from entering the SM module. Even if they were inside waiting for her, she'd use her tools and Shep's knife to fight back. Shakily, she punched at the controls that started the pressurization process.

Air flowed into the airlock chamber, slowly filling its volume. Kimberly stared at the pressure gauge. It seemed to take forever for the levels to build up as the analog needle quivered across the dial. She felt as if she couldn't catch her breath. She tried to force herself to wait, but when the gauge showed 30 kilopascals of pressure she started to remove her helmet.

She bounced off the side of the chamber as she struggled to pull off the clear bubble of polycarbonate plastic, frantically twisting it back and forth and kicking her legs until the helmet finally came off.

Gasping, panting, she saw that the pressure dial registered only slightly less than five pounds to the square inch, about the equivalent of being on the summit of Mount Everest. But the pressure was rising. Kimberly tried to draw in deep breaths, pull more oxygen into her starved lungs as she watched the gauge slowly, slowly continue to rise.

The needle finally passed 100 kPa, right at the 14.7-psi sea-level standard throughout the station. Still, she sucked in deep lungfuls. And tried to convince herself that her reaction now was more psychological than physical. She should have plenty of air now, more than enough to breathe normally—unless the terrorists had somehow tampered with the gauges and they were now displaying false data.

She pushed that fear from her mind. These were *analog* dials, not digital. They were directly connected to pressure transducers embedded throughout the small chamber. They were immune to computer hacking.

And she realized that with that simple display of logic she was finally regaining her mental facilities.

Almost immediately she felt better. Her breathing slowed. Her mind really had played tricks on her. She didn't want to know how low her oxygen level had gotten; she hadn't shown so much confusion even during her astronaut hypobaric training in NASA's high-altitude chamber.

Instead of dwelling on that, she pulled Shep's knife out of her equipment pouch and crouched to launch herself out of the ПрК. With her free hand she slowly cranked the lever at the base of the hatch, rotating it counterclockwise . . . .

She tensed as the hatch swung open, praying that they weren't in Central Post; if they were, they'd only be fifteen or so feet away, just on the other side of the galley. Blood pounded in her ears as she readied herself for *any* type of response from Farid and Bakhet, from the two of them rushing her, to being hit on the head, even blindsided by some piece of heavy equipment. She pushed out with both legs as hard as she could, holding Shep's knife in front of her as she shot out the instant the hatch swung fully open.

Nothing. She was alone in the far aft end of the SM, by the Russian toilet, and Central Post was deserted.

She soared down the axis of the module and prepared to swing around the side of the vestibule as she exited the SM. If the terrorists weren't still down by the JPM, no telling where they were, but they'd still be trying to deorbit the station, and were probably furious because the thruster controls wouldn't work. They wouldn't have a clue that she'd physically prevented the hypergolic propellants from reaching the thruster motors. Most likely they'd be frantically combing through the software to see how she might have put another lock on the propellant control states.

So she'd have to start hunting them down, module by module, just as they did her when they first arrived.

She didn't know if she'd encounter one or both of them, but she figured she'd have the element of surprise. Her breath quickening, she rotated around the metal edge of the vestibule and flew directly into DC-1.

Bakhet was peering out the viewport, maybe looking for Mecca, just as that Saudi prince had done years ago when he had visited the station. Bakhet turned his head as she entered, his eyes flashing wide with astonishment. He started to yell while simultaneously ducking away from her.

Kimberly slashed out as she flew over him, barely missing him with Shep's knife. She spun around in midair by quickly jerking her hands and upper torso upward, forcing her legs to swing forward. Her feet struck Bakhet on the back of his skull, right above the neck. His head snapped against his chest and he cried out.

She spun forward from the hit and, unable to stop, sailed out of DC-1 and into the SM, straight into a large brown coarse fabric sack of supplies. As she tumbled she spotted the titanium prybar, wedged next to the laptop Bakhet had been using.

Could she reach the prybar before he did?

Bakhet came out of DC-1, holding a hand to his head. He lurched toward her, but with his inexperience in zero-gee he started to rotate forward. He reached out for the long Russian prybar; his hand swiped against it, causing the titanium tool to rapidly tumble away in a wobbly spinning motion.

Heading directly for Kimberly.

She tried to twist out of its way, but as she moved the bar's pointed end slashed against the top of her hand. Blood spurted from a vein, spewing out a stream of bright red globules. Gritting her teeth, Kimberly smashed against the pile of bungee-cord secured supplies. Shep's knife slipped out of her hand, spinning away in the opposite direction, toward the far end of the service module.

As she bounced, Kimberly reached out and grabbed one of the bungee cords, ripping it from its mooring. A mass of *mee-shauks*, large brown surplus Russian cloth sacks, floated out. She grabbed one by its back end and swung it at Bakhet, spilling out packets of nuts, buckwheat gruel, borsch, and tvorog Russian cottage cheese—creating a cloud of mini-asteroids in the center of the module.

Twisting in the air, she grabbed another bungee cord secured to the wall. With blood still pumping from her hand, Kimberly jerked the other end of the cord free, pulling out a heavy metal ring that fastened the cord to the module. The motion snapped her toward the wall. Hitting the module's insulated side, she whipped around and swung the long cord and its oval fastener at Bakhet.

The heavy metal ring struck him in the face. He screamed in sharp pain and doubled over, hands to his head. Shrieking, he rotated end over end and drifted into MRM-2.

Following him, Kimberly grabbed at a large white American MO bag that had been staged in the Russian airlock. She yanked open its zipper, emptying its contents. Clothing and blankets spilled out as she turned in the air. She hit the side of the airlock again and, holding the empty MO bag wide open in front of her, kicked off straight for Bakhet, still bleary and wailing from his injuries, floating in the middle of MRM-2. She hit Bakhet's head as she wrapped him in the bag.

He started to kick, rotating them both in the center of the module.

Ignoring her hand's bleeding, Kimberly rapidly closed the bag as Bakhet punched fruitlessly against the heavy cloth he was enclosed in. Dark red stains grew on both sides of the white fabric— on the inside from his blood, on the outside, hers.

Bakhet yelled hoarsely, frantically kicking and punching the sides of the MO bag, trying to escape. The bag looked as though a series of random eruptions was jabbing it from the inside.

Kimberly heard Farid shouting from the far end of the station, down by the JPM. She didn't have much time. She kicked off the wall and hit the pulsating bag with her outstretched hands, roughly shoving it toward the far end of MRM-2. The bag careened off the metal wall, further inciting Bakhet, as Kimberly coolly moved out of the open Russian airlock.

She slammed the hatch closed, trapping him in MRM-2, where the Soyuz craft was docked. Then she pushed off for the titanium prybar that was still slowly bouncing from wall to wall as it tumbled through the air. Grabbing the long metal bar, she pulled up and used it to pin the hatch shut, locking Bakhet inside. Although injured, she now had one terrorist down, trapped in the Russian airlock.

She kicked back for Command Post to find Shep's knife as Farid's yelling grew louder. He sounded as though he was almost at Node 1. As she flew through the air she grabbed one of the Russian shirts that floated in the module and wrapped it around her hand, slowing the bleeding. She felt incredibly weak and she didn't know if it was from the exertion or the loss of blood. In any case she had to keep moving, get to Shep's utility knife—

Farid soared into the module, screaming, his face red as he hurtled through the air.

Kimberly instantly grabbed her knees and ducked her head, balling up as small as she could. Farid's hand whacked her side as she sailed past, knocking her into the insulated wall.

She bounced off at an angle, spinning into the FGB. Extending her body, she grabbed at the vestibule leading to Node 1 and spun off into the module, toward Node 3, leaving Shep's knife somewhere behind her.

She had to find something else to fight with, but what? She had to search one of the tool pouches stored near the Joint Airlock, find one of the long screwdrivers or heavy wrenches to use as a weapon.

She heard Farid behind her. He must have been able to change his momentum before hitting the end of the SM. His curses reverberated throughout the station.

She didn't have time to change her own direction for the Joint Airlock. She careened off the side and kicked as hard as she could, entering Node 3 and flying toward the exercise equipment moored to its side.

Reaching down, she grabbed the handrail that ran across the treadmill. She rotated around, stopping her motion. She quickly scanned the module, but couldn't see any tools, or even extra equipment that might have been stored in one of the bungee-cord jails set against the wall. What could she use? There wasn't even a VAJ pressure hose she could use to evacuate the air in the vestibule and barricade herself inside, as she'd done in the JPM.

She felt her heart rate start to skyrocket. Maybe there was something she could use in the Bigelow module. At only ten and a half feet in diameter and accessed through a small hatch in Node 3, the experimental inflatable module was well past its mission life and was now used for overflow storage. The hatch was loosely held in place with only two hand-tightened bolts to guard against the module suddenly developing a leak; she felt a rush of cold air tumble out of the small, dark module as she opened it. The Bigelow was not powered or heated. Could she hide in there, hoping Farid might miss her?

Too late. Farid flew through the vestibule, arms outstretched, heading straight at Kimberly. His face was contorted with rage, his eyes blazing with the sole purpose of killing her.

Kimberly kicked back, out of his path. Flying backward, she put out a hand to brace herself against the module's side when she spotted one of the Portable Fire Extinguishers secured next to the hatch. She quickly rotated in midair by pitching forward and pulling her feet in. Kicking out, she hit the module's side and bounced directly toward the oval-shaped orange PFE. She opened the metal door, ripped it from its mooring, flipped the safety switch, and turned the nozzle toward Farid. A sudden spray of liquid carbon dioxide spewed from the extinguisher, instantly turning into a frigid, white, smoky gas.

Farid screamed and clawed at his head, his face nearly flash-frozen. His eyes were squeezed shut as he shrieked, his fingers digging into his flesh as though he were trying to pull off his frost-bitten skin as he spun, howling, toward the center of the module.

The momentum of the spray kicked Kimberly backward as she fought to keep the last few pounds of liquid CO_2 focused on Farid. Her head hit the metal side of the vestibule and the PFE went tumbling out of her hands.

Kicking the Node 3 wall, she pushed off as hard as she could, heading straight for Farid. Ducking her head, she hit him squarely in the chest like a battering ram.

He gave an audible *oof* at the impact and snapped back violently against the Bigelow hatch, hitting his head against the edge of the metal entrance as he tumbled inside the Kevlar-sided inflatable module.

Kimberly quickly bolted the hatch cover shut, sealing him inside. She scanned Node 3 for something to secure the hatch. She couldn't see anything she could use, but she knew that inside the dark, unheated module Farid wouldn't be able to access any of the station's controls, or unfasten the bolts and escape. Still, just to be safe, she needed to ensure that he'd never get out. She could depressurize the inflatable module by using the ISS's graphical interface. Let him breathe vacuum, she thought grimly.

She felt drained, and couldn't quite believe that she'd trapped the two terrorists in separate locations. She was dead tired from the exertion and lack of sleep, not to mention the stress. And now, though she'd bought a little time to try to re-boost the station, she knew she couldn't stop to rest on her laurels. She wasn't through yet, although she felt she could finally see the end of this nightmare.

Kicking off the side of the module, she left the Bigelow and pushed out of Node 3, heading toward Central Post. For the first time in days she moved without tensing up. Part of her wanted to look for Shep's knife; merely holding it gave her a feeling of confidence. But the logical part of her mind insisted that she first needed to ensure that the two terrorists couldn't escape. What she really needed was something else to make sure they stayed locked in. And after that she'd have to go EVA again to de-crimp the thin propellant line so she could boost the ISS to a higher altitude.

The station had already lost significant altitude, and now that it was in a lower orbit it was encountering more atmospheric drag. Kimberly knew that normally the ISS lost more than a hundred meters per day, mainly from drag created by the big, ungainly solar panels. If she had time, she'd pull up the mission control numbers on the ISS system to see how much altitude they'd already lost, but every minute she waited, the lower the station would drop.

At least this time when she went EVA she'd be in one of the old, self-contained spacesuits that didn't need an umbilical cord for oxygen. And there'd be no pressure from the terrorists.

She glided past the MRM-2. Glancing at the airlock she saw that the titanium prybar was still pinning the hatch shut. She'd love to evacuate the air in there as well as the Bigelow, but the controls were on the inside of the airlock and there was no way she was going to risk opening the hatch.

She tried the prybar; it was secure. Now to ensure that Farid would *never* get out of the Bigelow.

SOUTH PACIFIC OCEAN, NORTHWEST OF THE SOLOMON ISLANDS

The cruisers USS *Lake Erie*, USS *Decatur*, and USS *Russell* positioned themselves for an optimal launch of their Aegis antisatellite missiles. Their captains coordinated their movements so that no debris from the launch, or an unexpected missile malfunction, would threaten the ships of the small armada.

The ocean had calmed considerably since they'd arrived on station: clear visibility, fair winds, and following seas gave them near-optimal conditions.

The cruisers ran drills using the military's space-sensing network, a chain of radar and optical telescopes spread across the world that provided them with precise timing and aiming coordinates for the ISS. Awaiting the command to launch, the crews were trained, well rested, and ready to launch their ASAT weapons.

Eight thousand four hundred miles away, in Washington, D.C., and fifteen hours' time difference from the Solomon Islands, the U.S. State Department finished coordinating a top-secret agreement with China for the Chinese to provide a backup with their own state-of-the-art ASATs, Dong Neng-3s, only if the U.S.-launched Aegis missiles failed.

Russia would not guarantee that its own antisatellite weapon would work, because unlike the U.S. and Chinese, the Russians had never tested their ASAT system—high-powered, ground-based iodine lasers—against active satellites. But the Kremlin did agree not to interfere with whatever actions the U.S. or China undertook.

Once the agreement with China was reached, the State Department sent confirmation over classified channels to the National Security Council that the Chinese were ready to step in and help—but only if officially asked by Washington.

The stage was set, and the results were presented to a Principals Only meeting in the White House Situation Room, where all NSC members at the Cabinet level were present—with the notable exception of the NASA Administrator.

Reading the updates, the President relaxed slightly, thinking perhaps he had finally found a path for preventing massive loss of life because of the ISS deorbit. Things were already escalating wildly with the news being leaked that terrorists were trying to crash the space station somewhere along the U.S. eastern seaboard, and contaminate the entire east coast with plutonium.

The President realized that all he had to do was to pull the trigger . . . or not. There were pros and cons for acting immediately, as well as for waiting. He glanced at the clock hanging on the Situation Room's rear wall, irritated that the NASA Administrator was still hung up in traffic. He'd give her a few more minutes, but whether she was present or not, he didn't have time to wait. No one did.

At least now, with everyone else in the NSC assembled, within minutes he'd have the best advice his most trusted and senior advisors could give.

Yet, despite all the fail-safe plans, the President couldn't escape the nagging feeling that he was about to give carte blanche to a process that could quickly spiral out of control.

CENTRAL POST, INTERNATIONAL SPACE STATION

Kimberly floated in front of the laptop that accessed the ISS's graphical interface. Although she felt pressed for time, she concentrated on ensuring that there was no way that Farid could escape from the inflatable Bigelow module, for once she went EVA she'd be completely vulnerable. And with no one on board to help her, this was her last chance to re-boost the station.

As she called up the schematic of the Bigelow to depressurize the inflatable, she heard a faint thud, as if something heavy had hit the side of the station. Looking up from the screen, she felt a sudden chill as she saw the Russian prybar float through the SM. It slowly tumbled through the air, hitting the metal edge of the vestibule with a clang as it drifted across the Service Module.

It no longer pinned the MRM-2 hatch! Bakhet had somehow freed himself from the MO bag and had gotten loose! Since the airlock was not depressurized, there was nothing to prevent the terrorist from kicking against the airlock handle and dislodging the titanium bar.

Kimberly reacted instantly, knowing that Bakhet would appear any second.

She kicked away from the laptop, toward the prybar, still tumbling slowly in the middle of the module. Reaching the four-and-a-half-foot-long bar, she grabbed it out of the air. Her momentum took her past Central Post and she hit the bungee-cord-secured supply bags.

She heard crashing sounds from outside the module. Bakhet must be searching through MRM-2, looking for something to overpower her. He'd be wary of getting too close to her, so she wouldn't be able to use another bungee cord as a bola-like weapon. And when he saw that she had the prybar he'd certainly keep his distance. But, she thought, she *could* impale him with the rod's pointed end, nail him with it like an ancient warrior pinning an enemy with his spear.

With her injured hand, though, she wasn't sure she could throw the massive bar with enough velocity to transfix him, but she had an idea of how to do it.

Keeping an eye on the hatch, she rummaged through the bungee cords and rapidly untied three of the rubbery, elastic lines. Kicking back down to the laptop, she removed the small computer from its U-shaped base, then she swiveled the stand and looped the ends of the bungee cords around the U-shaped metal poles.

Her hand still hurt from being slashed earlier as she placed the curved end of the prybar against the cords. Then gaining purchase with her feet, she pulled back on the bungees as hard as she could, using the elastic lines and the U-shaped laptop stand as a makeshift crossbow for the prybar bolt, aiming the pointed end at the hatch.

The titanium rod quivered as she waited. She heard Bakhet moving closer and gritted her teeth as she pulled back harder on the bungee cords, stretching them to the limit as she waited, waited . . .

Bakhet suddenly flew into the module, his arms outstretched. In one hand he carried a long screwdriver. He sailed through the air, coming straight at her, snarling.

His eyes went wide as he saw the crossbow; he tried to pull up and rotate backward. He shouted—

Kimberly released the cords. The elastic lines snapped forward, hurling the prybar toward Bakhet.

The long titanium bar arrowed across the module, but its curved rear end started to rotate upward. For a second Kimberly thought that the metal rod might hit Bakhet on its side and not straight on—but before either one of them could react the prybar's pointed end slammed into his chest, piercing his clothing and skin. The momentum from the impact spun him slowly backward in the air, head over heels.

He hit the opposite wall and Kimberly saw a look of astonishment flash across his face. He flailed his hands. Blood gurgled in his mouth.

Kimberly quickly unwrapped the bungee cords from the U-shaped stand and started preparing a bola-like weapon as she watched Bakhet grab at the long metal pole. Using both hands, he gave a weak, halfhearted tug, trying to pull it out of his chest. Then his arms drifted off to his sides. His eyes turned glassy and stopped moving. Still rotating slightly, his body bumped against the far wall and bounced weakly back toward the center of the module.

Kimberly's breath caught in her throat as she watched, carefully, to make sure there was no more movement. After a few seconds, she cautiously pushed off toward him, keeping the makeshift bola at the ready.

She reached Bakhet and grabbed the curved, crowfoot end of

the prybar. Grunting, she twisted it several times, to make sure he was lifeless. He didn't respond.

He's dead, she thought. I killed him. She expected to feel guilt, remorse. Instead, a voice in her head exulted, *Better him than me.*

Finally certain that Bakhet was really dead, she pushed him back into the MRM-2 airlock. She closed the hatch and again used the prybar to secure the handle, unwilling to take any chance that he might somehow have survived.

She frantically rummaged through the debris still floating in the SM from when she'd torn the bungee-cord jail apart. She spotted Shep's knife; feeling relieved, she kicked off, grabbed it, then sailed along the station's axis to Node 3. Holding the knife out, she entered the module, expecting the worst . . . .

The hatch to the inflatable Bigelow module was still secure. She floated over to it and checked the entrance to the rubberized plastic of the module. It was still locked, bolted shut. And quiet. Once again she tightened the screws. Farid wasn't banging around inside; probably his flash-frozen face was still painful, Kimberly thought.

She thought again about depressurizing the Bigelow, using the graphical interface. But she'd already lost enough time dealing with the terrorists, and she still had the EVA to accomplish. And although contacting NASA was supposed to be her first priority, Kimberly decided they would have to wait. They couldn't do anything to help her, anyway.

She turned for the Joint Airlock. Gliding into the area, she started preparing the EVA suit that was equipped with the Extravehicular Mobility Unit so she could exit the station and de-crimp the propellant line. As she checked out the suit, she thought that now with both terrorists out of the picture, donning the EMU-equipped suit would be the hardest thing she had to do.

17TH STREET AND CONSTITUTION AVENUE NW, WASHINGTON, D.C.

Stuck in the honking, steaming traffic mere blocks from the White House, NASA Administrator Patricia Simone fumed at the delay and debated leaving her chauffeured limousine and walking the rest of the way. But the sidewalks were jammed, too, with angry, frightened people pushing and yelling at one another. And they glanced skyward, as if expecting to see the ISS dropping out of the heavens and falling on them.

The whole city was in gridlock, everyone trying to get away, panic rising higher by the minute.

Normally, the drive from NASA Headquarters to the White House didn't take more than ten minutes, fifteen at the most. But she'd been sitting in the car for more than a half hour, barely inching along in the honking bumper-to-bumper traffic. She decided she'd give it another five minutes and then she was out the door, no matter what her Chief of Staff said.

The LED TV screen embedded in the backseat console showed multiple windows of different national and cable news broadcasts: camera shots of traffic crawling out of the nation's capital, computer-generated graphics of the paths of the mass evacuations taking place up and down the eastern seaboard, rioting in New York City, Boston, Washington, Atlanta, and even Miami.

Sitting next to her on the backseat, perspiring despite the limousine's air-conditioning, Simone's Chief of Staff, Mini Mott, held up a red-bordered sheet of paper with the words TOP SECRET/ SCI stamped at its top and bottom. The normally optimistic ex-Marine's round face was flushed, scowling.

The TV screen suddenly blinked and the words *Breaking news from the White House* scrolled across its bottom, beneath the Presidential seal.

Simone sucked in a breath. This can't be good news, she thought. But how can it get worse?

"What do you have, Mini?"

Mott pulled a second page from the limo's secure portable printer. "The National Security Council has just signed off on the decision paper."

"Couldn't they wait another five minutes?" Simone complained. "They only called the meeting ten minutes ago and I was already on my way!"

Simone fumed, but she realized that with the speed with which things were moving, there was no use even lodging formal protest. Damn! She realized that she should have stayed camped out in NASA's cramped office in the Old Executive Office building so she could have made this last-minute meeting. But with the Dragon returning to Earth and the Starliner still approaching the ISS, she needed to make certain that Kimberly had the resources of NASA and the rest of the government at her disposal to stop those SOBs.

She took the classified document from Mott's hand and rapidly scanned it. Thank God her secure limo served as a rolling SCIF: her level of political appointment included this mobile Sensitive Compartmented Information Facility to allow her to view the highest-classified documents no matter where she was.

Mini said in a choked voice, "The news release at the bottom of the second page has gone out to every major national and international contact, and the President is going to hold a press conference at any moment now."

Simone looked up sharply. "But this is illegal! This news release reveals an ongoing military operation. And they've bypassed the interagency review! They've bypassed *me!*"

With a shrug of his shoulders, Mott countered, "To stop the rioting and panic spreading up and down the eastern seaboard, the NSC urged the President to announce that he's approved Operation Burnt Haunt. He's ordered the Navy to shoot down the ISS on its next pass over the south Pacific."

"But that's only one of several options."

Mini shook his head. "No, ma'am, not anymore. You'll see that the Decision Memorandum concludes it's better that the President goes public immediately with Burnt Haunt. It recommends he convince the American public that once the ISS is shot down, the station will fall harmlessly into the Pacific Ocean. They're hoping that the announcement—and the shoot-down—will dispel the panic and the rioting and things will return back to normal."

He jabbed a finger toward the TV screen in the back console. The display showed the President sitting at his desk in the Oval Office, looking as though he was about to speak.

Simone slumped back in her seat. "So he's going to kill one of our own astronauts just to dispel rumors and irrational fears."

"The rioting is real," Mott said quietly. "Hundreds, maybe thousands of people will die if we don't do something. The press is reporting the possibility it may be in the millions . . . ."

"But the chances that it'll hit New York—"

"That doesn't matter. It's the radiation, Patricia—the plutonium. People are scared shitless. They're starting to act like animals! The President's got to stop that. Now!"

"It's the wrong decision," Simone insisted.

"Yes, ma'am, I agree. But that doesn't change anything."

The NASA Administrator fought back tears of frustration. "Except that my best astronaut will be killed, along with this nation's space program."

JOINT AIRLOCK

Kimberly's side ached and her wounded hand throbbed as she pulled on a thin layer of long underwear, then her custom-fitted liquid cooling and ventilation garment. The garment was threaded with clear plastic tubing, looking like veins running through its skintight length. She felt warm as she dressed, but she knew that once suited up, chilled water would flow through the thin flexible pipes, keeping her temperature down.

She was behind schedule, having programmed a script for the ISS to rotate 180 degrees and engage the thrusters exactly nineteen minutes from now.

To save time, she'd skipped putting on the modified incontinence diaper she'd normally wear when suiting up. She remembered going through a few diapers she'd found in the JPM and hanging them up to dry; if she really had to go she'd wait until she could get back to the zero-gee toilet. She'd be on EVA only for a few minutes, she reasoned, hopefully no longer than she'd taken to initially crimp the fuel line. Plus, she'd been so dehydrated that she hadn't even peed for half a day. So bypassing the MAG, or maximum absorbency garment, was a small risk to take.

Her injuries seemed to have gotten worse: she felt stiff and achy, and incredibly tired. She tried to ignore the sullen pain, knowing that she would have plenty of time to attend to her wounds once she'd re-boosted the station.

Suddenly puzzled, she wondered where the cooling garment had gotten to. It should be right here, beside the spacesuit's outer shell . . . .

Then she realized she was already wearing it. Stupid. But she remembered that confusion and loss of mental acuity was one of the first signs of the bends.

I've got to hurry, she told herself. Get this job done before the bends really hits.

She thought about using SAFER, the cold-nitrogen emergency jet pack. But she'd have to fasten it to the back of the suit, and she was running out of time. Feeling weak, she winced as she struggled to pull on first the lower torso assembly and then the fiberglass hard upper torso.

Fighting against exhaustion, she took three tries before she finally connected the liquid cooling and ventilation garment's umbilical to the suit's water supply. Then she locked the upper and lower parts of the suit with the body seal closure before pulling on her gloves and the clear-bubble helmet.

Finally sealed in the EMU, she heard the suit's regulator and fan whining away at 20,000 rpm as she prepared to evacuate the air from the Joint Airlock. She rotated her arms and twisted her torso, trying to elevate her heart rate. Work as much nitrogen out of your bloodstream as you can, she told herself.

She knew she should have pre-breathed pure oxygen to purge her body of nitrogen to prevent the bends, but because she was so pressed for time, once again she had skipped the normal three-hour pre-breathing routine and opted for the abbreviated in-suit exercise. It was a risk she'd have to take, but in the scheme of things she decided she'd rather chance the possibility of decompression sickness than have the station slip below the point of no return as it continued to drop in altitude.

With purposeful care, she made certain that she was tethered securely and had both Shep's knife and the EVA-modified vice grip in her equipment pouch. Then she closed the airlock's inner hatch and started evacuating the chamber, pumping the lock's air back into the station. Her suit ballooned slightly as the pressure dropped. When it fell below 1 psi she vented the lock and opened the outer hatch.

It swung slowly open. Using the handrails on the station's outer skin, Kimberly pushed slowly out into the airless depths of space. For a moment she blinked in puzzlement, trying to recall how she could best find her way to the access panel. Then she got her bearings and remembered: it's on the FGB, the next module over. She thought she must have flashed to where she had exited the JPM through the small experimental lock; with all that had happened since then, the change in her location had momentarily confused her.

She pulled her way forward. Being tethered to the station, she could move faster than she had when she'd been in the second-generation suit. She knew she could take more risk by getting as quickly as possible to the panel where she'd crimped the line.

Bending at the edge of the module, she worked her way toward the FGB, hand over hand, with the long safety tether trailing behind her, playing out as she moved toward the axis of the station.

She reached out with a gloved hand and snagged one of the conformal thermal radiators. Her spacesuited body rotated gently as she moved across the station's outer skin toward the FGB access panel.

Her heart started thumping faster. She knew this shouldn't take nearly as long as her last EVA; the access port was already open and the Joint Airlock was closer to the FGB than to the JPM, located at the opposite end of the station's axis. All she had to do was de-crimp the thin stainless steel line to allow the dimethylhydrazine fuel to flow to the thrusters. A piece of cake, really . . . but for some reason she was finding it hard to concentrate on what she needed to do.

Pulling out the vice grip, Kimberly looped its tether around her right wrist, then grabbed the panel with her free hand. She pulled herself close, until her helmet was almost inside the opening, then carefully pushed the vice grip past the layers of mylar thermal blankets that insulated the line.

A sudden sharp pain pierced through her upper chest and neck, as if stabbing through the suit. It felt as if an army of ants crawled underneath her skin, across her elbows, chest, and thighs. Had she been hit by something on the station, or maybe a piece of space debris? The pain spiraled up in intensity: she could hardly think straight.

She started to pull the vice grip out of the access panel to see what had happened, but a vague thought seemed to grow in her mind. Her suit wasn't breeched or even struck by some outside object: she must be experiencing the onset of decompression sickness, the bends. Her two EVAs had not allowed her to sufficiently purge the nitrogen from her bloodstream, and now all she could feel was the incredible pain of nitrogen bubbles growing in her veins. Kimberly knew she'd be incapacitated unless she got back inside the station and into a higher-pressure environment.

But she couldn't leave. Not yet.

Gasping from the pain, her vision blurred as she refocused on de-crimping the fuel line. She had to fight through this. She wouldn't have a second chance if she returned to the airlock and the safety of the ISS's normal air pressure. By the time she'd overcome the decompression sickness the station could very well be so low in altitude that it would be beyond the point of ever returning to a higher orbit.

Her gloved hand shaking, Kimberly opened the vice grip and pushed it over the stainless steel fuel line. She barely tightened her grip as she moved the wrench slowly down the tubing. She felt a sudden indentation and stopped. It was where she had crimped off the flow.

Tears in her eyes, she carefully rotated the vice grip until it was nearly 90 degrees from where she'd previously crimped the line. Slowly, she closed the handle. Gently, she worked the grip back and forth. She rotated the tool, trying to ensure that the tube was now as symmetrical as she could make it.

She pulled the grip out of the panel. Grunting through the pain that enveloped her, she pushed her helmet close to the hatch's opening. She tried to see if she could spot any indentations on the line, but she couldn't focus her eyes that clearly.

Her skin crawling, burning, it was hard to think straight. She had to see if she needed to try again—

She felt a low vibration run through the FGB as she gripped the edge of the opening. She shook her head inside her helmet, trying to clear her vision. The engines must have engaged, she realized, commanded by the script she'd written prior to going EVA. The thrusters are working!

An incredible sense of relief swept through her pain and fatigue and growing weakness. She'd succeeded, but now she needed to get into the station as quickly as she could as the script she'd written started rotating the station 180 degrees, preparing to boost to altitude.

She used both hands to flip herself over. Floating above the FGB's outer skin, she started to drift away from the station; the tether securing her to the ISS snaked out as she floated farther and farther away.

Gritting her teeth, Kimberly reached down and grabbed the line with both hands, then started pulling herself hand over hand to the slowly rotating space station. It was revolving so gradually that even through her pain she knew she'd be able to pull herself back to the airlock before the station started ascending—but the effort seemed nearly impossible as the decompression sickness burrowed deeper into her exhausted body.

Little by little she pulled herself toward the Joint Airlock. The station's low acceleration had moved the ISS so that she had drifted until she was nearly on top of the inflatable Bigelow module. She tried to pull out of the way and avoid hitting the module. Glancing through the Cupola window in Node 3 she saw a faint glow coming from the Bigelow hatch window. Had Farid somehow gotten his hands on a light in the inflatable module? A laptop or something else that he was using to illuminate the supplies stashed in it?

As she laboriously pulled herself along the tether, Kimberly felt an overpowering fear that Farid would somehow get loose, free himself from the Bigelow and escape into the ISS.

A chill of fear swept through her.

With the thrusters now working, he'd be able to rotate the station back again and start it deorbiting once more. At the very least, he'd be able to close the Joint Airlock hatch and prevent her from ever getting back inside.

And if she couldn't get back inside the station she'd die from her oxygen running out, or from the bends, or—if she survived long enough—from the station's fiery plunge back to Earth.

Breathing hard against the incredible pain lancing through her, Kimberly opened the equipment pouch belted to her waist. A screwdriver, needle-nose pliers, and a wrench all floated away until she finally found what she needed: Shep's knife.

Stabilizing herself just outside the Bigelow module, she gripped the ultrasharp knife firmly, pulled back her arm, and stabbed the Kevlar-like fabric of the inflatable as hard as she could.

Again and again she stabbed at the material, working up a sweat until she finally broke through the white, reinforced siding. Small plumes of air spewed from the module, swirling as they vented through the openings. Kimberly kept jabbing, ripping, slashing with Shep's knife as deeply as she could.

She tore a ten-centimeter rip in the material. It split wider as air whooshed out. Small white ice crystals spewed out from the near-absolute-zero cold, clouding her view, until Kimberly could no longer see any sign of air still escaping the module.

She pulled close and peered into the inflatable module—then just as quickly pushed back.

Farid's face covered the rip from the inside, his mouth sagging open in a silent scream of death, his eyes frothy red from rapid decompression in the vacuum of space.

Kimberly turned away. Pain still crawling under her skin and inflaming her joints, she pulled to the Joint Airlock. Out of the corner of her eye she spotted Shep's knife tumbling slowly away from the station. The Navy astronaut's illegal utility knife had certainly earned its keep and served its purpose. It would probably never be recovered, just floating through the vacuum of space forever.

As she made her painful way back to the hatch, Kimberly knew she'd never have to use it again. But did she have the strength to get back inside the station?

NATIONAL SECURITY AGENCY, FORT MEADE, MARYLAND

The nondescript, low-slung warehouse was located just north of Mapes Road and east of MacArthur on Fort George Meade, HQ NSA. The windowless, concrete building was unmarked and could have been a maintenance facility for the U.S.'s premier cryptographic and communications intelligence and security agency. Buildings like this typically contained lawn mowers, fertilizer, grass seed, shovels, cement, lumber, and a wide assortment of spare parts used for the upkeep of a large government site.

Except a detailed, overhead view would reveal hundreds of thick power lines snaking into the facility. Outside, surrounding the structure's circumference were huge banks of fans and air conditioners, enough to provide cooling for tens of thousands of people—even though the parking lot in front was large enough for only a hundred cars. A dedicated cooling tower was located nearby. And despite being located on a secure U.S. Army base, four razor-wire fences surrounded the mysterious warehouse.

Inside the classified building the air-conditioning worked at maximum capacity, attempting to cool hundreds of supercomputers jammed into the massive facility. Over 40 percent of the world's entire computational capability existed within its confines, and today NSA's entire cyber system, enhanced by highly secure off-site cloud computing, was focused on breaking a Chinese encryption code.

State-of-the-art quantum computers simultaneously worked with massively parallel processors, all focused on discovering the one unique key that would unlock classified transmissions intercepted just days before from a deep, underwater cable. The purloined transmissions had been traced as coming from the highest level of the Chinese government, and were being sent to a remote space launch facility located in the South China Sea.

It was a herculean task, and only months before without the help of the still-experimental quantum computing capability, it would have been inconceivable to break such a sophisticated code.

But days into the calculation, the key was discovered.

OVAL OFFICE, THE WHITE HOUSE

The President straightened his tie and took a sip of water as they applied a last dab of makeup to his forehead, masking the sheen of perspiration that betrayed his uncertainty. In front of him, the camera crew's floor director held up a finger and mouthed the words, "One minute to airtime, sir."

The President glanced at the digital clock on his desk as it counted down the seconds, thinking that another, more crucial clock was ticking as well. The ISS was still deorbiting and there was incredible pressure for him to execute the Burnt Haunt anti-satellite option. Almost his entire cabinet was behind it, and the entire NRC urged him to shoot down the space station and put an end to this crisis.

He knew that if the antisatellite weapon was used, an American astronaut would die along with the terrorists: a *female* astronaut, who had a Middle Eastern background. And while that might end the immediate crisis, he also knew he'd be accused of not valuing the young woman's life, because of her heritage. They'd second-guess him, and ask loudly if he would have made the same decision and ordered her death if she'd been Caucasian, not Middle Eastern, like the terrorists.

If he ordered the station shot down, at least the likelihood of any radiation contamination or damage from its reentry would be removed, the panic spreading all over the east coast would be quelled, the rioting stopped.

But he'd kill an innocent American woman.

Should he wait and give the young astronaut a chance, or should he act now and execute Burnt Haunt, perhaps saving hundreds of millions of people from the mayhem of this growing, uncontrolled terror? It's only one astronaut, one American. That fact weighed heavily on him, the worst part of this dilemma.

"Five seconds, Mr. President."

He couldn't wait any longer. *I'm destroying a hundred-and-fifty-billion-dollar investment.* Did he really need to sacrifice that astronaut?

"... and three, two, one." The floor manager pointed to him and mouthed, *You're on.*

The President looked straight into the camera. Its red light burned steadily just above the lens.

"My fellow Americans. Today I come to you with a heavy heart." He swallowed. "In ten minutes the International Space Station will be in an optimum position over the open ocean of the South Pacific for pre-positioned United States cruisers carrying state-of-the-art antisatellite weapons to end this grave threat to our nation . . ."

PENTAGON

There were more stars attending the meeting than were visible on a good night's viewing: It seemed as if every three-and four-star general and flag officer in the U.S. armed forces was present. It was standing room only in the relatively small room.

The U.S. military Joint Chiefs and their associated staff were assembled deep in the bowels of the Pentagon, in a highly classified vault known as the "Tank." The officers were in direct contact with Strategic Command HQ in Nebraska, and the eight other U.S.-war-fighting combatant commanders—Africa, Central, Cyber, European, Indo-Pacific, Northern, Southern, and Special Operations—were following the briefing in the background. A secure link to the National Security Council was being relayed directly to the White House Situation Room.

The NSA Director, an up-and-coming Vice Admiral, started speaking without being introduced. "Ladies and gentlemen, two days ago the USS *Jimmy Carter* had intercepted intelligence from the Chinese that reveals they are *not* going to stop their ASAT launches, despite their secret agreement with the State Department. No matter what happens—"

Someone interrupted over the secure link. "What the hell does that mean?" The link to STRATCOM blinked and refocused on the National Security Advisor, standing in the White House Situation

Room. "The President's announcing as we speak that he's ordering the station shot down—but he also has the capability to *stop* those launches within seconds if Kimberly regains control! Why would the Chinese launch their ASATs if the station's no longer a threat?"

The NSA Director continued, unphased by the interruption. "Even if Dr. Hadid-Robinson regains control, there is a finite probability that the ISS will impact China if it continues to descend at the same rate—there's no guarantee she can stop it from coming in. As such, the Chinese have decided to cut their losses by preemptively shooting down the ISS so that it falls in the Pacific, even if the U.S. calls off its launch. And a second, perhaps more important reason is that by destroying the ISS, the Chinese will then have the world's only active space station, the new Tiangong. A political coup in their eyes."

The Tank was quiet as the Vice Admiral pulled in a breath. "And in case Dr. Hadid-Robinson somehow does gain control, they plan to explain that their military was not informed that the terrorists on the ISS were neutralized."

A moment passed before the National Security Advisor said bitterly, "A breakdown in communications."

"Yes, sir. It happens all the time."

The National Security Advisor turned to someone off camera. "Get me my Chinese counterpart on our hotline. I'm going to let that bastard know what you just told me. That will stop their ASAT—"

"But, sir, in addition to revealing our capability to tap into their comm, your counterpart can still say there was a communications breakdown—and their Spratly launch site never received the order to stand down."

"Then what the hell else can I do?" He glared through the link.

The Chairman of the Joint Chiefs leaned forward. "I don't know, sir—but at least you can go ahead and try, just in case Kimberly pulls off a miracle."

JOINT AIRLOCK

Exhausted and nearly fainting, Kimberly closed the outer hatch and opened the re-pressurization valve to its EMERGENCY position. Immediately, air started flowing into the evacuated airlock so fast that she was lucky her eardrums hadn't blown out, which had happened to one of her fellow astronauts. Barely lucid, she still managed to hang near the controls as the stiffness of her suit began to subside.

She felt a sense of overwhelming relief as the air density in the lock rose past the density inside her suit, which meant that she'd soon be able to take off her helmet and allow the greater pressure to start healing the effects of the bends.

Her heart still thumped heavily and her skin still crawled; she felt like curling up into a fetal ball from the fatigue and soreness. But she still had to make sure that the station was rising, gaining altitude. She tried to focus on the panel readout by the inner hatch. Red digital numbers scrolled almost too fast for her to register. Suddenly the readout stopped at 14.7 psi.

Normal air pressure. She could take off her helmet.

It hurt like crazy to lift her gloved hands and flip the latch. Every joint in her body ached terribly. But once she lifted the helmet off it seemed as though the pain wasn't as bad. Probably a psychological reaction, she knew, but real or not the result felt wonderful.

Kimberly knew she could stay in the airlock and increase the pressure to more than one atmosphere, to accelerate the healing. But she had too many things to do. Despite the stress and even the effects of the bends, she still couldn't quite believe that she was all finished and the crisis that had started nearly a week earlier was finally over.

She punched at the controls and the inner airlock hatch popped open. It was quiet inside the station: no terrorists were lurking out there. Fumbling tiredly with her suit, she shucked the upper and lower torso units but kept the cooling and ventilation garment, as she'd soon be going EVA again to transfer fuel from Scott's Starliner.

She swam through the empty station, feeling a weird sense of uneasiness. She'd shoved Bakhet's dead impaled body into the Russian MRM-2 airlock, and she'd been only inches away when she saw Farid's lifeless face pushing against the hole she'd ripped in the Bigelow inflatable. But still she felt on edge.

Once in the Central Post, Kimberly grimaced as she brought up the comm link with NASA. She knew she'd still be feeling the effects of the decompression sickness for some time, but she couldn't allow that to keep NASA out of the loop. She needed their help to extend the station's lifetime.

At the very least she needed to learn the status of the Boeing Starliner resupply capsule that was on its way to the station. Although the terrorists were out of the way and the ISS was slowly regaining altitude, she couldn't allow the same fate to happen to the station that had occurred to the Tiangong-1, the old Chinese space station, several years earlier when it had deorbited and broken up into a swarm of tumbling, fiery meteors in the Earth's atmosphere.

Her legs extended weightlessly as she floated in front of the laptop and established communications with Johnson Space Center.

The laptop's screen blinked and then showed Chief Astronaut Tarantino. He jerked with surprise, his eyes goggling.

"Kimberly?"

"Present and accounted for," she said, forcing a smile and trying to keep from grimacing with the pain.

Tarantino turned and waved excitedly to someone behind him. Within seconds Kimberly saw a mob of faces crowding around the CAPCOM station.

"Kimberly, thank God you're alive!" Tarantino fairly shouted, gaping at her. "Are you all right? ADCO hasn't shown us the latest parameters. What's your status?"

Kimberly drew in a still-painful breath. She knew there was a small time lag between ADCO—the mission control desk responsible for tracking the ISS's attitude—and NASA's ground radar. She brought them up to speed, giving only scant details about Bakhet's and Farid's gruesome deaths, but professionally running through what she'd done to stop the station's descent and begin the re-boosting process.

Pulling over to another laptop, she ran through the ISS systems, squinting blearily at the screen as she reviewed the station's critical parameters. "Be advised, CAPCOM, that I'm close to bingo fuel. I'm going to need that Starliner here sooner rather than later to transfer fuel, so I can keep gaining altitude."

Tarantino muttered, "Hold one," then turned and had a quick, whispered discussion with several of the NASA team clustered about him. Two people rushed away from the crowd, obviously in a hurry to do something off-screen. Then someone put a hand over Tarantino's camera.

"Hey!" Kimberly yelled. "What's going on?"

Her joints ached and it was difficult to concentrate. She

certainly didn't have any time for games. She thought that she could easily return to the Joint Airlock, turn up the air pressure, and be healing much more quickly rather than put up with this crazy ground activity.

"*Kimberly!*"

Rubbing her forehead, she saw that whoever had blocked off the camera had removed his hand. Tarantino sat there, looking somber, worried . . . frightened?

"What?" she snapped.

"You're sure the terrorists are disposed?"

"Of course I'm sure!"

"And there's no way they could escape, get free, somehow re-take control of the station?"

Anger simmering inside her, Kimberly answered, "Absolutely. One of them is floating in the MRM-2 with a hole in his chest and the other is sucking vacuum in the Bigelow. Now what the hell is going on?"

CENTRAL POST, INTERNATIONAL SPACE STATION

Tarantino moved closer to the monitor, masking out the others crowded around him.

"Kimberly," he said, his voice lowered. "You don't have much time. ADCO hasn't yet confirmed that you're gaining altitude, as the change is much slower than you should be rising. In fact, we can barely detect any change at all. But we've passed your information on to Washington."

Frowning, Kimberly glanced at the ISS readout. Everything appeared to be working. As they used to say in the old days, all systems were *go*. She pulled up the Motion Control Group interface, which displayed the station's altitude to a resolution of about five meters. That's strange, she thought. CAPCOM is right, the increase in altitude is far below what she had expected, as though something was still obstructing the flow of fuel to the thrusters.

She said slowly, "Maybe I didn't fully de-crimp the line? That would explain the low rate of increase. I may not have returned the line to its original, fully open diameter." Setting her jaw, she continued, "I'll do another EVA, take more time to make sure there's no indentations in the line."

Tarantino shook his head. "No. No EVA. You don't have time."

"You mean because I'm approaching bingo fuel." Leaning closer to the laptop's screen, Kimberly said, "I'm going to need a fully functional fuel line when the Starliner arrives with its load. Once we transfer the fuel he's bringing we'll be able to boost up to altitude, but only if that fuel line is completely unobstructed."

She started to turn back toward the airlock. She certainly didn't relish the idea of going EVA again, especially without having recovered fully from her last one.

"Kimberly!" Tarantino's voice had a shrill urgency to it. "Scott's Starliner is due in less than an hour. But by that time . . . it . . . it'll be too late."

"What're you talking about? This re-boost is already giving us plenty of time. Sure, it's slow and I'm close to bingo fuel, but the altitude change has already given us another few hours at the very least—"

"You don't have time because the military's been ordered to shoot down the ISS."

"WHAT?"

Looking utterly miserable, Tarantino said in a rush, "We're passing the information you gave us about the terrorists to the NSC, and Headquarters is using all their channels as well. Patricia has just arrived at the White House and will be briefing the President with this new information. Plus, as we speak, Mini Mott is talking with the Joint Chiefs, trying to stop the shoot-down. But it doesn't look good. The military's targeted the ISS to bring it down on this orbit, and since the order's already been given they may have launched."

"But . . ." Kimberly spluttered, "but I'm alive! The terrorists are dead! ADCO's confirmed that the station's increasing in altitude—"

"I know. I know. But there's no possible way to stop the ASATs if they've already been launched. No one can stop the missiles once they're in flight."

"But why did they give the order? It doesn't make any sense!"

"I don't know if there's any good way to say this," Tarantino replied, anguished, "but if there was *any* chance at all that the station continued to deorbit and contaminate American soil, the President was forced to put the safety of the people over saving the ISS. There's rioting and mass evacuations down here, Kimberly. It's complete mayhem and he had to stop it."

"I . . . I . . ."

"It's exactly the same reason why the military shot down USA-193, our own National Reconnaissance satellite back in 2008," Tarantino said, almost whining. "But this is a hundred times worse. The mere chance that the million-pound ISS carrying plutonium might impact a populated area is causing mass hysteria. People have already died! The President is determined not to allow any more deaths or injuries because of public panic."

Kimberly couldn't believe it was true. "But . . . it's all perception! No way is the station going to deorbit if I can refuel it. And the probability of it contaminating a populated area is damned near zero."

"Perception is reality, Kimberly," Tarantino said. "That's what the President is struggling with. That's what's forced him to make this decision. We don't agree with it; no one in NASA does. But that's not the point. The simple fact is that the military has been ordered to shoot down the station to make sure it impacts over the ocean, and this is one of their last windows to guarantee success. After your next orbit the ISS will be out of range, so they have to act now."

Through the fog of pain that still shrouded her, Kimberly shifted her attention away from their reasons why her own country might shoot her down, to finding a way of ensuring that the ISS would survive.

And keeping herself alive.

"Copy. Now tell me everything you know about this shoot-down."

Tarantino's face relaxed minutely, as though he was glad that he'd finally gotten past this seemingly insane shoot-down rationale, and they could go on to the next steps.

He looked down and read from a sheet of paper, "They've targeted you on the upcoming pass, a southern Pacific ascent, so you've got less than twenty minutes. The ASATs might already be on the way, for a counter-orbital interception."

Kimberly swallowed. "Okay." *It is what it is.* "What else?"

Looking up again, Tarantino replied, "The good news is that our defense liaison has just passed on the info that some of the antisatellite warheads may go ballistic on their last thirty seconds of flight, and won't be under control by either ground or onboard sensors. Greater than thirty seconds out the ASATs will be maneuvering to intercept the ISS, using their onboard tracking radar. But once that thirty-second mark is hit the warhead is committed to its ballistic path. And even better is that your altitude is above the ASAT performance limits, so they may actually go ballistic sooner than designed."

"That's the *good* news? What's the bad?"

Tarantino hesitated a heartbeat. "If the warheads are equipped with Aerojet's throttleable divert and attitude control system, they'll be receiving updated targeting information from the Aegis cruisers, so they'll be able to home in on the station during that last thirty-second window. And there's a high probability that three or more warheads will be used, all launched from the Aegis cruisers in the Pacific."

"Great," Kimberly groused.

"Presently," Tarantino continued, "we'll only be able to give you crude approximations on the ASAT trajectories from our ground-based tracking systems, so the error bars may be large. That's all we've got, Kimberly. We're trying to give you a live feed of the tracking data, but it'll be at least half an hour before that interface is up and running, and that's too late to do any good. We're working this on all fronts, and we'll let you know if Patricia can turn this situation around—at least stop the Aegis cruisers from feeding their updated tracking corrections to the ASAT missiles."

She closed her eyes. "Understand."

"And Kimberly . . ." Tarantino hesitated again before continuing, "I know this is tough after all you've already been through, especially with so little fuel. There's very little time left and communications across all these different government agencies isn't anywhere near perfect, so don't count on anybody being able to divert those missiles. We'll let you know as soon as we hear anything."

She pushed away from the laptop, leaving the comm channel open, and tried to ignore the pain from the bends. Over her shoulder she answered, "Roger that, CAPCOM."

He was right, she knew. She didn't have much time and she had a lot to do. "Go ahead and patch through whatever ground tracking you have."

She swiveled two additional laptop screens so that she could simultaneously watch them and the video from the ground link. She couldn't afford to wait for TOPO or any other ground source to finish that interface for relaying tracking information on the incoming warheads; the time lag between their discovering details about the ASAT launch, transmitting the information, and providing their ever-changing orbital parameters would take much too long.

She needed to solve this on her own.

For an instant she felt that all she could do was to rearrange the deck chairs on the *Titanic*. But then an inner voice said, *Screw that! You've got a problem to solve. Get to work!*

CENTRAL POST, INTERNATIONAL SPACE STATION

Floating before the laptops' screens, Kimberly assumed that the ASATs would be using an optimized, direct ascent trajectory, much like the Dragon's approach that NASA's aborted rescue mission had used earlier. But the ASATs would be traveling much faster, approaching her head-on in a counter-orbital direction, and accelerating at a much higher rate of speed. Their speed would certainly be much faster than the leisurely, one-foot-per-second relative closure velocity of the Dragon—in fact, over *fifty-one thousand times faster.*

She'd have to program warning alerts into the software, first to calculate when the ISS started its southern Pacific ascent, and then when she had thirty seconds left until impact: when the warheads went ballistic—*if* they went ballistic. If they did, since the warheads wouldn't be guided any longer, or making course corrections, they'd be blindly programmed to hit the ISS where the station should be thirty seconds in the future.

Which meant that she'd have half a minute to dramatically

change the ISS's orbital parameters, so the space station would not be where the ASATs calculated it would be. Kimberly had practiced Predetermined Debris Avoidance Maneuvers before, but this PDAM would be like flying by the seat of her pants, especially since she wasn't even sure of the ASATs' trajectories.

So her window for evading the incoming missiles was about equal to thirty heartbeats.

Maybe my last thirty heartbeats, she thought.

She knew that the ISS could rise a kilometer in about three minutes, which meant it gained a little more than five meters a second when under thrust, about fifteen feet. So if the fuel line wasn't obstructed she'd be able to boost the station 150 meters higher in half a minute. In reality, she'd probably be able to goose it only one or two meters per second, max.

It didn't seem like much, but only a few meters' gain could make a huge difference, because the ISS modules had a relatively small cross section—except for the solar panels. But a missile would just drill right through the flimsy solar cells and keep on going without damaging any of the modules at all.

But if the ASATs *didn't* go ballistic and continued to home in until the final moment, Kimberly didn't know what she would do. With a tremor of fear, she realized she *did* know: She would die. Instantaneously.

If she didn't do anything she would certainly be killed. *It's too much,* said a voice in her mind. Who are you trying to kid? They're going to kill you—and the entire space program, as well.

And would they win? Kimberly snarled silently. You're going to let them win, to destroy everything we've worked for all these years? To put an end to humanity's reaching outward?

No, she told herself. Never. Not without a fight to the death.

She put all thoughts of failure out of her thinking. She was determined to survive. And to keep the exploration of space alive and flourishing.

She got to work.

Before programming the alarms she first cut the thrusters. She was approaching bingo fuel, and she would need every ounce of thrust she had left to rapidly boost the station out of the missiles' path. In an ideal world she might have enough fuel to hike the ISS out of the way, but with the fuel line still partially crimped, the engines might not be able to produce enough thrust to prevent the station from being hit.

On the other hand, she wouldn't have enough fuel now to move the station at all if she hadn't screwed up de-crimping the tube.

So maybe this was her lucky day, after all.

She snorted. Right. Lucky if you consider that three or more ASAT missiles will be converging on me in less than twenty minutes with one goal in mind: to blow the International Space Station out of the sky.

And me with it.

SOUTH PACIFIC
OCEAN: NORTHWEST
OF THE SOLOMON
ISLANDS

The encrypted signals arrived over the military's classified MIL-SATCOM satellite link. All three cruisers received the order simultaneously, confirming to the ship captains what they'd anticipated, what they'd trained for the past several days. The captains were part of the national chain of command, but even as masters of their vessels they didn't make policy decisions. They executed the legal orders of those appointed over them.

And their orders were clear.

Alarms hooted, and with the firing sequence initialized, all three cruisers executed their mission as one.

Within seconds, an Aegis antisatellite SM-3 missile roared from each ship, smoke billowing from its rocket engines as the kinetic-kill warhead arrowed into a counter-orbital trajectory to intercept the International Space Station.

Almost instantly, each cruiser launched another Aegis Standard Missile-3. However, one of the missiles exploded almost immediately after it cleared its pad, raining flames and debris over the ship.

As the cruiser's damage control crew moved to suppress the fires and clear the wreckage, a total of five ASAT missiles locked on to their preprogrammed, counter-orbital trajectories and headed upward on their mission.

Thirty-seven seconds after the last missile launched, the captains received an urgent message to belay their launch orders and stand down.

CENTRAL POST, INTERNATIONAL SPACE STATION

Kimberly stayed in Central Post, diligently watching the laptop screens for any sign of the approaching ASATs. She was breathing pure oxygen through a portable mask. Her symptoms of the bends were becoming gentler, bearable. She felt thankful that the BME—the biomedical engineering team—had recommended the pure oxygen treatment as she switched out her nearly depleted bottle of oxygen for a fresh one while keeping an eye on the screens she'd set up.

Normally, the station's changes in altitude would be controlled by TOPO in mission control, and coordinated days in advance with the Attitude Determination and Control Officer, the desk responsible for the station's four control momentum gyros. But now as Kimberly prepared to engage in a last-second maneuver, she knew that she'd have to respond by instinct, she wouldn't have time to validate her decisions through Houston, or have them confirmed by the flight center at Goddard.

She scanned the laptops, not fully trusting the timing alarm she'd programmed into the tracking system's software. TOPO, the mission control center desk responsible for tracking the ISS's orbit, had an open line with NASA's Defense Department liaison, and was able to pass along the status of the approaching warheads, despite such information being highly classified, since it referred to ongoing military operations. But she didn't rely only on that intelligence for situational awareness. So as she floated in front of her bank of laptops she kept shifting her eyes to as many feeds as she could.

She started to query CAPCOM for another update when one of the laptop screens started blinking red and a raucous clanging noise reverberated from its built-in speaker. As she moved to cut off the ear-splitting alarm, Kimberly wished that the ISS had approach radar—but only incoming spacecraft had that capability. She couldn't even eyeball the missiles: it was virtually impossible to see them until they were only about two to five kilometers away, much too close for her to react. NASA's ground-based radars had picked up the incoming warheads, and from the timing numbers scrawling across one of the laptop screens they were zeroing in on her at incredible speed.

A cold chill enveloped Kimberly as she gaped at the dizzying numbers. The missiles were racing toward her in a counter-orbital direction at 17,500 miles per hour. Add that to the station's own 17,500 mph velocity in the *opposite* direction around the Earth and you got a head-on collision at 35,000 mph—over 51,000 feet per second—enough to tear the ISS apart.

Her heart pounding against her ribs, her hands clammy, and her throat dry, Kimberly pecked swiftly as a madwoman at the graphical display. She'd integrated NASA's tracking data with her own algorithm to show a crude visual image of the incoming missiles. Another object appeared on her screen, then another one— and then two more.

They had launched not three, but *five* warheads, all of them speeding toward her.

Kimberly poised her finger over the icon controlling the thrusters' fuel line, ready to start the flow of fuel that would engage the engines. Not too soon, she told herself. Steady . . . steady. Inanely, she remembered a line from her school days: *Don't fire until you see the whites of their eyes.*

The warheads were not converging on the station, she knew, but on a future spot in the ISS's projected orbit, where the ASATs' computers calculated the station would be located a mere few seconds from now.

NASA's feed showed the five warheads flying in graceful shallow arcs, neither jinking nor otherwise behaving like anything except dogged, determined cheetahs utterly fixated on their prey. They moved in undeviating trajectories across the screen, their positions updated by her estimated timing program.

Kimberly knew that her software was automatically updating the incoming warheads' position and velocity. The laptop was using that data to instantly project each ASAT's impact point. Simultaneously, the software she'd written predicted when her thirty-second window would open for her to engage the thrusters and maneuver the station out of the warheads' way. She'd know within seconds if the ASATs would go ballistic or if they would continue to home in on the ISS, making last-second course corrections right down to the moment of impact.

Silently, she prayed that the warheads would all go ballistic and converge on their predicted target all at the same time. That would mean that in their final thirty seconds they would not be able to maneuver.

But if the missiles didn't go ballistic, her biggest fear was that she'd engage the thrusters too soon, giving the warheads enough time to change their velocity and intersect her new orbit. Then they'd impact the ISS, no matter what she did.

Seconds count, Kimberly told herself. *Micro*seconds count.

Steeling herself, she watched the ASAT warheads converge on their calculated future location of the ISS's position. Each warhead showed on her laptop screen as a tiny oval at the end of a dotted line. In less than a minute the station would be at that point in space unless she engaged the thrusters. But if she started too soon the ASATs could adjust their velocity to converge on the new impact point.

The longer she waited the more they'd have to change their momentum. She hoped that their final stages were designed more for finessing rather than making any large orbital change.

It was a waiting game. Seconds stretched into eternities. The tension in Central Post ratcheted up unbearably. Kimberly wanted to scream, wanted to shout for help from somebody, anybody. But there was no one except her. She was alone. The thought flashed through her mind that this wasn't only her own life on the line. The next few moments would also determine the fate of 150 billion dollars' worth of space infrastructure—and most likely the future of the entire human space program.

The blips showing the five approaching warheads jumped closer to the ISS's future location with every second as their final-stage rocket engines accelerated them. Kimberly held her breath as the digital clock on the laptop screen counted down the time to her thirty-second window.

Two of the warhead blips turned green. They were within the window.

Kimberly started to engage the thrusters as a third blip went green. Three of the warheads had gone ballistic.

She froze her finger above the console as a burden of fear

slammed into her. The other two warheads were making small, last-second course corrections! CAPCOM had said they might have throttleable divert and attitude control systems. Time seemed to hang suspended as she glanced at the clock: twenty-six seconds to impact.

She couldn't wait any longer. It was now or never. Kimberly punched the fuel line control state to ON, hoping she'd be able to boost away from the three ballistic warheads' calculated impact point.

She could barely feel the 100 micro-gee acceleration of the station as the thruster engines engaged, slowly pushing the million-pound station higher, a few scant meters every second. On the screen the dotted line displaying the ISS's trajectory seemed to creep leisurely as it veered slightly off from the old, projected orbit to a new, longer arc.

I

CENTRAL POST, INTERNATIONAL SPACE STATION

Kimberly's eyes widened as she watched on the laptop's screen two of the approaching ASAT warheads blink and make a course correction. They now aimed for the updated future intercept point of the ISS's new, higher orbit. They would hit in less than twenty seconds.

Kimberly felt her stomach turning over. The two warheads were maneuvering, heading for the station's new position. She had mere seconds to live.

Suddenly the fourth and fifth warheads' color blinked green. The approach radar showed that they were no longer accelerating. But even with the station's new orbit, the ASATs had already made their final course correction and were still arcing toward the ISS's new, future location.

Unless she could once more change the station's orbit.

She glanced at the clock. Less than fifteen seconds to impact. She'd have to wait until absolutely the last moment, giving the station enough time to rise above the orbit that the three ballistic

ASATs were aiming for, and then cut off the flow of fuel, so the station was no longer rising. With any luck the station wouldn't reach the spot calculated by the more advanced, fourth and fifth warheads; the change might be too much, too sudden for them to counter . . . .

Kimberly's chest was aching as she counted down the final seconds. It would be close, terrifyingly close, but she couldn't afford to keep increasing the station's altitude. She just hoped that the fourth and fifth warheads had been programmed to impact the station along its main axis, so they'd have a chance to miss.

At the seven-second mark she cut the fuel. The clock continued to count down as the station settled in its new, higher orbit—but not as high as it had been thrusting toward for the last twenty seconds. Would the warheads miss by only twenty meters?

The clock hit zero and Kimberly felt a shudder run through the ISS.

She heard no sounds of explosive decompression, no tearing of metal or whooshing of escaping air. The station was intact!

She slapped at the graphical interface and pulled up an outside view of the station. The aft array of solar panels had a gaping hole ripped through its middle, looking as though the ASATs had torn through the thin Kapton without exploding. Kimberly realized the warheads were the "hit-to-kill" type, relying on their massive kinetic energy of impact to destroy their targets.

She glanced at the crude feed from the ground, still showing the warheads as they shot past the ISS. Three of them appeared to have flown under the station, while the other two had barely sailed above the main body. Their control systems must have homed in on the broad radar-reflecting cross section of the solar panels.

"I did it!" she shouted. She'd threaded the needle and survived.

Kimberly's whole body felt as if it were glowing from within.

She wanted to turn summersaults in midair. She felt an indescribable elation of relief as she pulled in deep breaths of oxygen.

But the rational part of her mind quickly resumed control. Glancing at the fuel indicator, she saw that she was almost at bingo fuel. At least Scott would be showing up in the Starliner with the extra fuel supply. For the first time in days Kimberly felt that the station would survive. With her in it.

She called up the MCC link and was immediately switched to CAPCOM. Chief Astronaut Tarantino looked as if he'd aged five years in the past few minutes, but a huge grin split his face.

"You did it, Kimberly!" he praised. "Thank God!"

She replied, "I'm ready for Scott to bring in the Starliner. Then we'll have plenty of fuel to boost back up to altitude, even if the fuel line is still crimped." She glanced at the clock. "His ETA is still twenty minutes?"

"Yes . . . but you've got to hurry."

"Hurry? Why?"

Tarantino's look of exaltation clouded over. "Patricia's learned that the State Department's engaged China to use their own antisatellite system as a backup, in case our ASATs failed."

Kimberly stared at the laptop screen. "You've *got* to be kidding!"

"I wish I were. The Chinese are preparing to launch their Dong Neng-3 ASAT at you on your next pass. You've got ninety minutes. Maybe less."

"What the hell is going on down there?" Kimberly yelled at the screen. "Our own military didn't stand down and now China's jumping into the fray? They don't even have a dog in this fight: the ISS is a U.S. and Russian asset, not Chinese."

"After China lost their first station when their Tiangong-1 went down, it's not clear how long they intend to keep the new Tiangong on orbit. I guess that's precisely why they're so anxious to help us get rid of ours."

"I need that kind of help like I need a bullet in my brain," Kimberly growled. "I've still got to de-crimp that line so we'll have enough fuel to boost to a higher altitude."

She tried to rein in her emotions, still not fully recuperated from her session with the bends. Now this. At least she'd been pre-breathing pure oxygen now, she thought, but that's been to help recover from the decompression symptoms, not to prepare for another EVA.

Tarantino's expression turned stony. "Whatever their motive, State is desperately trying to wave the Chinese off. Defense is working on the issue as well, as well as the President's National Security Advisor. We're also trying to get to them through our NASA channels, but the Chinese National Space Administration is giving us the runaround. You've got to kick the station as high as you can after you unload Scott's fuel, so we can convince our own government to step in at the highest level and stop this insanity. But you can't assume they'll stop the Chinese from launching."

"Copy," Kimberly said sullenly, afraid that if she tried to say more she'd explode. Without another word, she turned her back on the laptop's screen and kicked off for the Joint Airlock. Scott might not arrive for another twenty minutes, but she couldn't afford to waste any more time. As much as she still ached from the bends, she needed to prepare for another EVA, this time to finish the job by completely de-crimping the fuel line.

Before she did that, though, she'd have to transfer fuel from Scott's capsule after he'd docked to the Node 3 IDA. Nothing was turning out to be simple on this flight.

At least Scott was a big boy; once he docked he could start boosting the station as soon as she de-crimped the line. So she had to suit up.

She kicked off for the Joint Airlock and glided to the SAFER unit secured to its wall. The nitrogen-propelled Simplified Aid for EVA Rescue backpack fit onto the outside of her EVA suit and provided a safer, albeit much smaller and less powerful way of moving through space than the old Manned Maneuvering Unit. With time running out, she'd need all the help she could get de-crimping the line.

The SAFER unit had twenty-four small thrusters, each capable of less than a foot-pound of force. They weren't able to be throttled; instead the units were controlled by a hand switch. She'd have only thirteen seconds of nitrogen propulsion available, but at the rate she was squandering time, that might not give her enough leeway to de-crimp the line and re-boost the station.

It was tough enough just putting on the suit by herself, but installing the SAFER unit would make donning the suit an order of magnitude harder; usually a partner astronaut assisted with the task. So, reluctantly, Kimberly chose to forego the propulsion unit.

Her body still sullenly aching, Kimberly started to pull on the EVA suit's lower and upper torso units. She glanced at the time.

They had less than a full orbit until the Chinese ASATs would appear, no more than ninety minutes. Boy, was Scott in for a surprise when he arrived.

INTERNATIONAL DOCKING ADAPTER, NODE 3

Outfitted in her EVA suit and tethered outside the station, Kimberly held on to a handhold on top of Node 3; with her other hand she held a long, 1½-inch-thick fuel transfer hose that floated behind her. Myriads of stars hung around. Despite the close proximity of the shredded solar panel and debris slowly tumbling from the ASATs' near miss, Kimberly felt as if she were staring into a spangled infinity.

As she waited, Scott's Boeing CST-100 Starliner crept into view, gradually growing from a barely visible point of light to a fully three-dimensional spacecraft. Slowly it approached the ISS through the debris.

Kimberly felt a sense of relief, almost gratitude, flood through her. Scott's here, she thought. I'm not alone now. But she kept her emotions in check. With Scott's capsule and his load of fuel she'd soon be able to transfer his fuel to boost the ISS far above the approaching ASAT ceiling and at last put this long nightmare behind her.

Within minutes the Starliner floated outside the Node 3 IDA port, barely a meter away from the station, but didn't approach any closer.

Kimberly waited a few moments, but the CST-100 capsule still didn't move relative to the station; stars crawled behind them as the ISS and capsule continued their orbit. *That's odd.* The Starliner had routinely mated with the International Docking Adapter before, resupplying the station. The only difference this time was that a person was on board—and that shouldn't have made any difference . . . .

Kimberly spoke into her hot mike. "Starliner, Station. You're cleared for docking."

The comm clicked and Scott's clipped voice came over the link. "Station, Starliner. Ah, slight problem here."

Frowning, Kimberly said, "Go ahead, Starliner."

"The radars are FUBAR," he said, using the astronauts' expression for Fouled Up Beyond All Repair. "So are the backups. Might be affected by all this debris floating around."

Straining to keep her voice as neutral as Scott's, she answered, "Copy, Starliner. It looks like you're lined up with the IDA. Can you proceed?" But she knew the answer before she'd even asked . . . .

"Negative, Station. Unsure of alignment." Which meant that if he tried to dock manually, the capsule might end up damaging the ISS. "We'll have to wait until mission control shoots us a work around."

"Negative," Kimberly said. "There's already been too much excitement up here. And the bad news is there's more to come. We may have some Chinese ASATs up here in about an hour."

Scott responded with two quick clicks of his mike. "Then what do you suggest. The clock is ticking."

She realized she didn't know how long it had been since she'd

even seen a mechanical clock that ticked. Scott's attempt to remind her of the time squeeze merely caused her to focus on fixing
the problem, and not getting into a useless argument with her
ex-husband.

With barely fifty-five minutes until the Chinese ASATs arrived, she couldn't afford to go down any blind alleys. She was
running out of time and she still had to bring Scott's capsule in,
de-crimp the fuel line, pump the Starliner's load of fuel into the
station's tanks, and then boost the ISS's altitude.

She briefly thought about trying to connect the fuel transfer
hose to Scott's capsule as it floated freely outside the ISS, but that
effort might impart momentum to the Starliner and make it float
away—or worse, collide with the station; she couldn't even use
the robotic arm, as the CST-100 didn't have a grapple fixture. So
if the Starliner couldn't dock, the capsule couldn't provide the
fuel to boost the station to a higher altitude.

So *she* had to bring it in. That left only one thing to do.

"Going to plan B," Kimberly said. She secured the fuel transfer
hose with a safety lanyard, and locked her tether's auto-retract; it
snaked out behind her as she used the handrails to move hand
over hand toward the end of Node 3. She carefully pulled herself
along across the module's metal surface, making her way hand
over hand, unwilling to risk losing her grip and flying out into
space, despite the safety line. She didn't want to waste time haul-
ing herself back in with the tether, and she knew that she needed
to conserve her strength for bringing the massive Starliner into
its berthing port.

"Plan B?" Scott's voice took on an edge. "Say again?"

"I'll be pulling you in."

"Wait, Station. What're you going to do—"

His voice trailed off as Kimberly reached the edge of the module, overlooking the International Docking Adaptor port. There

was nothing Scott could do to help, and she wasn't about to let him try to talk her out of what she had to do. The logic was clear in her mind. The Starliner couldn't dock on its own, and since his radar wasn't functioning, she had to pull the capsule in, using her muscular strength to close the meter-wide gap. It was as simple as that. There was no other way.

If she'd had more time, she'd ask MCC to shoot up a work around. But with more warheads on the way, and the Chinese in the equation, she couldn't afford to wait. She was at bingo fuel and she couldn't move the station an inch higher in altitude unless she had access to the fuel on Scott's Starliner.

It was going to be incredibly tough to pull the massive Boeing capsule to the IDA docking port, but she had to try. There was no other way. Although the Starliner was weightless, its mass endowed it with plenty of inertia, nearly ten tons that she'd have to move a little more than three feet. Squeezing her eyes shut for a moment, Kimberly remembered tugging her father's sailboat into its lakeside dock. It was essentially weightless on the water, but it took every ounce of her strength to budge it even a little. Her father had to get out of the boat and splash over to the dock to help her.

Opening her eyes, she looked down at Scott's capsule, saw what she had to do: hang on to the station with one hand next to the IDA port, and grab the Starliner with her other hand, then pull the flat-nosed cargo vessel in. She'd heard about astronauts doing similar dockings during the Shuttle era, so she knew it wasn't impossible. Just incredibly tough.

Scott's voice sounded tired. "Anything I can do to help?"

"Can you bring the capsule closer? I'm going to manually guide you into the IDA." To herself, she added, *I hope.*

A long moment passed. "Negative. This is as close as I can safely get."

"Then just sit tight," she said.

"Copy. Maintaining radio silence." A hesitation, then, "Good luck."

Thank goodness Scott volunteered to leave her alone, she thought. She didn't need his encouragement right now, or anything else that would interrupt her concentration. She'd want his assistance soon enough, when she'd need him to help guide the vessel the last few centimeters into the international docking adapter.

She realized she was breathing too rapidly: All she could hear in her helmet was her own panting breath. She tried to force herself to calm down, slow her heart rate. She knew she was pressed for time, but she couldn't afford to make a mistake in her haste to dock the capsule, transfer the fuel, and then de-crimp the fuel line. Any error at this point was nonrecoverable. And now there was Scott's life on the line as well as her own.

She started working her way down to the IDA, her back to the capsule. The ripped Kevlar of the Bigelow inflatable was to her right; the module retained its voluminous shape despite the rip she'd slashed into its white siding, which was clearly visible with Farid's unmoving body behind it.

Reaching the IDA, she turned. Waiting patiently a meter from the Node 3 International Docking Adapter floated Scott's white Boeing CST-100 capsule. Resembling an overgrown Apollo module, its curved, forward aero-shell had been ejected, showing a flat nose that angled out to a cylinder serving as its base; rectangular viewports were set around the capsule's diameter, midway between the nose and the base.

Puffing, she stopped momentarily to glance inside Scott's capsule. She caught a glimpse of him squinting through the thick viewport windows, looking as if he was trying to spot her. She knew that without any lights on her she was nearly impossible to see, especially against the black background of space. Once she moved closer he'd probably be able to make her out, but Scott was basically helpless inside the supply vessel, unable to come outside and join her in an EVA, not even able to assist her by moving the capsule closer to the station.

Holding firmly to one of the station's handrails with one hand, Kimberly engaged the tether's auto-retract as she positioned herself next to the Node 3 IDA. She didn't need her safety line getting in her way. The International Docking Adapter's opening was a large target, but she'd still have to make sure that whatever momentum she imparted to Scott's massive capsule would be perpendicular to the module; otherwise she might cause the CST-100 to drift into the side of the IDA and perhaps recoil backward—or even damage the station.

Still holding tight to the handrail, she slowly swung out and grasped a handle on the Starliner's flat nose. The distance looked short, but once she started pulling, Kimberly wished it was only three microns instead of three feet.

She spoke into her hot mike. "Starliner, Station. I'm in position. On my count I'll start pulling you in. Keep me apprised of your motion."

"Copy, Station. On your count."

She stared straight ahead and drew in a breath. "Ready . . . ready . . . *engage!*" With one hand on the station's handrail and the other on the capsule, she grunted, closing her eyes as she tried to bring her hands together like a weight lifter. She pulled her arms inward in the heaviest dumbbell fly she'd tried in her life. Her triceps and biceps felt as though they would pop.

Sweat broke out on her brow and her whole body started to tremble. Grunting with exertion, she felt incredibly warm, roasting, despite the water-cooling filaments in her suit gurgling away like a babbling brook. Her chest and arms flared with red-hot pain.

Still she kept on pulling, tugging, while counting to twenty under her breath. She drew in deep lungfuls of oxygen, gasping. She couldn't tell if she'd made any progress at all.

Scott's voice came over the link, high with enthusiasm. "We have motion, Station! Estimated approach velocity is . . . not quite a centimeter per second. And that's a guess."

Kimberly gasped, "How's . . . the alignment?"

"Can't tell yet. But at this rate Starliner should contact the alignment guides on the IDA in about two minutes."

"Copy." Kimberly drew in a deep, painful breath. "I'll maintain position until you're berthed, in case I need to make any alignment changes."

Scott responded with two clicks of his microphone.

Still clasping the station's handrail, Kimberly tried to change position as the Starliner inched toward the Node 3 IDA. It appeared to be barely moving. The docking port had plenty of wiggle room, though, and as long as the Starliner's flat nose managed to enter its wide opening she wouldn't have anything to worry about—except for attaching the fuel transfer hose, finishing the de-crimping, and re-boosting the station.

Oh yeah, she thought. And avoiding the incoming Chinese ASATs.

OUTSIDE NODE 3, INTERNATIONAL SPACE STATION

Scott's voice interrupted Kimberly's thoughts. "Ah, how far until contact?"

She immediately snapped alert. "Foot and a half, max."

"You'll need to apply some pressure on the nose, move it toward the JPM. I'm starting to yaw and come in at an angle. All I'll need is a little nudge."

"How far off are you?"

"Not much, but we're running out of time."

"Copy," said Kimberly. "I'll give the nose a tap, stop the yawing."

"Roger that. Just keep your suit out of the way. The capsule may not be moving very fast, but it still has enough momentum to crush you if you get between the Starliner and the IDA."

Kimberly didn't reply as she pulled herself up to the station. Sore and aching, she could see the capsule's flat nose slowly inching toward the IDA's rim. But it would miss the dock entirely unless she changed its gradual yawing motion. She must have pulled it more off-axis than she thought. Its nose was slowly turning toward the left.

She saw that the nose was starting to inch beyond the port. She quickly leaned in to push it back and saw Scott staring through the viewport, looking worried.

"Kimberly! You'll get hit—you don't have enough room to escape!"

"Little astronaut, big capsule," she said. Still hanging on to the station's handrail with one hand, she extended her right hand directly in front of her, intending to nudge the Starliner's nose. She pushed as hard as she could, trying not to slip against the station.

The capsule's nose gradually swung back just before it cleared the International Docking Adapter's port. Still gliding slowly, it appeared to be swallowed by the IDA's yawning metal entrance.

"That's it!" Scott exulted. "We're in!"

Kimberly didn't have time to celebrate. She immediately turned her attention away from Scott's capsule and started back for the fuel transfer hose. Afterward, she'd find the best path to the FGB, so she could reach the access panel and the partially crimped fuel line.

"Don't wait for me," she said into her helmet mike. "After I connect the hose, start transferring the fuel. I've got to de-crimp the line. I'll join you shortly."

"De-crimp what?" Scott sounded surprised, almost annoyed.

"The hypergolic fuel line to the thrusters."

"What the hell's been going on up here?"

"It's a long story. We'll have plenty of time to catch up—if I can get back to work. You transfer the fuel and I'll explain later. And check with MCC about the status of those ASATs!"

"Copy," Scott replied. Kind of sullenly, she thought. And the link went silent.

Her arms and chest still aching from struggling with the fuel transfer hose and opening valve, Kimberly reached Node 1 and started pulling herself across the outside of the module, heading for the access panel on the Russian FGB. She still felt weak from her brush with the bends, but at least that and the pressure of dealing with the two terrorists were behind her. The only worry she had now was that she might not be able to fully de-crimp the small-diameter fuel line.

The Earth continued to rotate below, showing no sign of the approaching ASATs or the turmoil wracking the U.S. eastern coast. But she couldn't dwell on that false serenity. She was under a fast-shrinking timeline.

She spotted the metal access cover, still poking up vertically from the FGB's outer skin as she pulled herself across the module. Securing her booted feet, she took out the vice grip, looped its safety line around her wrist, and pushed her helmet over the open access port.

She spotted the millimeter-thick tube that carried fuel to the thruster engines still buried in the layers of insulation. Trying to steady her breathing, Kimberly slid the pliers inside the small compartment. At first she could barely feel the small indentation, but her pliers abruptly caught as she gently ran the tool along the length of the tube. There was no question about it: she hadn't fully de-crimped the line.

How did I miss this when I was out here before? She thought she'd checked to see if the tube was symmetric after she'd initially de-crimped it. She must really have been out of it, she thought, when she'd been out here earlier. But after struggling through the bends, she knew she'd been lucky to get back inside the station, much less partially fix the line.

She rotated the tool, then lightly squeezed the compound pliers, turning it in a circle around the line's circumference. Then she slid the long-nosed compound wrench back and forth several times until she was absolutely certain that she had fully de-crimped the tube. She debated calling Scott to have him test the flow, but she needed him to transfer as much of the precious hypergolic liquids as he could—and they needed to assure the ground that they had successfully refueled the station.

With her safety tether retracting in, Kimberly started to make her way back to the Joint Airlock. Once again she left the access panel open, not because she thought she'd be back, but this time because every second counted.

JOINT AIRLOCK

Kimberly struggled to shimmy out of her suit before heading down to Central Post. She had red chafing marks around her elbows, collarbone, and the tops of her shoulders from her skin rubbing against the suit. She knew the irritation would fade away in about half an hour, but she looked like a sweaty, slimy worm that had just crawled out of a tight enclosure. What a way to feel when seeing her ex-husband for the first time in nearly a year.

Still wearing the tubed cooling garment, she kicked off to the side and caught a glimpse of Scott's arm as she glided down the module's axis. He'd already changed into his habitual blue-and-silver polo shirt with the Air Force Academy football logo. She thought that he wore it to let people know that even after a successful career as a fighter pilot and astronaut, his college experience as a defensive back was one of his personal highlights.

Then she thought, Or perhaps he remembered that it had been *her* favorite shirt when they were married.

She rotated around the hatch as she entered Central Post and pulled to a stop in front of one of the consoles. Floating upside down relative to her, Scott wore a headphone and a mike. He nodded as she entered, but continued talking as he ran through the fuel transfer checklist with mission control.

Fighting a sudden impulse to throw her arms around him, Kimberly nodded back as she turned to the laptop and focused her attention on the ISS graphical interface. She called up the station's housekeeping parameters. The fuel tanks were already more than a third full, so she started keying in the commands for the engines to start boosting.

They needed to start gaining altitude without delay. Atmospheric drag had been increasing almost exponentially, especially since she'd hit bingo fuel. They were so low that raising the station's orbit would be a real fight between atmospheric drag and the engines' thrust.

She immediately set the control states, and watched as the hypergolic fuel made its way through the lines. She couldn't feel any sense of motion from the minuscule 100-microgee acceleration, but there was a faint, unmistakable shudder as the thrusters fired. A low, barely perceptible vibration permeated the ISS.

She called up the fuel flow indicator: it was almost back up to normal. A sense of relief gusted through her: her efforts to decrimp the fuel line must have worked.

Seconds passed. Scott waved for her attention, then gave her a thumbs-up. "ADCO confirms we're climbing, right at five meters per second. They're forwarding that information both to our defense liaison and the State Department channels, to get it to the Chinese."

"But is our altitude increasing fast enough that we're no longer a threat to crash?"

"I would think so. As long as we keep going up."

Kimberly scanned the systems readouts, still not quite able to believe they were out of hot water. "What about the Chinese? Have they stood down their ASATs?"

Scott spoke to CAPCOM once again, relaying her concern. Kimberly saw that they had now transferred more than half the

Starliner's fuel; the station's tanks were well above their mini-mum levels.

She ran through the whole list of diagnostics, checking the various housekeeping functions as well as the sensors scattered through the ISS. The only anomalies she saw were that the JPM's power was still off, and the small experimental airlock was still open to space.

They'd eventually have to perform another EVA to close that outer hatch, Kimberly realized, but right now that ranked near the bottom of her priorities. Getting the ISS high enough so that it was no longer a threat to crash back to Earth, and ensuring that the Chinese had stood down their antisatellite missiles was at the top of her list.

Scott motioned for her to come over to the link he had set up with mission control. Kimberly swam to him. Grabbing his shoulder to steady herself, she saw on the screen Chief Astronaut Tarantino. He looked ragged, but incredibly more relieved than he had looked the last time he'd spoken to her.

"Kimberly," he said. Then he stopped, choked up. "You've been through a lot. We can't thank you enough—"

"The ASATs," Kimberly interrupted. "Have they called them off?"

"The answer is yes and we don't know. Our Aegis cruisers have stood down from launching additional missiles," Tarantino said, glancing at a sheet of paper at his side. "But we're still trying to find out the Chinese status. We received confirmation on the U.S. systems while I was getting an update from Scott. You don't have to worry about them anymore. As far as STRATCOM is concerned you're now in a stable orbit, and even if Scott hadn't brought along the extra fuel, the station has plenty of supplies until the next Russian Progress resupply vessel docks in another month. You should come home now, both of you. Return to Earth."

Kimberly's shoulders sagged. *Is he telling me to give up? What about the Chinese ASATs?*

Tarantino continued, "The military has confirmed that your altitude is continuing to increase, and with Scott validating that the terrorists are no longer a threat—"

"With *Scott* validating it?" Kimberly said slowly. She glanced at her ex-husband. His normally dark, ebony face showed a shade of red. "You didn't take my word that the two were disposed of?"

"I believed you, and NASA did," Tarantino replied, looking decidedly uncomfortable. "But the NSC, they wanted a separate confirmation. Otherwise, they didn't know if you were actually being held under duress, perhaps being forced to say the terrorists were no longer a threat. They could have turned the tables at the last moment, after we had put down our guard."

Kimberly set her mouth in a hard line, feeling her innards turning to fury. Her own government hadn't believed her. She could understand their point, but what did they want her to do, drag Farid's body into Central Post for everybody down there to see?

And what would they have done if Scott had not confirmed that the terrorists were indeed no longer a threat? He may or may not have seen Farid's dead body, floating in the Bigelow inflatable. And Bakhet's lifeless, impaled body was locked inside the Russian MRM-2 airlock, completely out of sight.

But Scott believed me, she realized. He took my word that both the terrorists were taken care of. He could have very well wasted precious time methodically searching the ISS for the two, but he *trusted* me, didn't even look for them. Staring at her ex-husband, she felt a happy glow dissolving her anger. And now he was showing more than trust. *Finally, he respects me.* She wanted to hug him.

Tarantino's voice sounded calmer as he came back over the

link. "Kimberly, this wasn't about trusting you. It's about ensuring that our station is completely safe and stable—"

"But I thought you said the military has stood down."

"Yes, yes, they have." Tarantino picked up the sheet at his elbow and waved it at the camera. "Patricia reports through separate channels that the President will be making an address to the nation later tonight—"

"And the Chinese," Kimberly interrupted coldly. "You're avoiding the issue. What about them? Have they stood down their ASAT capability as well?"

Mopping his forehead, Tarantino replied, "NASA, Defense, and State are working the problem. They're all on the same page—"

"Kimberly!" Scott's voice interrupted them.

She glanced at him. Scott looked grim. She saw that his laptop had a live, open link to TOPO, the Trajectory Operations Officer. It appeared that MCC had gotten that interface with NASA's ground tracking facility fully up and operational.

"What is it?" she asked.

Pointing to the laptop's screen, Scott replied, "The left window is from Goddard. The right is a delayed view from one of STRATCOM's Space-Based Infrared System satellites at GEO. Vandenberg declassified this geosynchronous SBIRS feed before shooting it to TOPO. You'd better take a look."

Kimberly pushed away from the link with MCC and peered over Scott's shoulder. The left window showed a standard view of the ISS's orbital trajectory, fed from NASA White Sands. The right window displayed a high-altitude image of Earth, broadcast from geosynchronous orbit 22,236 miles above the ground.

Scott pointed at two icons on the outer edge of the SBIRS image, overlaid atop a smoky-gray picture of Earth, typical of an old, but high-resolution infrared sensor. Dotted lines showed the icons' projected paths: they both intersected on the right-hand edge of the image.

Scott said, "STRATCOM just detected two Chinese SC-19 launches from their facility in the Spratly Islands."

"Can't be." She shook her head. "They launch out of the Korla Missile Test Complex in western China."

"That would be too obvious. Their Spratly port is an unacknowledged site. I . . . flew escort for a Navy P-3 surveillance plane when we were gathering intel on it when it was being built."

Kimberly's breath gushed out of her. *Oh no! After all this!* "What did they launch?"

"Not sure yet," Scott said tightly. "The intel's not in. But if they're carrying Dong Neng-3s, those are state-of-the-art exo-atmospheric missiles. ASATs."

"You're sure they're Chinese?"

"Doesn't matter whose they are. They're on a counter-orbit interception. At the rate they're approaching, we've only got fifteen, twenty minutes at the most before they impact us."

CENTRAL POST, INTERNATIONAL SPACE STATION

Kimberly felt as if she'd been hit by a piece of space junk.

"But . . . but CAPCOM said our military and the Chinese were both in the loop to stand down their ASATs."

Grimacing, Scott replied, "And how many times in our own government does the right hand not speak to the left? These are huge bureaucracies, and they've been on hair-trigger alert for days."

Kimberly kicked back to her laptop, where she immediately started running through the graphical interface. "Keep me updated on those incoming trajectories. We're going PDAM," she said, as she called up the Predetermined Debris Avoidance Maneuver.

"Kimberly!" Bluish-gray light from the laptop's open link reflected off the sheen of fine sweat that covered Scott's face. "PDAM's half-meter-a-second delta-v will never push us out of the way in time. You heard CAPCOM: we've got to abandon the station, evacuate in the Starliner."

Kimberly was struck by his worried expression. She'd never seen her normally cool ex-husband look so concerned.

"*Extended* PDAM," she corrected. "A longer, high-velocity extended burn for a lot more delta-v. I did it to evade our own ASATs, I can do it for theirs."

"It'll never work. Dong Neng-3s can maneuver up to the point of impact. They'll be making last-second course corrections—"

"Help me solve my problem, Scott!" she insisted. "Don't tell me that I can't do it. I'm not giving up. The station's too important."

She refocused on preparing as much as she could for the last-minute maneuvering. Although they had not yet completed transferring all the fuel from the Starliner, they had plenty for giving the station more delta-v, so that was not a concern.

But if Scott was right, and if the DN-3s could really home in until the last second, then even with a tank full of fuel it was going to be tight timing—incredibly tight. So what else could she do to throw off the incoming warhead sensors?

Scott pushed over to where she was preparing for the extended burn PDAM. They'd have to work with TOPO later in order to get back in their safety box so other pieces of orbital debris wouldn't accidentally hit the ISS. But at the moment that was the least of her worries.

Scott watched her for a moment. Then he said quietly, "They're just over twelve minutes out." He studied her face. "This station means more to you than saving your own life, doesn't it?"

She continued working the laptop, not looking up at him.

Scott went on, "Look . . . I knew what I was getting into when I pushed Patricia to send me up here. And you're right: This piece of space metal is too important to abandon ship. So what can I do to help?"

Still without looking at him, Kimberly said, "Give me an idea on how to spook the warheads, get around their course corrections. I cut the thrusters when the Aegis ASATs went ballistic and I was able to sneak between their paths. Can I use that tactic to confuse the Chinese warheads?"

Shaking his head, Scott replied, "The Dong Neng-3s were designed to overcome that tactic. They probably lifted the idea from our own latest-generation air-to-air missiles. But we countered those improvements with electronic spoofing, and metallic chaff before that: you know, clouds of radar reflectors."

As Kimberly continued to prepare for an extended PDAM, it hit her that Scott had actually been schooled in this spy-versus-spy stuff, including countermeasures and everything else one adversary might throw at another to get a leg up on the opposition, to gain even a small advantage that might allow you to sneak through the other guy's tactics. If there was anyone who knew how to out-strategize the opposition, it was her ex-husband. And what was it he was rambling about . . . ?

She looked up suddenly. "What did you say about chaff?"

Scott lifted an eyebrow. "That's old school, confusing the enemy with a fake of the head, a feint. Electronic countermeasures give you more finesse, a wider range of outcomes. Why? Do you have any ideas for generating electronic chaff? Like using that traveling wave tube you brought up to stimulate crystal growth, maybe beam it at the ASATs?"

"That's already served its purpose," Kimberly said, remembering both Farid's and Bakhet's surprised reactions when she'd hit them with the burning millimeter waves. "But there was something else you said. It was just at the tip of my tongue."

She closed her eyes, thinking as hard as she could. She realized that Scott agreed with her, and he was right. The survival of the ISS was much more important now than just about anything else, even though Chief Astronaut Tarantino had already told them they should abandon the station and use Scott's Starliner capsule to return to Earth.

"The Starliner!" Her eyes snapped open. "And the Soyuz vehicles!"

She reached out and shoved Scott back toward the MRM-2 Russian airlock. "I've already expended all the fuel in the Soyuzes, so you'll have to eject them both manually."

"Eject them?" Floating backward toward the port, Scott's eyes widened as he followed her train of thought. "You mean send them out as free-flyers. Use them as chaff!"

"Right. Since the Soyuz at MRM-1 is docked at the nadir, when you eject it, it'll go into a slightly lower orbit than the station—"

"Meaning it'll be traveling faster than us, and out in front, the same direction that the ASATs are coming!"

"Like chaff in front of us," Kimberly agreed. "It'll have enough delta-v to start physically drifting from our orbit, and we can start it transmitting on whatever RF frequencies you can bring up to really confuse the incoming ASATs. Ejecting the other Soyuz at MRM-2 zenith, and the Starliner at Node 3 zenith, will make them both go higher and slower than us. So between the two Soyuzes and the Starliner, the DN-3s just might home in on them instead of the station's big optical or radar cross section. And when the ASATs are too close to us to commit to a large delta-v course correction—"

"You'll execute your extended PDAM and maneuver out of the way, beyond the ASATs' ability to recover and home in on the ISS." Scott kicked off the side of the module and headed off for the closer of the two Soyuzes. "We've still got at least ten minutes before the DN-3s arrive. I'll power up the Soyuzes, override their three-minute emergency scuttle, and eject them as soon as I can. The Starliner may take a little more time—"

"Just do it, Scott. And make sure the RTGs are all secured in

MRM-1 when you eject the Soyuz—we don't want to lose any of them."

"Copy."

"And when you're through, grab a pair of binoculars and get up to the Cupola. Start looking for the ASATs, get a visual to give me a few seconds' warning for the PDAM."

"Yes, ma'am." Turning, he gave a curious look at the prybar sealing the hatch to MRM-2; he quickly removed it before disappearing into the airlock leading to the Soyuz that brought up the two terrorists and kicked off the whole debacle.

Kimberly went to Scott's laptop to watch the SBIRS feed of the approaching ASATs. He'd said the images were being scrubbed by STRATCOM before being chopped over to TOPO, so she didn't know how up-to-the-moment they were. So she didn't know how much time they had left. But if Scott could scuttle the three space capsules to serve as a cloud of chaff, it might be enough to confuse the ASATs, even if it only gave her a few more seconds to try to quickly maneuver out of the way.

Moments later, Scott appeared at the hatch, his eyes wide. "The MRM-2 Soyuz is ready to scuttle . . . along with a dead body."

Kimberly threw him a glance. "Thanks." She didn't have any remorse for Bakhet, not after what he and Farid had done; Scott didn't ask what happened, and she didn't try to explain.

He shrugged, and before turning to head off for the other Soyuz docked at MRM-1, said, "I'm . . . sorry. I didn't know you had it in you. Nice work . . . ."

Kimberly grunted.

Scott grinned at her as he turned and started for the Soyuz.

Kimberly smiled to herself as she turned back to the laptop. Inwardly she felt a warm glow: that grin was more recognition than he'd ever given her—or anyone else, for that matter.

She forced herself to focus on the screen, running through her options. The Chinese DN-3s had the capability of making last-second course corrections. With their velocity, and the station's limited capacity for delta-v, that translated into perhaps the ASATs missing the ISS by less than a meter. But again, if Scott was right and those missiles actually were hit-to-kill and not filled with explosives, then all she'd need was for them to miss by millimeters, not meters.

It was like horseshoes—a miss was as good as a mile.

But the consequences of not missing was killing herself, her ex-husband, and most likely America's space program.

CENTRAL POST, INTERNATIONAL SPACE STATION

Kimberly kept her eyes glued on the updated link from MCC as Scott stood watch in the Cupola, searching for any sign of the approaching ASATs. A smattering of debris from the last ASAT encounter still enveloped the station in a thin cloud.

The emergency crew return Soyuz now flew in front of the station in a slightly different orbit. The zenith-docked Soyuz that the terrorists had arrived in, as well as Scott's Starliner followed slightly behind the ISS, at higher orbits. All three capsules broadcast their positions in an attempt to fill the electromagnetic spectrum with radio frequency interference. In addition, hopefully they would provide optical, infrared, and radar clutter to further confuse the incoming ASATs. With all that, Kimberly steeled herself for radically changing the station's own position.

She tried not to think that in some ways this was exactly what Scott had been trained to do in the air during his fighter pilot days. He should be at the controls, she thought. But realistically, she had more recent experience; it was up to her to evade the incoming warheads.

Her one consolation was that she'd never know if she'd failed. Her own death, Scott's, and the station's would be nearly instantaneous.

MCC's voice came over the comm link. "STRATCOM reports two ASATs at station forward. Estimated time to impact . . . twenty-two seconds."

"I'm scanning in that direction," Scott said over the internal comm.

Kimberly concentrated on trying to integrate all the information rushing toward her: the uplinked visuals, the SBIRS feed, Scott's monotonic voice, the digital readouts, the Soyuz and Starliner tracks, a dozen other parameters. It was as if she were totally immersed in the world's most complex video game, one with thousands of lives and billions of dollars at risk.

Suddenly the comm went out, the graphical trajectories blinked off, and the screen went blank.

"I'm blind!" Kimberly screamed. She turned to another laptop and ran through the graphical interface.

"What happened?" Scott's voice came from the Cupola. "Can I help?"

"No. I'm flying blind. The Ka-band's down."

"Must be handover from TDRSS East to West," Scott said. Tracking and Data Relay Satellites relayed the station's communications to NASA ground stations. When comm handoff changed from TDRSS East to TDRSS West a blackout of up to thirty seconds was normal.

Kimberly felt sweat beading her brow and her stomach was clenching sourly. She counted to herself, assuming the missiles' velocity would change only minutely as she estimated the time she had left.

"Ready . . . ready . . ." she muttered. She punched at the graphical interface and immediately felt the low vibration of the thrusters as she engaged the hypergolic fuel controls. She hesitated, then rapidly stopped, then restarted the controls in a random sequence.

The comm blinked on again, displaying the ASAT trajectories. TDRSS handoff was complete. The two approaching missiles appeared to make a course adjustment, but Kimberly couldn't tell if it had really happened or if it was her imagination. And the latency of the data being transmitted from the ground made it all the worse.

Are they moving away from us or toward us? she screamed silently at herself.

The station's system was not built for fire-control or assessment. The purely emergency nature of the PDAM maneuver was considered a last-ditch procedure for the astronauts to haul the massive ISS out of the way of incoming space debris, like pushing a stalled race car off the track at Indy. NASA's "Plan B" in case the PDAM maneuver didn't work was for the astronauts to quickly scramble into a crew rescue vehicle and flee from the station, getting as far away from the incoming space junk as possible.

But with the two Soyuz and the Starliner capsules now serving as high-tech chaff, hopefully masking the ISS, there was absolutely no way for them to find refuge in case of a mistake.

"Tallyho!" Scott yelled. "Incoming! Incoming! I have visual at station forward!"

The laptop screen showed both missiles hurtling right at them.

"And now!" Kimberly jabbed again at the controls, just as the approaching icons converged on her position. Time seemed to hang suspended as the station lurched upward at a little more than five meters per second.

An open window on the adjacent laptop showed a splash of

light. An instant later her ears popped from a sudden decrease in pressure; the deathly sound of something ripping its way through the station's framework reverberated through the ISS. One of the warheads hit the station; the other must have slammed into one of the decoy Soyuzes flying behind and above them.

Kimberly stared at the controls as an alarm clanged. "It's DC-1!" she shouted.

She kicked off for the adjacent module, hit the access hatch, and grabbed the inside of the vestibule to swing herself around and face the airtight entry door. She pulled down the cover and hurried through the steps to seal the DC-1 module. Was there any other leak? Something that might have hit the station, but would only work itself loose and cause them to lose their air?

Seconds ticked by. Scott floated in, his expression questioning, and hovered beside her. Kimberly ran through the sequence of safety checks, gradually convincing herself that the breech in DC-1 had been the only serious damage the ISS had sustained.

There was no sign of another impact, no indication of air escaping anywhere, no power failure or anything else that might indicate a dangerous collision had occurred. Only the DC-1 was void of air.

She tried to smile at Scott. "We made it."

He nodded shakily.

Kimberly felt her chest raise and lower as she pulled in breaths. The sound of blood pounding in her ears overwhelmed anything that Scott or MCC might have been saying.

The nightmare was over. She, Scott, the ISS, and America's space program were very much alive.

CENTRAL POST, INTERNATIONAL SPACE STATION

As much as Kimberly had been through during the last week, she had a feeling that in some ways the hardest part might be just around the corner.

After they spoke with the thoroughly grateful and praising President, the comm switched to the NASA Administrator's private office. Models of rocket launchers, memorable space capsules, the Space Shuttle, and the ISS bedecked the bookshelves behind the Administrator's desk and dangled from the ceiling. Patricia Simone sat on the sofa off to one side of her desk; the only other person in the office was her Chief of Staff, Mini Mott, sitting quietly at her side.

Simone smiled tiredly into the camera, and Kimberly noticed tiny crow's-feet in the corners of the ex-astronaut's eyes.

"I don't know where to start," Simone said, her voice husky with emotion. "What you've done for the nation, the space program . . . I . . . I can't begin to say how wonderful it is to see both of you, alive and safe."

Floating beside Kimberly, Scott glanced at her before answering. He cleared his throat. "I think it's fair to say that it's all due to Kimberly, ma'am. Anyone in the astronaut corps could've ridden the Starliner up here. Saving the station was all her doing. She's an incredible lady."

Kimberly thought, *Now that's a first.* "It was mostly luck," she said simply.

"Luck didn't have anything to do with it," Scott insisted. "It was anticipating and being proactive. Not reacting or waiting. What astronauts are trained to do."

Kimberly felt puzzled. What had gotten into him? First him showing respect, and now this? Usually Scott was the first to try to grab the glory.

Mini coughed. He looked uncharacteristically embarrassed. "If we're through with the accolades, I don't want to overwhelm you kids with too much trivia, but this is an opportune time to boost the popularity of the nation's space program, call in some well-deserved chits."

Uh-oh! Alarms went off in Kimberly's head. "Meaning?" she asked, pulling closer to the laptop.

"Meaning that, believe it or not, you two are the most popular people on the planet," Mott replied. "Especially you, Kimberly. More admired than Hollywood types and even royalty. As such, I've put together a proposed schedule of events for interviews, ghostwritten articles, backgrounds for your biographies, and daily live updates from the station while you're waiting—"

"Hold on." Kimberly waved a hand, cutting Mini off. She shook her head. "This sounds like you've scheduled us for a month-long publicity stint up here. How long will it take for the Russians to get an emergency Soyuz launch to us for a rescue mission? A week or so, at the most. Right?"

Back at NASA Headquarters, Mini coughed and threw

a glance at Patricia. "Uh, do you want to take that, Madam Administrator?"

Simone leaned in to the screen. "The Russians are completely revamping their launch facility in Kazakhstan with the discovery of Farid Hazood's radicalization. This is very closely held, but they're not even sure if any other cosmonauts or launch site crew workers may have been involved, so they're doing a complete, top-to-bottom review of all personnel backgrounds, including equipment inspections and in-depth interviews with everybody on their launch teams."

"Sounds more like interrogations, comrade," Scott murmured.

Undeterred, Kimberly asked, "Then what about U.S. spacecraft? Isn't there a manned Dragon launch that can be accelerated?"

Simone shook her head. "With what we've been through, that's at least three months out. It will take a month just to get a new launcher to the Cape."

Kimberly glanced at Scott, but her ex-husband kept his expression stony.

Simone continued, "However, the Russians have assured us that a Progress resupply vessel can be expedited to launch within three weeks, and a manned Soyuz a month after that." She pursed her lips momentarily. Then, "So I'm sorry, but that's the best we can do for you. In the meantime . . ."

"You want us to participate in the equivalent of a publicity tour," Kimberly said.

"That's one way to put it," said Mini. "Look, Kimberly—in reality these publicity events won't take up that much time. You've both been through it before. You know, the old grip and grin PR boondoggle for NASA. You guys'll have plenty of time to start repairing the station, bring the JPM back online, maybe even complete some of the experiments you started."

"Only if Kimberly sets the agenda," Scott said. "And the timeline."

He turned to her and lowered his voice. "Think of this as having another pair of hands to help you finish your projects. Since I was a last-minute addition I certainly didn't have the normal prep time to come up with my own set of experiments."

That was certainly unexpected, Kimberly thought. At a loss for words, she shifted her attention back to Simone, and noticed that the Administrator was wearing a tight smile. "You were going to say something, ma'am?"

"Just take advantage of the time," said Simone. "In addition to Mini's point about exploiting this opportunity for the space program—including getting a significant increase in the human space budget—you'll not only have less of a constraint on completing your experiments, but it will be good for my two best astronauts to, uh, reacquaint themselves."

Kimberly pulled back, suddenly self-conscious. Keeping her eyes riveted to the laptop, she asked, "Is that all, Madam Administrator?"

"For now. You've both had a long day—and you, young lady, have had an incredibly hard week. One for which the whole nation is grateful. Why don't we pick this up tomorrow, and then Mini can go over the first few items on your new schedule."

"With Kimberly's approval," Scott insisted. "As long as we also publicly acknowledge the sacrifice made by the six that died."

"Agreed." Simone nodded. "You can give the schedule thumbs-up or -down."

"Copy," said Kimberly. Without asking Scott if he had any other questions, she leaned forward and cut off the comm.

She pushed back from the laptop as Scott killed the link to MCC. *Two months!* That was an unusually long time to extend a mission, on a par with what had happened with the unfortunate

Columbia disaster, back in the Space Shuttle era. But she knew that nothing she, or anybody else, could do would get them home faster.

As frustrating as that might be, though, at least she still *had* time, instead of having her life prematurely ended.

Outside the ISS, orbiting behind them were the Boeing CST-100 Starliner capsule and the surviving Soyuz. There was no way they could get to the two vessels. And with the small but noticeable atmospheric drag, without being boosted up to a higher altitude, within months both capsules would meet their demise with final, fiery entries into the deeper atmosphere.

So now we have three weeks before the unmanned Progress resupply ship arrives, Kimberly told herself. And at least another month after that—nearly two months total, alone on the ISS—until a Soyuz rescue craft arrives to take them back home.

Two months alone with her ex-husband. In zero-gee.

At least Scott didn't seem as arrogant or self-absorbed as he'd been when they'd broken up. But had he really changed? And if he had, what had motivated his turnaround? Is it for real? And most important, will it stick?

So Patricia was right. And it didn't take the NASA Administrator, or her being an ex-astronaut or even a three-star Air Force general to tell her: two months alone on the station was more than enough time for her and Scott to get reacquainted.

Kimberly smiled to herself. *And hopefully very well.*

ACKNOWLEDGMENTS

Thanks to John Silbersack, our agent, and Bob Gleason, our editor.